THE RIVER DISTRICT
THE MERCULIANS   BOOK 6

CARO SOLES

Marlo followed Triani into Eulio's dressing room, slightly out of breath. "What do you want to show me?" he asked, looking around.

"Those." Triani pointed to a large bouquet of black flowers tied with a huge white satin bow.

Marlo peered more closely at the flowers and reached out a hand to touch them.

"Careful," warned Triani. "They have thorns."

"What are they?"

"Roses." Triani paused and laid one hand on the dark curled petals. "They're a Terran flower."

Marlo leaned closer but didn't touch.

"I had a Terran boyfriend long ago," Triani went on. "He used to send me red roses every opening night, whenever I was close enough. He said red was the color of passion." Triani paused again and turned away for a moment to collect his thoughts. Images of Lucius rushed into his mind and he felt a stab of loss so strong it made him dizzy. He blinked hard. Now was not the time for memories. "Anyway, he told me about the different colors of this flower and what they meant. Black was not good."

"What does black mean?"

"Death."

Marlo sat down abruptly. He looked again more closely at the flowers. "Technically they aren't really black," he said slowly. "I'd say more a very dark purple, don't you think? So maybe you're wrong?"

"I'm not wrong!" shouted Triani, anger pushing out all other feelings. "Something bad has happened to Eulio and you have to find him!"

ONE

There is always something special about coming home, Beny thought, even for a journey as short as this one. He glanced at Eulio, curled up beside him, still caught by surprise sometimes to realize he was now married to this beautiful, talented dancer whom he had loved for so long. Far below their air-car, the sun sparkled on the lakes and rivers of their glorious planet and glinted on the distant towers of Merculian's capital city.

Eulio leaned forward. "Look, there's Triani's place. The gardens look gorgeous, don't they?"

"I never understood why he needs such a huge property," Beny said, watching the estate slide into the distance below.

"Status," said Eulio.

Beny laughed. Eulio knew his famous dance partner very well.

"Maybe we should have let Dhakan know we're coming back a day early," Eulio said after a moment. "Shall I contact him now?"

"Don't bother. He'll just get all upset and start bustling about for no reason."

Eulio went back to reading the messages tied in ribbons that had been tossed onto the stage after his farewell performance at the festival last night. "Look! Here's another one of those weird ones! 'The sun that shines on you will soon go down to darkness.' That's...strange."

Beny swallowed. "It's nothing to worry about, love. Someone's trying to be poetic, I suspect. You know, one great day of glory ends then starts another day of glory. That sort of thing." But this was worrisome. It was the third oddly disturbing message Eulio had received this way lately, the first two after performances in Cap City and now it seemed the creature had followed his spouse all the way to the Festival in Darsona. The last note had referred to Eulio as 'she,' so perhaps it was some off-worlder confused by the traditional use of the pronoun 'he' to refer to the hermaphrodites of their planet. Yes it was misleading, but what can one do? Traditions are strong on Merculian. Beny sucked in his lower lip. Perhaps he should report this threat to the authorities. He thought of the investigator Marlo Dasha Bogardini, the Regulator who had been so successful solving other problems for Eulio's family not so long ago. Whatever he decided, he didn't want Eulio to worry about it. It might be nothing. Then again...

Below them the capital city nestled like a colorful jewel, cradled in the semi-circle of gentle hills surrounding it. The air-car driver had slowed down considerably and dropped to a lower altitude, adjusting coordinates to the stricter flight paths inside of the city limits. Eulio packed away his ribbon-messages in his shoulder bag. Beny glanced around to make sure his beloved *klavalo* was still firmly attached to the float with the rest of their baggage.

Ten minutes later they were home, walking together under the entwined branches of the two trees planted on either side on their front door to mark this a house where a married couple lived. It was an old custom that many people didn't bother with anymore, but Eulio was from a First Order family, and they kept to all the old traditions, something Beny liked. Recognizing their touch, the door swung open at once and they went inside, standing aside to let the preprogrammed baggage-float hum by, headed to Beny's music studio.

Beny had just changed into his comfy velvet beaded slippers and was joining Eulio in the garden for a quick drink when he heard a scuffling behind him and Dhakan appeared, out of breath and doing up his top buttons. His copper eyes gleamed desperation.

"Excellencies, I am so, so sorry! I not know you come here soonest. Everything no ready!"

"It's alright, my friend. Everything's fine. We don't expect anything special when we come home."

"But I go clear away all things from the reception rooms tomorrow morning!" he exclaimed. "Not yet done."

"Come and sit down with us," Eulio called from the garden.

"Oh no, excellency! Much work now to do."

"There's no rush. The reception isn't for a week." Beny patted the man's arm, feeling from his touch the poor Kolari's distress. Not being a touch empath like the Merculians, the alien male could not sense the sympathy and caring Beny was sending him so strongly. Beny wished the man would stop using the term 'excellency' with them, but at least it was better than 'master,' which is what he had started out with on his arrival from Abulon years ago.

"I bring *pamayo* juice? Sherry? Mint wine? Biscuit, maybe."

"Yes, thank you. And then join us." Out of the corner of his eye, Beny thought he saw a slim figure disappearing around one of their braided rope trees at the side entrance, but he wasn't sure.

"You were right," he said, joining Eulio. He threw himself into the embrace of the mossy-green chair, which promptly fitted itself to his frame. "I should have contacted him."

Eulio grinned smugly. "His language skills have deteriorated rapidly under the strain."

Beny had wanted to unpack his instruments and go over some of the music he had recorded at the festival but now he would have to stay and reassure Dhakan that all was well. He pushed a *twyla* vine aside. It chirped at him.

Not quite a servant, not quite a friend, Dhakan's place in their home was problematic. He had learned to take the role of Keeper, though he did not wear the Key of office around his neck, yet they consulted him on many things a regular Keeper would just be told about. He worshiped Beny, who had been the one to deliver him from his horrible life back on the planet Abulon, and he took great care of Eulio because Beny loved him.

Twenty minutes later they were all in the main reception room and Dhakan was asking for instructions on what to do with the pile of wedding gifts still scattered over the tables and a few chairs.

"I was planning to put them all in the storeroom off the main patio but perhaps you would like to go through them first?" Dhakan now seemed more at ease, his language skills reappearing as he slipped into his familiar role.

Eulio sighed. "They're nearly all from alien embassies who refuse to pay attention to our rules about no gifts except from the inner wedding party. I don't even know what some of these are!" Eulio held up a long roll of heavy rope-like lace. "Hang it on the wall? Put it on the floor? What?"

"We can look it up, I suppose," Beny said, eyeing it dubiously. "I think it's from the Blavonians, and they're not coming to the reception next week so let's put it in the cupboard."

They relegated nearly all the rest to the cupboard except for the water globe from the Ectarians, who might come to the party, and the ornamental fire sticks, which could go on the main courtyard in case the Schtandezets made one of their rare appearances. You could never tell with them.

"And of course, that awful painting thing from the Terran Ambassador has to go up on the wall in a prominent place," Eulio said, glancing around. "I think I stuffed it out of sight somewhere."

"It's very valuable," Beny reminded him, "and I like it. A little."

"But it's so dull and only two dimensional."

"It's several hundred years old, the Ambassador said," Beny pointed out. "I think he has an exaggerated idea of our importance."

"We *are* important," Eulio objected.

"I mean in the international world of diplomacy sort of way."

"It's far too valuable for a wedding gift anyway," Eulio muttered, checking behind a curtain.

Beny wandered off to look through all the storage cupboards. He could hear Eulio banging doors as he searched, even checking the gardens, though why, Beny couldn't say.

And then Eulio screamed. "Orosin!"

Beny ran towards the sound, but Dhakan got there first. He let out a high yelping noise.

"I'm coming!" shouted Beny.

As he ran around the door of Eulio's dance studio, he saw the big elaborate gilt frame leaning against one wall.

Empty.

TWO

Something was brewing in the River District. Marlo could feel it in his bones, even before the frenzied call from Eulio about the stolen painting. Of course, there was always some trouble or other in this area of the city where misfits and scofflaws took refuge from the Regulators and plied their questionable trades, but this time it was bigger than usual. And it was growing.

For one thing, there were a lot more robberies and slick pickpocketing going on, and a lot less of the playful snatching of relatively inexpensive objects which then turned up a few days later back in their place. These were carried out as a test of one's mettle or sometimes as a sort of initiation. But this was serious, and the Regulators were busier than usual trying to keep it all under control. On the darker side, there were rumors of a new drug making the rounds which had a bad effect on the young party-loving Merculians, putting a few under the Healers' care. And then there was the sudden appearance of strange graffiti, a visible sign of something alien in the area. It was a puzzle several of his team were working on. And now this painting business. It was all very troubling

Com Marlo Dasha Bogardini loosened his belt and munched on a handful of *chaico* chips as he surveyed the latest haul retrieved from yesterday's raid on the back room of Lardini's, a questionable bar on the fringes of the River District. Several tables were piled high with purses and jewels, hair ornaments, and expensive bracelets.

"This looks like a *cimbola* dagger," he said, picking up a slim blade and pulling it out of its scabbard. "Look, here's the name. Big Stendi's crew would know better. There's no market for these personal items. We may be dealing with some other bunch setting up shop down there. Mostly Terrans these days, right?"

"Or maybe a young crew getting out of hand." Eldred frowned.

"Or someone just made a mistake," Oslani suggested. *"Cimbola* daggers aren't always obvious from the outside."

Marlo shook his head as he picked up another beautifully inlaid scabbard and pulled out the blade. "Anything's possible," he murmured. "But anyone from here would know about the name being engraved on a coming-of-age dagger. Most would recognize the style of inlay and jewels on the pommel, too."

"I don't know, Marlo. That seems a stretch." Eldred picked up another dagger and studied it. "I expect there's a way to remove the names. Any jeweler would know how."

"But not many would do such a thing. Check that, would you?" Marlo picked up a clearly high-priced jeweled hair comb. "Maybe we're not asking the right questions. Who's in the quizzer room?"

"Just now there's Liola."

"Still?"

An image of Liola's innocent-looking cherubic face instantly sprang into Marlo's mind. He had already drilled the youngster without result. He sighed. Maybe someone else would have more luck. The kid talked a lot but never seemed to say anything useful. "I can't decide if he's too low in the hierarchy to know anything or just too cunning to let anything slip. You try for a while, Oslani. Someone just back from baby leave might unnerve him."

Eldred laughed. "Maybe the kid likes milk-filled breasts."

"They turn you on, do they?" Oslani threw back his shoulders and arched his back to show off the aforementioned new and temporary part of his anatomy.

Marlo shook his head. "Remember what we really need," he murmured. Apart from his boss, only Oslani, Eldred, and himself so far were aware of the great painting heist and he wanted to keep it that way as long as possible. He had great faith in Oslani's questioning technique. Before wandering back to his office, he gave the order to haul in Cushna, a villain who was higher up in Big Stendi's organization. He usually knew everything that was going on but rarely let on, unless it would benefit him somehow. Marlo would have to think about that.

It felt like a long day already and it was only just after lunch. He was about to sit down when the name on the last dagger registered. Of course! Orelin Travesi Canilor, the well-known *epicantare* singer who performed as part of the troupe at the new theater in the Wave Entertainment Center. Marlo had often seen him perform. He had a memorable face, with startling blue eyes, shoulder length black hair and pale skin. His voice was sweet and clear in the higher registers but lacked real power. Still, Marlo adored singers and singing in general and would love to meet him, so he decided to take the dagger to him personally. He hurried back to see if there might be anything else belonging to the singer in the haul but nothing else had been identified.

It didn't take much digging to find out the singer's address in a surprisingly modest area of the city. Marlo took a Ring Car, the old-fashioned mode of transport amusing him as it swung through the old town, tooting jauntily as it arrived at each station. He climbed down at his stop and looked around at the narrow streets and brightly colored houses with their high walls covered in flowering vines. Easy to climb up, Marlo thought, looking at the many open windows on the second floor. Few people thought seriously about security around here, apparently.

The front door was down an alley so narrow he could almost touch both sides at once. But flowers spilled from the second story windows and the autoclap on the door was brightly polished. He touched it and activated the hollow clapping sound he could hear reverberating inside. After a moment, Travesi Canilor opened it himself, dressed in deep blue velvet with lace at the sleeves and neck and a cloak tied with a silver cord over one shoulder.

"Yes?" His voice rose dramatically, stretching the short word into three syllables.

Marlo bowed. "I am Marlo Dasha Bogardini, investigator with the Cap City Regulators," he began. "And a fan," he added.

The singer flung the door wide open. "Do come in!" he exclaimed.

"I don't want to disturb you," Marlo looked at the gorgeous outfit, but the singer seemed quite at ease. "You look stunning," he added, unable to control his admiration. Those sparkling blue eyes!

"Oh, I'm having my portrait oil-painted by that famous Terran artist everybody's talking about," he said, tossing the cloak back over his shoulder. "We can talk while he paints, if you like. He doesn't have a lot of time."

He led Marlo down a corridor. "My Keeper has the day off," he said, pausing at a door on his right. "You can sit here in the doorway. The Maestro doesn't like anyone to watch him at work." The singer pointed to a stool just inside the room.

Marlo dutifully picked it up and placed it in the doorway, trying not to notice the odd smell in the room. It was harsh enough that he tried to avoid taking deep breaths. Apparently used to the sharp smell, the singer went inside, mounted a platform and took a dramatic pose. Head back, one leg on the floor, his right hand held high as if pointing to something in the distance, the singer looked faintly ridiculous.

Marlo smiled at the Terran male artist behind the large canvas. The man paid no attention, frowning in concentration as he mixed colors on his palette. He had thick white hair short at the back but falling over his high forehead at the front. His bushy eyebrows and a long aquiline nose gave him an unexpectedly fierce look.

When Marlo sat down, most of his view was cut off by the large canvas, placed at such an angle that he could see nothing of the artist now, but he could see the singer. The sun shone brightly from the one window over the artist's right shoulder, which, Marlo decided, must give him lots of light.

"Have you noticed anything missing lately, *chai*? Jewelry? Daggers? Anything valuable?"

The singer turned his head for a moment then resumed the pose. "Now that you mention it, yes. My *cimbola* dagger. I hardly wear it anymore, since I have a beautiful presentation dagger that was given me when I won the Notable Competition. See? I'm wearing it now."

The noise of throat clearing came from behind the canvas.

The singer lowered his voice to a whisper. "This is meant to bring to mind my role as the valiant Sibilene in the *Songs of Valor Cycle*."

"Oh, I see. Very nice." Marlo realized he was whispering, too.

"And there's meant to be a dragon at my feet and a cherub of some sort as the Guide. The drawings for the Guide are right behind me. See them?"

"I never realized the Guide was naked," remarked Marlo.

Something resembling a snort came from the unseen artist.

Unperturbed, the singer went on: "In this scene I'm meant to be leading the hosts of the dragon's acolytes to free him from his ensnared state. You noticed the golden sandals?"

Marlo nodded He was thinking they were none too practical for leading hosts of any kind.

"I think they should match the cord on the cloak, but the Maestro here says he'll just paint the cord gold, so it'll be alright."

"I would love to see you in that role," Marlo said.

"Unfortunately, I won't be singing that part in the next performance. You have no idea how difficult things are in my line of work. All the juicy roles go to the *Meshsdravi* singers. It's so unfair." He dropped his arm and turned to Marlo, his pale face flushed. "They're no better than I am! Some not as good even. Jealousy! That's what it is."

That's what it is, all right, Marlo thought. "I had no idea," he said out loud. He got to his feet, moved by a sudden desire to get out of the narrow little house with this big ego stuffed inside it and the odd smell permeating the small room.

The artist made a growling noise, and the singer sprang back into position.

"Listen, *chai*, I have to go but I'll leave the dagger right here on the stool and if you find anything else missing, just let me know."

"Fine. You can let yourself out."

Marlo did. Quickly. He was hurt by the insults hurled at the *Meshdravi*. His lover Calian was really the only one of the group he knew well, but he had met plenty of others and found them all generous and fair to a fault. And they were all great singers.

He closed the door softly behind him and hurried down the narrow street. He was so wrapped up in his thoughts about the resentful singer he almost fell over the figure of a young Merculian slumped at the entrance to the alley.

"Are you all right?" Marlo lowered himself to one knee and raised the young Merculian's face to the light. He was pale, almost grey, his round, light brown eyes dull and unfocused, his mouth a strange shade of greenish blue. There were traces of vomit on his tunic and leggings. Marlo recognized the signs of Corvian Bram poisoning. He had seen it often enough lately among adventurous Merculians looking for a new experience and drinking the near-lethal brew coming from the bars close to the River District frequented by the young.

As he contacted the Health Unit to pick up the pour soul, he wondered what had happened to the youngster's friends? Had they been too sick themselves to care about their drinking companion? He shook his head and sat down on the ground beside the now moaning youth to wait. What was happening to his city?

THREE

Triani had just purchased a necklace of rare colored *mantino* stones at a very good price from Scando's, the jeweler his manager had told him about, and was feeling particularly pleased with himself. He wore the necklace over his wine-red tunic so that he could glance at it from time to time as he strode past the north end of the Labyrinth in the Pleasure Gardens. The tall blue-green hedge completely hid the winding paths and pleasant bowers inside, but now and then he could hear small cries of pleasure which made him smile. He was taking a short-cut to the theater where he had a rehearsal. There were few people about and no vidster newshounds to leap on him unawares with their pesky personal questions, usually about his love life and when he was going to dance again with his young sibling, both types of questions annoying to one of Merculian's greatest dancers. Triani was still not completely used to having a sibling at all, let alone one who was a subject of as much curiosity as he was himself.

Triani paused to check his messages as a short figure came rushing out of the narrow entrance to the Labyrinth, pursued by another figure shouting at him to come back. Triani's grin turned to a frown when the first runner turned round, saw him and rushed right at him.

"Holy shit, Rio! What are you doing here?"

"What do you think? It's the Labyrinth, isn't it? But he wants to be paid for sex! That's not right, is it?" Rio was indignant, tossing back his dark curls and drawing himself up to his full height, which was not very tall, although he was almost to Triani's shoulder.

"For fuck's sake! This is the north end. It's called the Back Door and people coming here expect to pay."

"Why?" His young sibling looked genuinely perplexed. Coming so recently from the Colony Planet, he still had a lot to learn about living in the capital.

By now the other young Merculian had caught up to them and stood there, waiting. He obviously recognized one of the planet's greatest dancers, but he said nothing, only bowing when Triani looked at him.

The dancer sighed in exasperation. He didn't have time for this. "Look, it's mostly much older people coming here to be with young people. They pay to get what they want with no strings. You should have come in the front way, where the signs are." Triani looked at the youth, who on closer inspection was probably younger than Rio by a few years but obviously street-wise, as he himself had been at that age, when he was doing exactly the same thing to provide the luxuries he craved. "Sorry, kid. He's had a very sheltered life up to now."

"I didn't know he was a virgin," the kid said.

"I am not!" said Rio indignantly.

The kid just smiled.

Triani took off two bangles and handed them over. Before he let go, he said quietly, "It was good for him?"

"Very good, *chai.*"

Triani released the bracelets and turned away. "Look, I've got a rehearsal, Rio. Try not to get in any more trouble."

"I have an audition."

"For a paying role?"

"Of course! I'm a professional! Honestly, Triani, all you think about is credits."

"Holy shit! Somebody has to! And don't tell me you have credits. Who paid for your sex just now?"

"Shit, Triani! I didn't know, okay?"

"Front entrance from now on. Save credits." He strode off towards the theater without a backward glance, fingering his new necklace.

By the time he arrived at the theater, he had forgotten his momentary spurt of anger at Rio and was concentrating on this afternoon's rehearsal for his role as the Night Bird in the new production. He had been skeptical of the hot new director everyone was talking about, and sure enough, right away he had caused a furor among the principals by announcing they would all be switching partners and, also, they would have to share their roles with another dancer—one night on, one night off. This was not the custom here. Eulio was furious but Triani didn't really mind, especially about switching partners, until he found out he was paired with Alesio, the willowy red head he had teased so mercilessly when he had joined the company years ago. Alesio had terrible stage fright. Once he got onstage, he was fine, but that initial quivering near-tears state Alesio went through in the wings every single time exasperated Triani and this just made things worse.

After that little bombshell, however, Evalindo was making all the right moves and he was handling the big names like himself, Eulio, and Lumasine with an impressive mixture of diplomacy and respect, starting with the initial meeting with each of them individually when he had been charm itself, combined with an encyclopedic knowledge of each dancer's awards, repertoire, gala events, and quirks of style.

Except for his first greeting to Triani.

"I grew up enthralled with your artistry," he had exclaimed, in his dramatic way, his steepled hands held just under his chin.

Triani leaned back and smiled. "Does that line ever work for you, sweetie? You know, by the time you'd have had the rare chance to be enthralled by any part of me, you'd be well past your growing days."

And the director had covered his face and laughed and apologized and asked him his opinion of the new costumes.

They said that Evalindo had desperately wanted to be a dancer in his youth, but his body would not cooperate. He had wide shoulders, a heavy torso and short legs and lived in constant fear of getting ill. He habitually wore a warm scarf wrapped around his neck and pinned with a large silver broach in the shape of a E studded with crystals. He also wore fingerless gloves and woolen leggings in bright colors that matched the scarves. As a director, though, he was that rare breed who did it all: designed the set, the costumes, the lighting, and picked the choreographer to work with whose style would fit his vision.

Triani was under no illusions about him but after the first few bumps he hadn't had any real trouble, each of them testing each other out carefully as they went along.

Triani had just entered by the stage door when the director himself appeared. "My dear Triani, how lucky to run into you! Could you spare a few moments?"

"Sure, sweetie. What's up?" Triani leaned against the wall.

"I feel so lucky being able to work with you! You know that."

"And?"

"And I have just one teensy request. You know how hard I'm trying to get the right look and feel for my vision. You're a major part of that. You are a near perfect Night Bird, my dear Triani." He paused.

"*Near* perfect?" drawled Triani.

Evalindo's sensual mouth curved into a slow smile. "In our art form can anything be perfect?"

Triani shrugged. He wondered what all this was leading up to. Evalindo wanted something and he wanted it badly. Triani spotted a light sheen of sweat on the other's upper lip.

"I'm trying for a sleek production and need to trim a bit here and there. I've already talked to a few of the others and we're all in agreement. So I suggest leaving out your solo after the second Red Bird dance in act two and not repeating the trio at the end of act one. That will move things along beautifully." He smiled again, his intense grey eyes completely concentrated on the dancer.

Triani straightened up. "So you're all in agreement about my time on stage?"

"No, no!" Evalindo stepped back, patting the air in a conciliatory gesture.

"Look, just because I've been all sweetness and light with you up to now, don't think you can take liberties with me, sweetie! Cut someone else's time but don't mess with mine."

"I didn't mean–"

"Yes, you did. If you want to claim time for your new sex buddy Foraline, that cutie in the chorus I've seen you with, do it from someone else. And one more thing. Fori isn't worth it. He's enthusiastic in bed, take it from me, but he has fluff for brains!"

Triani walked away from the stunned Evalindo and made for his dressing room.

He was almost there when Eulio waylaid him and pulled him inside. "The most awful thing has happened," Eulio breathed.

"You're damn right! That so-called genius director tried to cut one of my solos! He's a sly fucker."

"What? Wait. Tell me later. I've–You've got to promise not to tell anyone what I'm about to tell you! Not even Parla!"

"What are you talking about?"

"You've got to promise."

"Okay, okay. I promise."

Eulio was wringing his hands and walking back and forth in a way that was quite unlike him. "You remember that old 2-D painting of the female dancers the Terran ambassador gave us for a wedding present?"

"Vividly. It takes a bit of getting used to, but I like it, in a weird sort of way. What about it?"

"It's gone," Eulio whispered.

"Gone? As in not there?"

"This isn't funny! Someone stole it!"

"Holy shit. Why?"

"Exactly. Orosin is deathly afraid of this causing a diplomatic problem."

"So he's given up pretending he has no direct connection to the diplomatic corps, has he?"

"That's not helpful."

"Look, sweetie, why don't you call that chubby Regulator. What's his name? Marlo. Why not call him? He's proved he can be discreet."

"I did that already."

"Then what do you want from me?"

"Sympathy."

"Sweetie, I've got my own troubles."

"It's always about you, isn't it!" Eulio sniffed and stomped out.

Triani closed the door behind him and began looking for his rehearsal tights. Eulio often overreacted, he thought. He had no children, and he was married, so no worries there. A spouse was the last thing Triani wanted but it would be nice to have his problems solved as easily as Eulio's seemed to be. Sometimes Triani thought that if Eulio wasn't his best friend he would really dislike the *conte* Eulio Chazin Adelantis.

FOUR

Beny had been staring at the oblong red box with the Merculian state crest in the middle for more than fifteen minutes. Every now and then he would turn away, muttering to himself, but he never went far, and he always came back.

"Bloody damn," he said loudly, staring at the box again. "This can't be good!" But there was no way to send a Government message box back to sender. He glimpsed Dhakan crossing the courtyard with someone he didn't recognize but resisted the urge to call out to him. No one should be present when a Government box was opened. And open it he must. He closed the door, took a deep breath and placed his hand over the crest. The box began to vibrate. He snatched his hand away just in time before it sprang open, and a bright beam of light hit the ceiling, releasing a hologram image of an older Merculian in a long red tunic, black stockings, and red shoes. He wore a sparkling dagger at his waist and a large slouch hat with a rosette on one side.

"Orosin At'hali Benvolini. May blessings shine on you." A small hand sketched a circle in the air.

Beny stepped back, almost as if trying to avoid the hand. Not sure how or even if to respond, he said nothing.

"As you may know," the figure went on, "the InterPlanetary Alliance is experiencing problems with one of the freeports under their aegis. Station 59XD32, known as Rozemar, needs a negotiating team to settle some disputes between the Terrans, Merculians, and some late arrivals from Eksaverria. Because of your sterling record, we are appointing you as a second for this team."

"Sterling record!" shouted Beny, unable to contain himself. "Come on!"

"You have been successful acting on our behalf before. We

need you again. To make your answer known to us, you will speak now."

"No," said Beny, promptly. "I do not wish to go. A second gets all the blame, for one thing, and besides, I just got married. And I have work to do here. Musician's work."

There was a moment of silence. Then a clicking sound.

"That is a great pity," the figure said. And then it vanished and the box itself collapsed and disappeared in a flash of light.

"Bloody damn," said Beny, sitting down. He had been making use of his diplomatic connections for years, listening in on chatter he had no right to hear, commenting on things he had no right to know. This was the result. "I should have known better." But at least they knew now that he wasn't interested.

He wished Eulio was home, but he was at the theater where apparently some of the principal dancers were still having problems with the new director. He would hear all about it soon enough.

Thinking of Eulio reminded him that his spouse was still receiving those vaguely threatening notes. One more had arrived after the performance last night, but again Eulio had refused to report it. Maybe Marlo would take care of that, too. Beny needed action after the strain of the message box. He dug out is com-dev and punched in Marlo's code.

He caught the Regulator on his way back to HQ, but he agreed to drop by as soon as Beny mentioned the painting. Apparently a possible diplomatic rift with Terra if the painting was not found had more weight in Marlo's mind than any number of vague threats, Beny thought bitterly.

Dhakan, who came in halfway through the discussion, made grunting noises of disapproval. "The Regulator should see threats are more important than a piece of missing property," he said at once when Beny put away his com-dev.

"This painting represents more than just 'a piece of missing property.' I'll show him the notes when he gets here, though," Beny reassured him. "By the way, who was that I saw you with a moment ago?"

Dhakan looked down, his copper eyes troubled. "I am sorry. I should have asked permission before—"

"No, no. If it's a friend of yours, he's welcome. This is your home, too." Beny put his arm over Dhakan's broad shoulders in a gesture of comfort and sensed the embarrassment and anxiety the man was feeling.

"I wanted to introduce her the day you arrived home early, but she is shy."

Beny smiled. So, he *had* seen someone scuttle out through the side garden. And *she*. Was that just a slip of the tongue? Perhaps it was just how Dhakan saw the person or was she really a she and not Merculian? "We're just glad you've finally found someone," he said at last. It must be a sexual sort of friend, taking into account the man's deep embarrassment.

"Thank you. You have done so much for me. Leading me into your beautiful world—"

"Please, that was years ago. This is your world now."

Dhakan had calmed down enough by the time Marlo arrived to bring a tray of snacks and then went back to fixing the food synthesizer.

"I have nothing new to report about the painting, I'm afraid," Marlo said, choosing a pink biscuit from the tray beside him. "On the way over, I just heard that one of my team has a lead, but it might not pan out as we hope."

"I know you're working on it, Marlo, and you know how important it is. What I wanted to talk about is—well, these." He spread out the messages on the table, pushing the tray aside as he did so. "I see these as veiled threats. Six of them now. Eulio won't take them seriously and doesn't want to report them. What do you think?"

Marlo studied each of the dark poetic messages with a frown. He reached out for another biscuit absently, then read the notes again.

"One of them even arrived when we were at the Music Festival," Beny said, watching Marlo anxiously. "He followed Eulio to Darsona!"

"Definitely a stalker," Marlo said, "and definitely the same person. Look how similar the phrasing is—here—and here—but it's hard to say how serious a threat he is. It could just be he wants to be noticed."

"I'm noticing him all right!" exclaimed Beny.

Marlo smiled. "Not by you."

"Of course not. So what will he do if Eulio keeps ignoring him?"

"That's hard to say." Marlo picked up one of the message cards again. "I don't see how we could find out who it is. These things are really untraceable, unlike contact messages, say, and Eulio and you have both handled them quite a bit."

Beny sighed. "So you can't do anything?"

Marlo glanced at the tray and, apparently realizing there were no more pink biscuits, looked away. "I'll see if I can get permission to set up a surveillance cam inside the theater. We might be able to tell who throws the messages and check them out. It's a long shot but it's all I can think of at the moment."

"Thank you, Marlo. It's comforting to think something's being done. And of course, you'll keep working on the painting situation. There isn't much time before the reception. If it's not here...well, many important government people are coming. No one must be embarrassed."

"I understand. I'll be in touch the instant there's any encouraging news."

Beny watched him go with a frown. Did the Regulator really understand the importance of getting the bloody damn thing back? "I wish off-worlders would read the Merculian Manual before coming here," he muttered. "It clearly states no wedding presents!"

FIVE

Most of the soloists with the Merculian National Dance Company were gathered in the small rehearsal hall, sitting on the floor or against the wall, wrapped in colorful shawls and legwarmers. Triani sank down between Durina and Eulio and rubbed his left calf muscle to ease a cramp.

"What's this shit all about? Has Evalindo pulled some other stunt?"

"Not with me." Eulio was sewing elastic on a dance shoe. Cutting the thread with his teeth, he began on the next one.

"He has with me." Durina wrapped cotton around his big toe. "He insists on me doing that added business at the end of act one even though now it makes no sense, since he cut the scene before."

"Did you hear what he tried to pull on Triani?" Alesio looked around brightly.

"Everyone's heard about that."

"Yeah," said Lumasine. "The shit tried to get me to agree to cut one of my solos by saying Triani was doing it."

"He told you I'd agreed?" said Triani incredulously.

"Well, he implied it. The thing is, I know you too well to fall for it."

Triani laughed.

The door opened and Nevon walked in, rubbing his hands in a way Triani recognized. He was nervous.

The chatter stopped at once as they all looked at the theater's managing director expectantly.

"It's nice to see all you soloists together for a change," Nevon began with a wide smile. "Due to the large cast for this production, with everyone rehearsing in different places, I haven't had a chance to drop in on you individually the way I like to. I called you all here today just to check in and make sure everything's going well."

"Just peachy," said Triani.

"If you have any problems, anything that isn't working out for you about the production, please come to me directly." He paused and looked around at the raised faces.

"Oh yes. What a good idea," muttered Eulio, flinging a shoe into his dance bag.

Durina started to stand up, but Triani pulled him down. "Don't be an idiot, sweetie. You can't win this one."

"I'm told the set will be arriving later today so the loading dock and that whole area back there are off limits until further notice. As you can tell from the model, parts of it are huge, so keep out of the way for your own safety. On another subject," Nevon went on, ignoring Durina, who was still trying to get his attention, "I just want to add something about tonight's performance. By special agreement, there will be float cams in the theater. They might be there for several nights. Don't let them distract you."

"What are they for?" Alesio asked, instantly alert. His stage fright was well known and anything different would be bound to upset him.

"Don't worry, Alesio. It's nothing to do with the stage. They'll be trained on the audience. Some kind of security check thing I was told. So, that's it from me." He waved a hand in dismissal.

As they all filed out, Nevon called Triani over. "A quick word," he said, turning away from the stragglers.

Triani dropped his dance bag. "Did I say anything against the precious genius?"

"Not yet, no. But it's not about that. He wants to bring in about ten youngsters to join the chorus. Most of them have just graduated or are about to."

"Chories."

"Exactly. Keep your hands off them."

"What?"

"You heard me, Triani! I don't want a repeat performance of what happened two years ago."

"He was NOT underage!" spluttered Triani. "His parents were just overprotective busybodies!"

"Maybe, but mark my words if this happens again, there will be hell to pay."

"Holy shit, Nev! What if I have to dance with one of the little dears?"

"Dance, not sex."

Triani raised an eyebrow. "Dance, not sex. Got it."

"By the way, someone left this for you at the stage door." Nevon handed over a bangle with a large yellow jewel dangling from it.

Triani slipped it on. "Pretty. No note?"

"Nothing."

"Let's hope the adoring fan is of age, sweetie." Triani grinned and strode out of the room, humming the theme from *The Night Bird*.

That evening Triani and Eulio danced their way through another performance of *Prindi Nan*, a production they had danced many times before. The crowd loved it, deluging them with flower garlands and mini messages tied up in ribbons. Triani was beginning to think a reimagining of this one might be a relief as he walked off stage, his arms full of flowers.

Parla, his gorgeous lover, was waiting for him in the large, beautifully appointed star dressing room. He was Eulio's cousin but had not been a real dance fan until seeing Triani across the room at lunch one day at The Terrace over a year ago.

"I took Giazin on a tour of the Terran art show this afternoon," he said as Triani came in and threw himself into his favorite armchair.

"Why?"

"He wanted to see the flat paintings some of the other kids were talking about at school, and Govsy had a day off."

"Shit, Parla, he's only seven."

Triani's dresser helped him out of his costume. "I saw that exhibition last week," he said, shaking out the red spangled shift. "I thought it was weirdly fascinating."

"So did Giazin," Parla said, and they all laughed.

"Maybe I should take a look at this stuff." Triani thrust his throbbing feet into the bucket of soothing 'blue goo' and began taking off his exaggerated stage make-up. "You want to go again next week, Parla?"

"Certainly. But I have to leave now, remember? My parents are home finally and the whole family is gathering. I'll stay in the city tonight."

Triani pulled his lover's face close and kissed him good-bye. "See you."

He was trying to remember what Parla's parents looked like as he wiped off the last of the makeup. He had met them a few times but always felt slightly ill at ease with them. Damn First Order Merculians, even if one was his best friend and another his lover. His street kid background would always be a hidden barrier that kept him from being fully at ease.

Hearing a gentle clapping at the door, he called out, "Five more minutes!" and began to repair his face, concealing lines of fatigue and putting back color to his cheeks and lips. He pulled on the tight black satin pants, his purple silk blouse. A wide silver belt cinched in his narrow waist. As a final touch, he snapped a small black lace ruff around his neck and slipped on his flashy rings and the new bangle.

At last, he nodded to his dresser to open the door, letting in a chattering group of his admiring fans, all of them feeling very special at being allowed to visit with their adored star dancer for a few minutes.

At the back but head and shoulders above the crowd of Merculians, an arresting blond Terran male watched Triani with intent grey eyes. The dance star was always generous with his fans, spending a lot more time with them than many other big names of the dance world. But tonight it was harder than usual, his mind on the interesting Terran, who appeared to be hanging back. Triani kept sending him encouraging smiles and winks until at last, the man was in front of him.

"A very interesting night," the man said, sitting down on the other chair. "This was my first introduction to Merculian dance and I'm a convert."

"What exactly did I convert you from?" Triani leaned over and laid a hand on the man's chest, picking up the usual feelings of curiosity about dual-gendered Merculians. And something else he couldn't quite place.

The man laughed, a series of loud booming sounds. "Guess that was the wrong word. Anyhow, I liked it a lot."

"I think I like you a lot, too, sweetie. Want a drink?" He picked up a bottle of Crushed Emeralds and poured two glasses, holding one out to the Terran so he could hear the singing sound the expensive drink made as it settled.

"My name's Max Kolinski. I'm a dancer, too, back on Terra. A ballet dancer."

"So that accounts for all those muscles." Triani ran an appreciative hand down the man's arm and onto his thigh.

Max moved back and tossed down the Crushed Emeralds in one long swallow. "Thanks for the drink but my friends are waiting for me outside. Perhaps we can talk later? Have coffee or something? Here's my contact info." He dropped a card on the table.

Triani glanced at it. "Coffee?" Obviously Max didn't know the effect of coffee on Merculians. "Look, sweetie, I've got a better idea. How would you like to come with me to a reception on Friday? There's supposed to be an old Terran painting there on display and lots of interesting people. Then afterwards we can get away somewhere private and get to know each other better."

"Sure. Sounds good." Max stood up.

So did Triani. Although he was tall for a Merculian, he barely came up to Max's shoulder. He tried to lean against the man for a moment, but the Terran turned away. "See you, Friday," he called over his shoulder and disappeared. Triani shrugged and picked up the info card. At least he would have a chance to get a lot closer on Friday and arouse the apparently sleeping fires of the handsome blond dancer from Terra. And *he* was definitely not underage.

SIX

Marlo was not pleased with the way things were going. He now had a second case featuring the Adelantis-Benvolini couple and he hadn't even solved the first one. He was almost out of breath as he reached the investigative unit, having taken the time to pay a quick visit to his friend Euvi on the Drugged Drunk and Disorderly unit.

"Found Cushna yet?" he asked, tucking up a sleeve he just noticed was unravelling.

"More by good luck than anything else," said Eldred. "He's in the quizzer. You want me to start?"

"No. Let him stew for a while longer." Marlo went into his office and sat down, staring out the window. Do whatever needs to be done, his boss had said. Marlo put one hand in his pocket and winced, feeling the soft bag of alien bubble dust he had just picked up from his friend in the DDD. He had never done anything like this before. Even the thought of what he was about to do was frightening. It was crossing a line he had only played with before. But apparently, if that damn painting wasn't found and returned at once, it could become one of those events that has far-flung and deadly serious consequences. He knew Cushna must know something about it, tied into Big Stendi's network as closely as he was. Even if Stendi wasn't mixed up in it, Cushna had to know something. He was the only one Marlo could count on to have the all-important information. Marlo had to get it any way he could.

He took his hand out of his pocket and stood up. Through his door he could see his boss's office and had the fleeting thought that he should bring him up to date on what he was about to do. He soon thought better of it. Even Old Livid wouldn't approve of what he had in mind. As Marlo made his way down to the quizzer, he felt slightly queasy. He stood in front of the one-way glass and studied the dapper thief.

Marlo wasn't sure of Cushna's exact age, but he was no naïve youngster. He had never been actually charged with anything, since he always managed to wiggle out of it somehow, usually trading information for his freedom. He was successful in his dubious occupation partly due to his stylish good looks. Today his long blond hair was neatly brushed to the side as usual, and he wore a well-tailored short jacket over his sparkling white tunic. His manicured hands were bereft of rings, probably so nothing would snag as he withdrew some valuables from someone's pocket. There was nothing flashy about him. He aimed to fit in.

Marlo felt the bag of drugs in his pocket again and sighed. He touched the glass and the door opened before him.

"Nah! What for ya want me, ya razzer?" Cushna said at once, in his thick nasal River District accent. "Lucky sticks I'm not on the clock fer ya!"

Marlo said nothing. He was used to the accent and the slang, unlike some of the younger investigators who were at a loss half the time, which was, of course, the point of it all. He sat down and surreptitiously entered the code to shut off all recording and viewing equipment. Then he leaned back in his chair and stared at Cushna.

"Nah! Lost yer talker?"

"Tell me what's going on in the River District these days," Marlo began conversationally.

Cushna shrugged. "Same old, codgia."

"No. It's not. I think someone's moving in on Big Stendi."

Cushna shrugged again. "No figgers what's on with you, razzer."

But his eyes were now a little wary.

"I don't give a flying fart about our mutual friend and his battles. What I care about right now is a stolen Terran painting. What do you 'figger' about that?"

"Nah, swerve it off, Marlo! I never!"

"I know you didn't take it. All I care about is—" Marlo took a deep breath. "Where is the damn thing?"

Cushna raised his eyebrows and stared back at Marlo.

"There isn't much that goes on down there that you aren't aware of," Marlo went on, his voice rising. "Pay attention. You're a villain who's often in the hold, without a record at the moment but if you don't tell me what I need to know, you'll be a villain in the hold *with* a pending record. Understand?"

Cushna studied Marlo, his head on one side. He wasn't used to this line of questioning and was obviously not convinced Marlo would follow through on his oblique threat.

He shook his head. "Nah. Tha's fog right there."

Marlo put his hand in the pocket of his tunic, slowly pulled out the bag of drugs and set it on the table in front of Cushna.

The thief paled. "Nah! Nah! You're thirsty, Marlo! Not mine and ya knows'er!" He appealed to the glass behind Marlo, assuming there were people watching.

Marlo felt a twinge of guilt but pushed the drugs closer.

Cushna sat on his hands. "Nah!"

"Who are the courts going to believe, Cushna?" Marlo said softly. "A known thief with an arrest record as long as your arm or a class A investigative Regulator like me? Just think about that for a few minutes." Marlo picked up the drugs and left the room.

Once outside, he stood and leaned his forehead against the wall for a few moments. He felt sick to his stomach and wished he hadn't eaten all those pink biscuits at Beny's. Hearing someone else enter the small room, he turned around.

"What are you doing, Marlo?" Oslani gestured to the opaque wall which should show Cushna in the quizzer on the other side.

"I have to find the damn thing before the higher-ups start riding me out the door."

"And the rules?"

"This is political, Oslani. There are no rules, remember?"

"Guess I missed that part in training. How can I help?"

Marlo threw his arms around his friend. "Thanks," he said, drawing away again. "You just did."

"By the way, I didn't get a chance to tell you something Liola said when I was questioning him earlier. He thinks there's an artist group of Terrans working in the River District. He says the small group has a stall in the ExPat Market where they sell the things to stock the new fad. He says they store the paintings in tubes. Not sure how that will help since it's not about an old painting," He shrugged.

"But it's the first actual eyewitness news about any painting at all. That's a start." Marlo took a deep breath and went back into the quizzer.

Cushna seemed to have shrunken. His face looked pinched.

Marlo sat down and pushed the bag of drugs across the table.

"I jus' slip the small stuff," Cushna said plaintively, recoiling as if from a poisonous snake.

Marlo said nothing.

"You do this, not jist the razz be against me but equal, my own crew."

"So talk."

"Don't…" His eyes filled with tears.

Marlo turned away to hide his own feelings.

Cushna sniffled. "Could be I hear maybe…something real snaps among the pipes under the Dragon bridge but is just chitters."

"How snaps?"

The thief shrugged. "Shiny." The fight seemed to have gone out of him.

A few minutes later, Marlo left the quizzer with a sketch, a kind of treasure map as it turned out, leading to the long disused water pipes under the old Dragon bridge.

There were more pipes here then Marlo was expecting, and in every one he and Eldred and Oslani found something of value, presentation daggers, hair ornaments, jeweled combs, even a few credit rings. Eventually Oslani found it—a long tube curled up in one of the bigger pipes.

Marlo breathed a sigh of relief. "Take the small paintings back to HQ. I'll be there in an hour." He rinsed his hands in the river and dried them on his tunic.

Twenty minutes later, he stood in front of Beny, somewhat rumpled but with the scroll of canvas in his arms. His emblem of office hung round his neck recording it all. "Could you please take a look and verify that this is, indeed, the painting that was stolen? We just need it official." He handed it over and watched as Beny unrolled it, with the help of Dhakan.

"Thank you, Marlo!" Beny exclaimed, relief in every syllable. "You have no idea how grateful I am! You're a hero! Please join me for some wine and biscuits to celebrate! You can tell me all about it."

Marlo shook his head. "I'm sorry but I can't do that, *chai*. I can't stay.' A hero doesn't threaten another Merculian with false charges that would get him ostracized by his own people or even worse, just to get a piece of canvas back in time for a party. It was all Marlo could do to keep himself from running out of the house.

SEVEN

It was late afternoon and the music balloons that Beny had spent hours tuning, swung in the gentle breeze, spilling out their merry greeting as the brightly dressed guests in their silks and satins and sparkling jewels passed by on the walkway up to the Adelantis-Benvolini home. It was supposed to be a small affair but as often happened when Eulio was in charge of the invitations, the list had grown longer, apparently of its own accord. By now, neither of them was quite sure who might arrive. Beny didn't mind. They both enjoyed parties. His only real care was to make sure the Terran Ambassador saw the bloody damn painting hanging in its place of honor, at least for today.

Many of the dancers invited arrived early and gathered in front of the painting in curious groups. Most shook their heads in confusion, but they all wanted to take a look. Terran oil painting was much in vogue these days but not everyone had seen any samples. Once they had slaked their curiosity, they moved on and picked up the buzzers and tranq sticks set about conveniently in bowls and on moving serve-bots.

By the time the ambassador and his wife finally arrived, elegantly prepared finger food was making the rounds and Beny was helping the musicians tune their instruments. Eulio led his guests to the work of art.

"Well, isn't that something! It looks real good here." His Excellency Earl Johnson Wayburn rubbed his hands together as he stood in front of the painting and rocked back on his heels. "It's the wife who's the real art appreciator here. Right, honey?" He turned to the skinny bleached blonde beside him, who looked as if she had been sewn into some sort of red curtain material. She had her pointed nails painted the same shade of bright red and wore very high heels, which made her as tall as her very tall husband. Eulio was getting a crick in his neck looking up at them both. "Shari Lee organizes all kinds of charity balls to raise money for art stuff, right, honey? She's the one who found this little gem. Some collector had fallen on hard times and had to sell, so it was a great price, too. Glad you guys like it."

"It was an amazing gift," Eulio said, glancing at the drab thing, then back to the beaming ambassador.

"A little bird tells me your spouse is an ambassador, too, or was at one point," chirped Shari Lee.

Eulio wasn't sure how to answer this and looked around for help. He was relieved to see Beny rushing to his rescue.

"So glad to meet you again, Your Excellency, and Mrs. Wayburn." Beny shook hands in the Terran manner and began to steer their guests over to a group of diplomats who had just arrived. "I'm afraid your little bird heard an exaggerated rumor. I served a brief time as a cultural ambassador, not really important. Have you met Excellency Frandori Solinar Porferindo from the High Council of the Praetan?"

"Do I have to kiss his ring, like you do the pope, hon?" Shari Lee half-whispered to her husband.

"That won't be necessary," said Beny quickly.

Eulio breathed a sigh of relief as he turned away, glad to leave Beny in charge of the Terrans and began to make his way through the chattering guests, exchanging a few words with everyone before passing on. Wondering why the flow of delicacies that had been so carefully prepared was no longer in sight, he went looking for Dhakan. It was unlike him to let this sort of thing happen. Thinking he may have been taking a break in his own quarters, Eulio checked there and was disconcerted to hear soft snores emanating from the sleeping chamber.

"Dhakan? What's wrong?" he said, moving closer. But the one curled up in the bed wasn't the stocky Kolari, but a slight Merculian with masses of fine reddish-blond hair. He looked very flushed and seemed to be sweating. Was this the shy friend Beny had mentioned? Eulio was just about to withdraw when Dhakan rushed in.

"I think your friend is sick," Eulio whispered. "We should call the healer."

"Oh, my, no. Please! She wants no fuss. Just to rest a while before she leaves." Dhakan closed the door softly behind them. "I was just fixing the serve-bot circuit," he went on, moving away from the chamber. "Is fine now. All will be fine with the evening."

"Thanks, Dhakan." Eulio decided to wait until after the party to contact anyone about the sick friend.

The reception was in full swing by the time Triani arrived, his hand clasping the large hand of the Terran male dancer Max, who seemed amused by the situation. Eulio saw them coming and made his way over to greet them.

"You finally got here," Eulio said, laying one hand on his partner's arm, the other on Max.

"Well, sweetie, we were delayed for a while, checking out a few dance moves." Triani winked.

Max laughed. "Our technique is quite different in ballet."

"I'm sure it is," said Beny smoothly, joining them.

"I'm sure the technique you're interested in has little to do with ballet," Eulio murmured to Triani.

"I have many interests, sweetie. So where is the main attraction? As it turns out, Max is a great authority on the artist. What's his name again?"

"Augustine Dégalas. My mom used to drag me to galleries all the time when I was a kid. She's an art restorer, and I was actually an art student for a while myself. She worked on some of Dégalas' stuff, if I remember right. He did a lot of paintings of dancers backstage or waiting in the wings."

"Sounds like ours. It's through here."

By now, most people had drifted off to the main courtyard where a group of Beny's friends were playing. Beny had spent some time transcribing a few popular Terran dance tunes for the event and the Ambassador and his wife were dancing to one of them. Only three Merculians were standing in front of the masterpiece. They stopped talking and moved away as Eulio approached. He had the feeling they had not been saying nice things about the art.

Max stood and stared at it for a long time. Triani began to

fidget, glancing towards the courtyard. He grabbed two glasses of wine as a serve-bot glided by.

"Cheer up and have a drink," he said, handing one to Max. "It's not that gloomy."

"It's not a Dégalas," said Max.

Eulio stiffened and glanced around. No one had heard. "Keep your voice down," he pleaded.

"I'm sorry, but it's not. I don't know what the hell it is."

"What do you mean?" asked Eulio, beginning to sweat.

"It's...weird. The brush strokes are pretty good. Could fool any casual observer, but it's too dark, too much varnish and craquelure. And that's not even the main problem. Just look at the dancers. They're supposed to be ballet dancers, like me. All the right costumes, long white net dresses for the girls and the guy in the background is dressed right. But some of the ballet positions are slightly wrong. And the anatomy is a little off. No dancer in my world could do what that one is doing." He pointed to the male. "Our bodies aren't that flexible.'"

Triani studied the pose and then recreated it. "Not hard," he said casually, jumping to his feet.

"Exactly. Not hard for you, but I couldn't do that." He tried to demonstrate and fell over backwards in an ungainly sprawl.

Beny and several others came running. "Are you all right? What happened?"

"He tried to do a dance move I can do," Triani said. "That's all. A little competition, sweetie, and I won," he added smugly.

Eulio grabbed Beny and held his hand, letting him feel his consternation.

"Let's all go back and do a few dance moves of our own," Beny suggested to the several guests who had followed him.

Once they were back and happily dancing, Beny returned. "What the bloody damn is going on?" he whispered.

"He thinks the painting is a fake," Eulio whispered back, pointing at Max.

"The models are Merculian, I suspect, although the artist has hidden it well," Max said. "Basically, it's a fraud."

"Bloody damn! This is even worse than losing it in the first place!"

They were silent for a few moments, staring at the painting. "The question is," Beny said quietly, "did the ambassador give us a fraudulent painting or was the real one exchanged for a fake?"

"No, no," Eulio breathed. "The question is, what do we do now?"

"We'll talk about it later."

EIGHT

After the reception, Triani was looking forward to taking Max out for a late dinner and then carrying on to his apartment. He had even considered luring him to his country house but remembered in time that Parla would probably be there, and his lover had only so much tolerance for this sort of thing. Besides, Parla was drop dead gorgeous and might stir up the embers of the man's lust in totally the wrong direction.

But the two only made it as far as Triani's air-car when Max asked to be let off near the ExPat District.

"Do I look like a taxi service to you, sweetie?" Triani demanded truculently, shoving a group of jeweled bangles up one arm.

Max leaned against the air-car's sparkling fender. "I guess I deserved that. Not my night, is it? First I accuse the ambassador of giving your friends a fake painting as a wedding gift, then I insult you. Sorry. I should have told you I have a date for later on with some friends."

"Yeah, you should have." Triani hopped into the car and slid the door open for Max. "Fuck it. Get in."

Max grinned wider and jumped in beside him. "Thanks. Look, are you dancing Sunday night?"

Triani perked up. Perhaps he was getting somewhere after all. "What have you got in mind?"

"Do you know what a 'flash' is?"

"A kind of secret party Terrans organize from time to time, right? I've heard rumors. You inviting me?" Triani was already scheming how he could leave the theater early.

"It's an afterhours event and there's one tomorrow night." Max dug a yellow-gold bracelet out of his pocket and handed it to Triani. "This will get you in. You can't tell anyone, though. Got it?"

"Got it."

"I'll send you the location when I get it. So, we're good?"

"More than good, sweetie." Triani was so intrigued by the illicit event with its hint of danger he would have forgiven Max for just about anything.

The more Triani thought about Max, the more he became interested in the man as a dancer. How different was this art Max was devoting his life to? The next day he spent hours studying rare clips of Terran classical ballet he had discovered in the theater archives, one of them with Max dancing a major role. He was, apparently, very well-known in his world, although why Triani was so surprised he didn't know. He knew Max's dance company was returning to Terra after being on tour and no one sends their second-string performers on the road.

What he saw was mesmerizing. It was similar, yet completely different. Even the music was different, though tuneful once he got used to it. He decided to concentrate on one short solo Max performed and he watched it in slow motion, jotting down rough choreography notes and then trying to duplicate what he had seen. It took a long frustrating time, because the whole thing was so different. When he finally got through the four minutes he was not satisfied. The image of himself doing the dance still didn't look right, and he had no clear idea how to fix it since he really didn't understand the technique. It was frustrating because he was usually a quick study and could have learned this short piece in a few minutes if it were a Merculian style dance.

He sat on the floor, staring at the leaping images: the lithe, graceful females dancing across the stage on tip toe in their odd, long pink shoes and the muscular males springing after them, lifting them into the air with such ease. Shutting off the music, he pulled his com-dev out of his dance bag and punched in the contact for Max. He needed to know more about this alien dance form. No one else here would have that specialized knowledge.

To his surprise, Max agreed to drop over to the theater and appeared half an hour later ready to work. He pulled off his sweatshirt and loose pants, revealing a faded T-shirt and black tights underneath. Then he slipped on a pair of dance shoes.

"You actually tried to dance that solo?" Max said, pointing to his own image projected on the wall. "I think you might do better with one of the ballerina roles."

Triani frowned. "I thought of that, but they seem to have special shoes or something, so I guess I can't."

"Yeah. Show me what you did."

Triani ran what he considered his best rendition of the dance and they watched in silence.

"Wow," said Max when it had finished. "Just wow. It ain't ballet but it's impressive."

"Thanks, but why isn't it ballet?"

"It's hard to explain." Max took a deep breath. "Okay, look. See that position?" He paused his own image, leaping, back arched, arms above his head, legs to the side.

"I did that."

"Yeah, but everything you do is really exaggerated because your Merculian body is so much more flexible than mine, so it's closer to your style of dance, judging from what I saw the other night. Look." He brought up the same position with Triani doing it, only the Merculian's body bent back so far his head was much closer to his feet, his arms almost perpendicular to the floor.

"It looks better to me," Triani said, studying the images.

"Maybe so. I'm just saying it isn't ballet."

"It's the first time I've tried this."

"Hey, I'm not criticizing! I think it's awe-inspiring you can do this type of choreography at all let alone after just a few hours. Your leaps are higher than mine, too! Not fair." He grinned. "Let me see your foot."

Triani sat down opposite him and put one foot on the man's lap, nudging his crotch inquisitively.

"Stop that." Max took the foot firmly in both hands and felt the toes through the slipper. "This shoe is stiffened a bit at the toe."

"So? We do some toe-dancing from time to time. It helps."

"Your feet feel different from mine. Shorter in comparison

to the long legs, for example, so again, more like a ballerina. And they're really flexible, too! By the way, why are your shoes tied like that?'

Triani shrugged. "Tradition, I guess."

"What are you two doing?" Rio came into the room, curiosity shining in his dark eyes.

"Well, hello." Max got to his feet, smiling down at Rio with much too much interest, in Triani's opinion.

"I'm Rio Porvan Erlindo," he said, ignoring his sibling. He glanced at the images that still danced across the wall, dropped his shoulder bag and leapt into an approximation of what he saw.

"Not bad," said Max, clapping. "Let's try a *pas de deux*. Like, a duet for two dancers, okay?" He clicked the clip farther on to where he was dancing with a smiling ballerina. "Watch," he said. "Can you do something like that?"

"Show me again and slow it down." Rio slipped off his shoes and watched intently while putting on his dance slippers.

Triani was furious. The little shit had only come to the theater to have a session with the company Healer and now he was stealing the spotlight! Besides, this could be dangerous. Rio had not been dancing much recently because of his health. And dancing the female part, too, without the special shoes. Triani scowled. "Weren't you on your way someplace?"

"I've got time. Okay, Max, I'm ready." He held out his arms to the man and was swept up into a dramatic lift, faster, higher than any Merculian could possibly manage. Rio let out an audible gasp but managed a graceful twist on the downward sweep and reached the ground on the beat, ready to go into an approximation of the graceful turns seen in the clip. They finished with Rio leaping into Max's arms and up onto one broad shoulder.

Triani watched, seething. The little shit didn't look as good at this alien art form as he had, but Max was all smiles.

"You're really cute," Max said now, setting Rio down. "Too bad you don't have any pointe shoes like the girls wear or we could really get into it."

Rio beamed up at him. "Thanks. That was fun, but I have to go. I just came to say I have a date for dinner."

"Good riddance," Triani muttered.

"Wait up. I have to go, too." Max pulled on his top. "Maybe I can give you a lift somewhere? I have an air-cab waiting."

Suddenly left alone, Triani threw a music cube across the room. Anger churned inside, mixed with confusion. He was angry at Rio for interfering, but a small voice asked if he should be worried about his naïve young sibling. Should he find out who he'd been going out with lately? Triani was all Rio had. That thought made him angrier, but this time at the parent who had so thoughtlessly dropped them both in this situation abruptly six months ago and upended his way of life.

Rio had been born on the Colony Planet and was still learning about how to live on Merculian, let alone in the teaming capital city. And in spite of wearing the dagger from his recent coming of age ceremony, he was still naïve and had no street-smarts, witness his mistake at the Labyrinth. Even knowing this, Triani couldn't help feeling resentful of the added responsibility. His own youngster Giazin was enough to deal with!

He waved off the lights to the studio and made his way through the quiet corridors of the theater to his dressing room. The bracelet Max had given him for the party was still on his dressing table. Looking at it, Triani smiled, his anger fading away. It was all very mysterious and exciting. Thinking about what this might be like, Triani gathered up his things, threw on a long pale green coat and went over to the apartment he kept across the street to take a shower. Sunday night he would finally have Max to himself.

NINE

"**Y**ou are not a bad person, Marlo dear." Calian had been saying soothing things like this for an hour or so. He had finally convinced his depressed lover to come with him on a walk to pick up some *istician* for their dinner. "I need it if you want me to make my special stew. And I won't go without you," he added.

Marlo sighed and pulled on his shoes, an effort that left him short of breath. "How can you care about someone who did what I did the other day to a poor soul from the River District?"

"That 'poor soul' is an admitted thief who works for a known crime boss," Calian pointed out. "Do you want some of that cinnamon twist before we go?"

Marlo took the offered treat and followed him out the door of Calian's house. "I went against the Ethics Code," he said mournfully. He sniffed.

Calian handed him a handkerchief. "You were doing your job. And you were successful, so I think that's enough moaning, don't you? Let's go this way."

"I'm sorry, Cali. This must be so—" He stopped, staring at a wall covered with graffiti in bright red, yellow, and pink neon colors. Black symbols of some sort were scribbled in any open space. It hadn't been there yesterday when he arrived.

"That's kind of pretty," Calian said, stepping back to take in the whole effect. "There are patterns to it." He moved farther to the right. "Look. Seen from this angle it looks almost three dimensional."

Marlo was peering closely at one of the black symbols. "This stuff is popping up all over town," he remarked. "I'm sure it means something, and something not good. These symbols all look very similar."

"You are such a pessimist!" Calian laughed. "Maybe they're just art student doodles?"

"Why now? Why are they appearing now and not earlier?" He took a picture of the wall. "For my collection," he said, but Calian had already turned to the open window of a spice shop.

While his lover checked out the spices on offer, Marlo continued to study the wall. He needed to see the others, to access all the tech he had available to him back at HQ so he could study them all together. He stuffed his handkerchief in his pocket and went after Calian.

"I need to get to work now, Cali," he said. "I'm sorry I've been so…well, no fun today."

"You were fun last night," Calian said, wrapping one arm around him as far as it would go. "By the way, you better change your socks. One of them is mine."

"Oh dear. Does it matter?"

"It wouldn't if they were the same color."

"Flying farts."

An hour later Marlo was hard at work, munching on the last cinnamon snack Calian had wrapped up for him as he peered intently at the graffiti images. He had tried everything he could think of, inverting them, turning them inside out, taking out the color, removing everything but the scribbly things, but nothing was coming together. Nevertheless, he was still convinced there was something there meant to be seen. Some statement or claim or even proclamation. Something!

"Still at it?" Eldred ambled into the team room and looked at the images. "It's all just nonsense. Bored youngsters following some new fad."

Marlo sat back and stretched his arms. "Maybe, but I don't think so. How's the float-cam image search coming along in the Adelantis case?"

Eldred shook his head and perched on the edge of the table. "It's pretty slow. I had no idea how many people throw those messages on stage in that theater. And it's nearly impossible to figure out who they're for!"

"Show me what you've got."

"Who says I've got anything?"

"You wouldn't be here if you didn't have something."

"Well, to be fair, it's Oslani who's got something."

Marlo hauled himself to his feet and followed Eldred next door where the others were still sifting through the float-cam feeds from the last few performances when Eulio was on stage.

Marlo sat down and studied the faces in the images. They were all shining with the joy of the recent shared experience. There were tears and open mouths and some even had their eyes closed. Flowers flew into the air, obscuring some of the faces as they moved past the cams and out of range.

"I should have ordered a few cams facing the stage," Marlo muttered. But it had been hard enough getting permission for these without saying why, and Beny had especially requested discretion. How he hated that word. "Fabulous," he muttered. This would take days, and even then they might not be any further ahead.

"Besides Eulio," he asked, "who were the stars performing that night who might get message ribbons?"

"Triani, Alesio, and Lumasine, mostly." Ever the dance fan, Ferdalin was quick off the mark with that answer.

"We figured out where they stood to take their bows," Oslani said. "Mostly by finding someone who was there and remembered." He grinned. "Very scientific."

"It'll do."

"Triani was far left, Eulio beside him, then Alesio and then the other one. So, we checked who was aiming for the left."

"Flying farts! That could just as well be for Triani!"

"No, no! I fixed that problem." Oslani pulled a flat box closer to him and tapped out a few keystrokes on top of it. "I coded a tracker graph to show the probable trajectory for each one. Sorry it's taken so long. It will only show a few at a time, to keep it as clear as possible. Let's hope it helps."

With the tap of a finger, the images were overlaid by a graph, tracing the path of a few of the messages as they flew through the air. It even showed an extension to the image where Oslani had sketched in the stage with stick figures representing the dancers, one of whom was hit in the head by a message.

Everyone laughed.

"I've seen that happen for real," Ferdalin said.

"So have I." Eldred smiled. "His Nibs was not pleased."

"Triani, I take it?"

Eldred nodded. "Look! I didn't think a Terran would throw message ribbons."

"Me neither." Oslani stopped the action.

Marlo studied the female Terran's face. Her perfect teeth, spikey black hair, and long dangly earrings. She was wearing a tight lowcut top with long sleeves which didn't hide her muscular arms. "Who was she aiming for?"

"Either Triani or Eulio. It fell between them."

"Too bad."

Oslani stopped the action again. "But these two fall right at Eulio's feet."

"Wait. I recognize them." Ferdalin stood up excitedly. "They're friends of my parents."

"I doubt either one of them is a stalker," Marlo pointed out.

Ferdalin sat down again, dejected.

Marlo sighed. "Thanks for this, Oslani. It'll still be a long list but a much more accurate one. And now we can cross those two off."

Oslani worked his magic and the two smiling Merculian dance fans disappeared from the image.

"Luckily it's only the ground floor seats that are close enough to throw messages and flowers," Ferdalin remarked.

"Can you cut that down by seeing only the repeaters who keep coming back over several nights?" Eldred suggested.

"You think we haven't thought of that?" snapped Oslani.

"Well, keep going." Marlo got to his feet slowly. "I'll contact the theater to see if it's possible to match names with seat numbers. Also, somebody there might recognize the faces we come up with. We'll get there."

And then what? he wondered. So what if it is a Terran female? What could they do to someone who follows their favorite dancer around and sends them dark poetry?

TEN

"*Chai* Triani, I would strongly suggest you do not wear that ring to this sort of…event."

Triani looked at his trusted driver and considered his words. "You got something to tell me, Vandari?"

"Just what I said, *chai.*"

The excitement Triani had been feeling about the flash was now tinged with a hint of caution, especially when he saw where it was being held. The alien casino had been closed down for months, ever since there had been a great explosion right in front of it. He had been involved in this in a minor way and the experience did not make him want to revisit the site.

He had put some thought into dressing for the event, careful not to put on any really expensive necklaces or hair ornaments. His silver-studded belt looked flashy but wasn't worth much, but the valuable *mantino* ring Vandari had noticed was one he wore a lot and he had forgotten about it. Without a word he took it off and slipped it in the pouch on the dash. His finger felt naked without it.

"I will be within call," Vandari said, staring right ahead of him.

"Thanks, sweetie." His inscrutable driver worked as his bodyguard when necessary and knowing he would be in the vicinity made Triani feel better.

It was late for a Merculian to be out and about and Triani had taken several stims after his nap to make sure he didn't fall asleep in the middle of the party. He slipped out into the shadows around the side of the Casino. It looked strange, the huge white building looming above him with boarded up windows and not a chink of light visible anywhere. Most of the building was surrounded by a high wall, put there by the city to keep people from getting inside, but ahead of him several tall Terran figures disappeared right into the middle of it. Obviously there was a door carved out by someone, maybe just for this event. Triani followed and came face to face with a hulking Terran male in a tight black T-shirt, leather pants, and a black and white striped cap.

"Hi, sweetie." Triani held out his bracelet and the man bent down, wrapped it around Triani's wrist with a practiced twist and pressed a clicker, logging him in. The yellow bracelet molded itself to his wrist at once and he moved inside a long dim corridor lined with rough wooden walls. Colored lights were strung along the low ceiling giving just enough illumination so he could see ahead of him. Not designed for Merculians, he thought. His people were not fond of shadows. The corridor twisted to the right and began to descend. So, going to the basement. Beneath his feet he felt the reverberation of loud music. He didn't see anyone else until he got to the heavy metal door which swung open as he approached, flooding his eyes with bright light and his ears with the thudding beat of ear-splittingly loud music. As he stood trying to make sense of it all, he wondered for the first time if he might be the only Merculian there.

The large room was full of gyrating sweaty bodies, mostly Terran, but eventually he made out a number of Merculians in the crowd. Several black-T-shirt-wearing Terrans with black and white bandanas around their necks walked around, exchanging handshakes with people. Drugs, maybe? Triani popped a buzzer in his mouth to help him get into the mood. Swirling black and white spirals whirled on the walls making him momentarily dizzy. The images were projected from a booth high up at the front of the room where a grinning female Terran with tattoos on her bare arms and headphones on, gestured and jumped to the music. Perhaps she was the one orchestrating it. He moved to the side of the room and leaned against one wall, scanning the crowd for Max as he opened his shirt farther. He noticed his yellow bracelet was now glowing, like the fingertips of the dancers.

"Looking for friends?"

He was surprised he could hear the female who now pressed against him suggestively.

"You can't have too many friends, sweetie." He leaned into her warm curves, his head on a level with her breast as she slipped a hand under his open shirt, moving slowly lower, only stopping when her fingers touched his belt.

Triani began to undo it, but she drew away, smiling. "It's on the house, darling. Enjoy." She moved away in her high heels, melting into the crowd.

Only then did he realize she had left a small packet of purple powder behind, stuck to his smooth skin. He opened it and touched a few grains to his tongue. A sharp jolt exploded through him, making hm gasp. For a minute he thought he would fall. He dropped the unpleasant purple packet to the floor and after a moment to regain his balance moved closer to the crowd whose idea of dancing seemed to be jumping up and down and swinging their heads around to the beat.

A tall young male loomed over him his grey eyes weirdly intense. "You want some Murch? Smackers? Lolly? Maybe buzzers? You guys like them, right?" He slipped a hand into his pocket.

"Hey, sweetie, what about ...you?" Triani laid a hand on the young man's thigh.

The man laughed. "I'm not on the menu, buddy. You want the other room. Go through there. Your VIP bracelet will get you in to the pick of the Wallflowers." He pointed across the room to a wide shadowed door and turned away to peddle his wares elsewhere.

Triani blinked, still feeling the aftereffects of the small amount of purple dust he had sampled. He took a last look at the crowd, but Max was nowhere in sight. For a few seconds he thought he glimpsed a familiar short Merculian leaping energetically, his dark curls and ribbons flying. Then he was gone. Triani shook his head. It couldn't be. He made his way across the gritty floor to the metal door. Ahead of him, two Merculians caught his eye. They were unusually tall, their blond hair flowing over their shoulders, their long smooth legs bare under a very short tunic. With them was a petite Merculian wearing red shoes.

"You're late!" snapped the door guard, slapping the back-side of the closest one. "Get in and get to work."

As they rushed inside, Triani caught a glimpse of an external ear on one of the tall ones. Mixed race? Interesting. He showed his bracelet to the black T-shirt, who grunted and waved him inside.

He had been expecting some approximation of the Labyrinth but what he saw under the red-tinted lights was quite different. There was nothing sensual or particularly erotic about this bare windowless room, but it was filled with the heady smell of raw sex and that alone was a turn-on. Terrans of both sexes were pressed together, whispering and moaning, completely unaware of the others nearby. Triani watched a drop of sweat drip down the bare back of the clos-est man. On impulse, he reached out and scooped it up on his finger, tasted its salty sweetness in his mouth. Then he noticed a few scantily clad Merculians, one of whom made a beeline for him.

"I can make you happy," he said in a husky voice, press-ing his small damp body against Triani. He slid to the floor, pulled the silver belt off, and was working on the tight satin pants when Triani pulled away.

"Back off, sweetie. This isn't what I want now." He looked down at the kid and realized he was very young and high as a kite. "How old are you anyway?"

"How old do you want me to be?"

Triani buckled his belt and moved away. Through a gap in the crowd, he glimpsed one of the exotic mixed racers in the arms of a tall Terran female. The slight Merculian in the red shoes who had arrived just before him, jumped up onto a plat-form in one corner and began to dance, turning seductively and showing an alluring hint of bare ass. Not bad, Triani thought, trying to inch his way closer, but he was abruptly cut off by three large Terrans.

Frustrated, Triani looked around and noticed a smaller room. Moving to the doorway he peered in and saw several nearly naked young-looking Merculians standing along the wall. A few older Terran males slouched on a low-slung couch, watching them. From time to time the kids would shift positions, one turning around, glancing over his shoulder enquiringly. It seemed almost choreographed. On a bench against the other wall, a completely naked youngster was laughing as he postured provocatively. At least this one looked engaged in what he was doing. He also looked vaguely familiar.

Without warning, the Terran male reached out to grab him in one powerful hairy arm. "Playtime's over, kid."

The kid danced out of reach. "What if I want to play some more?" The youngster pouted and raised his hands to his head, fluffing his curls over his too bright eyes.

The man yanked his arm roughly "You do what I tell you! I own you tonight, remember." The Merculian tumbled into the man's arms and disappeared from sight, pushed into the corner.

"Are the Wallflowers in here?" A female Terran shouldered Triani out of the way. "Yeah! I want that one!"

Wallflowers. Suddenly Triani lost all desire to connect with anyone here. The whole scene bothered him. He made his way back through the metal door into the main room to look for Max. Compared to what he had just witnessed, this scene looked perfectly normal. In a sudden break in the gyrating crowd, he saw the dark haired Merculian he had glimpsed here earlier and stopped in shock. Rio! It *was* Rio!

"Max, you shit," he shouted and ploughed into the crowd, getting pushed roughly and even struck once in the face by the mindless flailing dancers. He finally reached Rio, but Max was not with him. Triani grabbed Rio by the wrist. "We're getting out of here," he shouted.

"Fuck off!" yelled a sweaty male. "He's mine tonight!"

Without hesitation Triani stepped back and delivered a powerful kick between his legs. The man screamed and crumpled to the ground.

Triani grasped his sibling roughly and began to shove through the sweating bodies who seemed oblivious to the man writhing on the floor nearly under their feet.

"Let me go!" shouted Rio, trying to resist, but he was so high he kept losing his balance and Triani ended up half dragging him towards the exit.

"I'm going to kill Max," muttered Triani.

And then the lights flashed. Once. Twice. The pounding music faded away. Rio stopped struggling. Around them the drugged-addled crowd swayed to a stop and looked around the now colorless drab space, dazed.

Triani pulled Rio roughly through the door. He suspected there might be another way out but didn't want to stop long enough to find it. He had the feeling they wouldn't have much time. He began to run, stopping once to pick up the now sobbing Rio and throwing him over his shoulder. Behind him the crowd seemed to have woken up and was thumping after him, screaming, seeking a way out.

Suddenly bright lights blinded him.

"Halt! Stay where you are."

A Merculian voice, amplified almost to a painful level. The crowd behind him screamed louder. Triani blinked and flattened himself against the wall, yanking Rio onto his feet as a group of Regulators wearing protective headgear and carrying long taser clubs swarmed by, four abreast. One stopped and stared right at him.

"Out this way." He pushed at a seam in the wall, and it opened just enough to let them squeeze out. "Follow the wall and you'll come out near the bridge. Quick!" He popped back inside, leaving Triani and Rio on their own in the semi-dark.

"May all the gods of the universe bless dance fans," Triani muttered, starting along the narrow dirt path.

"My head hurts," said Rio.

"Your ass will hurt in a minute if you don't stop whining. And blow your nose, for fuck's sake."

"You can't talk to me like that!"

"You're lucky I'm talking to you at all, you little shit! Keep walking." Triani slowed down as the path moved into deeper shadow. He began feeling along the wall until it came to an end and a small exit appeared between the rough boards. He squeezed through and pulled Rio after him. "Come on! Keep holding my hand or we'll never get to the air-car."

"I don't want to!"

"Holy shit! You're worse than Giazin!"

Seeing a group of Regulators, Triani stopped himself from shaking his sibling and smiled in what he hoped was a pleasant manner. He put one arm around Rio. "Smile, damn it!" he snarled.

"I don't feel so good." Rio stopped abruptly and threw up. Most it landed on Triani.

"Fuck! Can't you even aim properly?"

Rio wiped his mouth.

"The air-car is this way, *chai.*" Vandari stepped out of the shadows looking completely unruffled by the scene. He reached down and scooped up Rio in his arms. The young dancer was too startled to protest.

As Triani followed behind them, he pulled off his smelly shirt, wiped the front of his pants with it and flung it behind the wall.

ELEVEN

Marlo was on the verge of a great revelation about the graffiti, when Old Livid rushed in, scowling.

"Stop staring out the window and get over to the Lindini Circle."

"But chief—"

"Take Eldred. It's bad." Old Livid paused, leaning one hand on the desk.

"How bad?" Marlo swiveled around and looked closely at his boss, all thoughts of the graffiti gone. "Is it... Eulio Chazin Adelantis?"

"*What*? What are you talking about! There's a body, Marlo. Get over there." He turned around and stomped off.

Marlo got up slowly. A body. He hated bodies. A person. Lying there broken, surrounded by invisible baggage; hidden links to people they had known and loved, things they had done, places they had visited, each one with some memories he and his team could never access. There were not a great many suspicious deaths in Cap City and most turned out to be tragic accidents. But not all. Perhaps his mind had gone directly to Eulio because of the veiled threats against him, or perhaps it was because his last murder case had involved a member of that family. That one had been very bad indeed. He looked around his office as if trying to find someone else he could send, but as a class A senior investigator, and the one with the most hands-on experience with suspicious death, he had to go. He called Eldred.

The Lindini Circle was on the other side of a wide boulevard leading to the Pleasure Gardens. A fountain danced in the middle and several life-sized statues of famous singers sat around on the edge, one with a hand dabbling in the water.

When Marlo and Eldred arrived, several Regulators in uniform were herding a small crowd of people back behind a hastily erected circular screen at one side.

"How do they find out about tragedy so fast?" Eldred said, scowling in the direction of the vidster newshounds, running towards them.

"They can smell it." Marlo stepped quickly behind the screen.

Several members of the crime scene team were taking images with different types of cameras for use later on in recreating the scene. They all wore sky-blue one-piece outfits.

Charlo sat back on his heels. "Hey, sweet cheeks. I hoped it would be you."

Marlo moved closer to look at the body lying on its side, sheltered on the left by the high hedge of *twyla* vines shielding everything from the street. He looked as if he had just walked here and lain down to sleep. He was well dressed in a multi-colored silken tunic and lacy white tights. One bright pink slipper was missing. His face was hidden by masses of long strawberry blond hair.

"Looks like he was coming home from a party," Eldred suggested.

"Where's the other shoe?" Marlo asked.

Charlo shrugged. "Not my department," he said, getting to his feet. "But I can tell you this is a very suspicious death. There doesn't seem to be a mark on him. Not in plain sight anyway. And I'm not sure yet if he is a 'he' in any sense of the word." He bent over and drew the hair back revealing an external ear. "Either a blender or a Terran, though maybe too short for a female Terran."

"*Blender*? Do you have to use such obnoxious language?" Eldred turned on the post death specialist angrily.

"Okay, okay." Charlo held his arms up as if threatened. "Mixed Racer. That better for your sensitive self?"

"Stop it, you two." Marlo was looking around at the pristine scene. The grass was smooth, the flowers undisturbed. If the poor thing had been attacked, there was no sign of it on the surroundings. He checked on the other side of the hedge. Nothing there, either.

"This is pretty close to the Pleasure Gardens and the Labyrinth," Eldred pointed out.

"Still, no reason for just lying down and dying. Illegal drugs maybe?"

"I can tell you that later, but you'll have to visit me in my lair." Charlo leered, or attempted to. It wasn't successful.

"Who found the body?"

Eldred pointed out a couple huddled on the white chairs always brought to a crime scene for anyone who might need aide. One was weeping quietly, leaning against the other one. They both looked old and were clutching worn ornamented cases for Merculian pipes in their arms.

Marlo went over and sat beside the crying one. "I'm Marlo," he said. "I'm an investigator." He gestured towards the badge, hanging around his neck on its multi-colored ribbon. "Could you tell me how you found that poor soul over there?"

The one beside him raised his watery blue eyes and peered at Marlo. "We were walking to the park to join our music group, you see."

"We play there every week at the same time with some friends," the other one put in.

"Let me tell it, Dasel. I saw him first."

"And you thought he was one of those party youngsters sleeping it off."

"It was a most credible assumption," said the first one, bridling.

"Quite right," soothed Marlo. "When did you realize he wasn't…sleeping it off?"

"Dasel didn't want to disturb him but then I saw…I saw a little bird—you know, one of those tiny colorful ones that sing three notes in a row over and over in the key of C."

"Key of C sharp," said the other one.

"Don't interrupt! One of them landed on the poor thing's hair! That would wake anybody up, don't you think?"

"It would wake me," Marlo assured him.

"So when it didn't, I took a closer look."

"Did you touch anything? Anything at all?"

"Oh no! I just looked and then…he wasn't breathing. I could tell." He began to cry again.

"Thank you." Marlo handed the couple over to a young Regulator with instructions to take them home and went back to the crime scene.

Charlo was packing up and the death transport team had arrived, their long white air-car hovering on the boulevard nearby.

"There was no shoulder bag?" Marlo asked suddenly.

"Not even a cred ring. I would have mentioned it."

"So we have no idea who he is."

"Or even what he is, at the moment. See you later, sweet-cheeks." He shouldered his bag of instruments and strolled away.

"The Crime Scene 'Bot Unit is on their way," Eldred announced, checking his com-dev.

"Tell them to look for another shoe. And send the report to me right away." Ordinarily he enjoyed watching the shiny metal sensor-like creatures crawling all over things, flashing and beeping happily as they gathered data from the most inaccessible hidden nooks and crannies, but not today.

"So I'm supposed to wait for them."

Marlo nodded absently. "I don't think he died here," he said, studying the place where the body had lain. "It's too tidy."

"Unless it's illegal drugs and he did just fall asleep and didn't wake up."

"How far away is the Labyrinth from here?"

Eldred crossed his arms and thought for a moment. "About a ten-minute walk. Fifteen for you," he added.

Marlo laughed and took off his badge of office. "Tell them to widen the search area that far. I'm going back to HQ. I can at least begin a search to see if anyone is missing the poor thing."

"Good luck," Eldred called after him.

Marlo wondered about luck. The poor dead soul had apparently run out of it and he, Marlo, would need quite a lot to figure out who, how, and why this terrible thing had happened.

TWELVE

Music spilled out of Beny's workroom into the garden where the clear notes of the *klavalo* mixed with the soft twitter of the birds and the sound of water falling into the pool just out of sight. There was a pause and then deeper sliding notes joined in, giving it strength. After a moment he added an odd, syncopated rhythm that made him smile. He was just about to layer in another track when he heard voices. Eulio was supposed to be at the theater this morning. Maybe something had happened to him! He felt the creative mood dissolve as Dhakan appeared at the door.

"I know you said—"

"What happened? Is it Eulio?"

"His Excellency Pamiano Charria At'hali is here," he announced gravely.

"*Now?*"

"How could I keep him out?"

No one could keep *Tan* Pami out if he wanted to come in, Beny thought. His *tatsi's* older sibling was a powerful force in government circles, with a seat on the Inner Council. "I wonder what he wants," Beny muttered, pushing away from his instruments reluctantly.

He found his visitor standing in front of the painting that still hung in its place of honor in the main salon. "Hello, *Tan* Pami."

His *tan* turned around and pressed one soft cheek against Beny's. "Always such a pleasure to see you, Orosin."

"And me, you. What do you really think of our painting?"

"It may be a work of art but frankly I wouldn't have chosen it."

"We didn't." Beny laughed, hoping there wouldn't be any questions about the authenticity of the suspect art. "Shall we go into the garden? It's such a gorgeous day."

"It was a lovely reception, dear," Pamiano went on, following Beny through the courtyard into the garden beyond. "Very smart to highlight the ambassador's gift like that. It was your idea, I expect."

"I don't remember, exactly. I do remember it almost didn't happen. Someone stole the bloody damn thing while we were away at the festival. Luckily we have a friend who is a Regulator. He got it back to us."

"That was lucky. Who was that male person Triani brought along, by the way? He seemed to spend a long time looking at your masterpiece."

"Some Terran dancer Triani picked up. They're exchanging notes on differing techniques of dance, apparently."

"I'm sure they are." Pamiano smiled archly, his sherry-brown eyes so much like Beny's, twinkling. "Does he fancy himself some kind of art expert as well?"

"I don't think so. He just likes it, apparently."

Beny curled up in his favorite chair and pressed the code for *pamayo* juice and plain biscuits on the table beside him. To his surprise it appeared almost at once. Dhakan must have done a good job on maintenance after the recent breakdown.

"I hear you received a red message box the other day," *Tan* Pami said, examining his biscuit.

"I did." Beny tensed. So this is what the visit was about. "And I said no, as you probably already know." He wished he had ordered sherry instead of juice, but it would be too obvious to add it now.

Pamiano shook his head sadly. "You rarely disappoint me, Orosin, and I have always been proud of you."

"*Tan* Pami, I am a musician."

"I know, dear, and you have composed and performed some beautiful music. I watched all your recent festival clips and enjoyed them thoroughly."

"Thank you." Beny put down his juice and waited for the 'but.'

"You and Eulio have contributed a lot to enrich the lives of all Merculians. This temporary posting is just another way to help your planet."

"I've turned it down."

"Well, the post on Rozemar is still open, dear. Our family has a duty to the state. You can still change your mind."

"No."

"Orosin. Please."

"No!" Beny jumped to his feet. "Look, I know how this works, Pamiano. This place is very far away, and the postings called temporary are rarely under a year, usually more like two, and that's not including travel time, which is almost a month as I recall. And I just got married!" He began to pace. "I've done many things I didn't want to do, many, because it was my duty. I went to the IPA Academy for three hellish years because I thought it was my duty. I was the only Merculian there and I wouldn't have survived without my Serpian friend Thar-von Del."

"I know, dear, and––"

"I'm not finished! I served my time on the InterPlanetary Alliance Starship *Wellington* because it was my duty and that nearly cost me my life! And then I accepted the post as an ambassador to Abulon, because it was my duty, and you know what happened there! No, Pamiano, I've done enough!" He stopped pacing.

There was complete silence in the room. Beny felt an odd tremor as his anger drained away. What had he done? A tiny bird lit for a moment on the edge of the table and gave his full-throated three note descending trill. Beny sat down and punched in the code to bring sherry. Who cared what time of day it was?

Pamiano was examining his fingernails. "I am aware of everything you've done, my dear. I, too, have made sacrifices and even lost loved ones, but I am a career politician. You are not."

"I'm a musician," Beny said weakly.

"What you have told me now is the perfect illustration of why you are such an ideal fit for this position. But if you have decided against it, so be it."

Beny looked at him, surprised.

"Don't you know that I love you, Orosin?"

"Of course, I do! And I love you, too! So much. You have helped me in so many ways, so many times I've lost count. This isn't about you."

Pamiano reached over and took Beny's hand and squeezed it. "There's something just perfect for you right here in Cap City, my dear. I should have thought of that sooner! You can make music, live here with your spouse, and still serve the state in this time of need."

"Need? What need? What are you talking about?"

"We're being overrun with off-worlders moving into our planet, mostly here to Cap City, and some of them are causing problems. Serious problems. That theft of your painting, for instance, may be an example. You know there is no prejudice involved on my part, but in this case these particular Terrans and their allies are part of a criminal element that threatens to strain our capacity to deal with legal offences. Someone with the experience you've just outlined, dealing and living with off-worlders for long periods of time, would be invaluable. And all you have to do is sit on a temporary commission to discuss possible solutions. Isn't that so much better? No long trips. No time apart from Eulio. Perfect." He clasped Beny's hand in both of his and smiled as if he had just given him a great gift. "And it would be such a help to me," he added.

That word again. Temporary. Beny sighed. "How much time would it take? A few hours now and then? Every day? A few times a week? What?"

"Just in the mornings, so plenty of time to compose."

"*Tan* Pami––"

"I knew you wouldn't disappoint me!"

The sherry had arrived. Beny took a long drink. Bloody damn. As he listened to *Tan* Pami chatter on, now about some mutual friends, he began to realize he had been completely out-maneuvered. Taking a stand had merely led to the desired outcome more quickly. Pamiano never really wanted him to go to Rozemar. He wanted him exactly where he now had him: in town, sitting on this new committee.

Beny poured more sherry.

THIRTEEN

Marlo and his team were getting nowhere in their efforts to identify the body discovered on Lindini Circle. The CSBU had not come up with anything useful and the teams sent out to search for the actual site of the death had also been unsuccessful thus far. Marlo had called for the sniffer 'bot tracers to be set to prowl the area, but they had not sent their report yet. The clothes which he had hoped would give them some clues, had also come up useless: no labels, no name stamped or embroidered anywhere inside. The lacy tights could be bought anywhere, and the full-skirted tunic seemed to be home-made, apparently a pretty good copy of a famous designer's work. The one shoe was no help either. There wasn't enough of anything there to trace. A search of the image data base came up empty. Whoever he was, it was almost as if he didn't want to be identified.

Charlo wasn't much help, either. "There's no injury anywhere. A few bruises, but not enough to cause death. And 'he' is a 'she,' though just barely. She's a real mixed racer. There are signs of minor surgery to remove vestiges of external male genitalia, which is not that rare, according to my experts, but the chest is pretty flat, so she could pass as a Merculian if she covered her external ears."

"How did she die, then?"

"Still no clue but for you, sweet cheeks, I will persevere." He winked. "And I respond well to sexual favors. Just saying."

"How do you respond to being fired?" muttered Marlo.

Charlo pouted. "Some people need more fun in their lives. And by the way, our mystery body had a lot lately."

"A lot of what?"

"Sex, baby. Great, hot, sex." He rubbed his hands gleefully.

"Fabulous."

"I'm not finished. There seems to be some sort of substance under her fingernails, but I haven't been able to pinpoint what it is yet. Likewise, some odd substances in her blood, besides the usual party drug cocktail."

"Keep trying."

"For you, always, sweet cheeks."

Marlo shook his head and went back upstairs. He found his friend Euvi waiting in his office with a bag in his hand.

"Did you bring me something yummy?" he asked, hoping for a snack.

"Sorry to disappoint you. Just evidence. You know about the raid we did on the flash last night?"

"I heard there's a lot of very hungover Terrans in the detainment area right now."

"Mostly Terrans, yes. Anyway, we did a thorough search of the area surrounding the casino and found lots of garbage, but also this." He pulled a filthy ruffled purple shirt out of the bag and turned it to show the label. In bright pink letters it spelled out the words: *Made by Yoni Designs for Triani.*

"Flying farts."

"Soooo, I want you to interview him for me."

"No, Euvi!"

"You know him!"

"Exactly. Look, he was probably at the flash, but that's got nothing to do with my case."

"You owe me one. Remember those drugs? And anyway, there could be a connection. Your stiffer is mixed race and we know there were a bunch of them there. So maybe..."

Marlo paused and looked out the window, thinking. "I'll interview His Nibs if you show the dead one's image to everyone in detainment. I need an ID."

"Done!"

Marlo grabbed the bag and wrinkled his nose in disgust. "It smells terrible."

"Vomit," said Euvi, just before he fled.

Triani was not at the theater or his downtown suite, so Marlo settled in for the long ride to the dancer's estate at Hanging Rock.

It was a pleasant ride and he nodded off after about ten minutes, to be wakened by the air-car telling him they had landed, and the door was open. Would he care to descend? Soon? He took a quick drink of wake water and climbed out.

"*Chai* Triani is not in to visitors today," announced the Keeper solemnly.

"This is not a social visit," Marlo said firmly, moving just enough inside the door so that it could not close.

The Keeper looked annoyed. He stared balefully at Marlo for a long minute. Marlo stared back. "Perhaps *Chai* Parla could help you," the Keeper said eventually. "Follow me."

Marlo followed, through wide hallways, several courtyards and eventually out onto a terrace where Parla stood in the sunshine in a loose smock, inspecting a large plaster model that looked like part of this sprawling house. His feet and legs were bare, but in spite of the casual attire he still managed to look elegant.

"I told him *Chai* Triani was not available," said the Keeper mournfully.

Parla smiled and waved the Keeper away. "Welcome, *Com* Marlo. Perhaps I can help you with something?"

Though obviously taken by surprise, Parla was ever the gracious host. He motioned to a nearby leafy chair and rinsed his hands in the fountain before joining him on the bench opposite. "I was going to put the finishing touches on the addition I've been building to Rio's suite, but he was out late with Triani and he's still sleeping."

"Could you tell me where they were?" Marlo asked.

Parla shook his head. "I'm afraid you'll have to ask Triani about that,"

"Ask me what?" Triani leaned in the archway, wrapped in a lacy shawl and looking unusually pale.

"Up so soon?"

Triani scowled. "What the hell do you want, Marlo?" He moved over and slumped down beside Parla, letting the shawl fall over his shoulders. "I feel like shit."

Marlo pulled the soiled shirt out of its bag without a word.

"Fuck. I threw that away."

"And the DDD search team found it. I don't care that you were at the flash. I just want to know who invited you."

"I'd like to know that, too," Parla said.

Triani closed his eyes. "Shit," he murmured. "Where's Giazin?"

"At school."

"Right." Triani sat up again and rubbed his eyes. "Max Kolinski, the Terran dancer I met backstage last week, invited me. There. You satisfied?"

"Not quite. What kind of an invitation was it?"

"He didn't lick it onto my ass, if that's what you mean."

Parla slipped an arm around his shoulders. "Just tell him."

Triani stifled a yawn. "Okay. He gave me a yellow bracelet and told me where the event was and that's all."

"Do you still have that bracelet?"

"I can't get the fucking thing off!" Triani stretched out his arm, showing where the yellow material still clung to his wrist.

Marlo opened his shoulder bag, snapped on his utility tool and the thing was released, falling on the ground. Marlo picked it up.

Triani rubbed his wrist. "Ask Max who gave him the extra bracelets. That's what I'm going to do."

"Please don't. Leave that to us."

"That fucker gave one to Rio. To my sibling, who had no clue what was going on there! No clue why he was really invited."

"Which was why, exactly?"

Triani pulled the shawl closer. "Because he's cute and looks and acts younger than he really is. Figure the rest out for yourself."

Parla handed him a tranq stick and murmured something into his hair. Triani pulled away.

"I know what I'm saying!"

Marlo cleared his throat. "On a completely different subject; do you know this person?" He showed him the manipulated image of the dead mixed-race female made earlier that morning. The art department had done their best to make her look life-like, but it was obvious something was not right.

"He looks pretty exotic. What's wrong with him?"

"Dead, I'm afraid."

"Oh shit."

"A mixed-race female."

"There were a few there, I do remember that, but I can't say for sure if this is one of them. It was crowded and the lighting was weird. Look, Marlo, I don't know who the hell she is. Now, if you're not going to arrest me for anything, I'm going back to bed."

"Thank you." Marlo followed Parla to the front door. Euvi would be pleased to find out about Max Kolinski, Marlo thought, but he himself was no further ahead in his search for the identity of the dead female.

FOURTEEN

"*Tatsi! Tatsi!* I'm going to be a star!" Giazin jumped onto the bed and straddled his sleeping parent.

"What the hell, Giazin! I know! Get off me."

"You told him!" Giazin glared at Parla resentfully.

"I didn't say a word."

"Tell me what?" Triani struggled to a sitting position.

"I'm going to be the star of the Junior Circle show on Founders' Day!"

Triani pushed the hair out of his eyes "That's wonderful, Giaz!" He opened his arms to his child and held him tightly, feeling the joy spilling over.

"You have to come this time, right?" Giazin looked at him anxiously. "Promise?"

"Tell me when, and I'll be there. I promise. Spit on my thumb, see? Now, better go to school, sweetheart." He kissed him and pushed him gently off the bed.

There was a moment's silence in the room while the child rushed out, his red sash streaming out behind him. Then Triani turned on Parla.

"So why are you finding all this out before me?"

"Because I was here."

"I was dancing!"

"I know. That's what I said. Giazin's been working very hard and getting quite good, too."

"He has?"

"Yes, and you know who you have to thank for that?"

"Both his parents are dancers and one of them is me! Of course, he's good!"

"Then why is this the first time he's distinguished himself? You have Rio to thank for this. He's been working with the child for months."

Triani stared at him. "Why doesn't anyone tell me anything? My own fucking family! In my own house!"

"I'm telling you now."

"Shit." Triani wasn't sure why he felt so irritated at what should be good news. It *was* good news. If he was being honest with himself, he had been concerned about why Giazin wasn't doing better at his dance classes. But he hadn't done anything about it. And now Rio had, and he was annoyed, not knowing what to do with his conflicting feelings.

"When is this Founders' Day shit? I expect you know that, too."

"In another two weeks. Plenty of time to get your under-study up to speed." Parla smiled annoyingly. "By the way, Rio has a lover."

"For fuck's sake! And you're telling me now?"

"You're here now."

"Have you met him?"

"He's been here overnight several times, so yes. Really sweet youngster. His name's Lio, I think."

Triani shook his head and strode across the room into the shower.

In a minute, Parla joined him, slipping his arms around Triani's waist. "Don't turn around."

Triani's first instinct was to twist round around at once to face Parla. It took an effort to relax his muscles and lean back against that familiar body, let Parla begin the slow, intoxicating dance that melted the bones and made him moan and cry out when the joining began. They both ended up on the floor, the light from the semi-opaque glass staining their wet bodies gold and red and pale blue, the water washing away all tension and strife. When Parla took him like this, Triani wondered why he bothered with anyone else.

Twenty minutes later Triani headed for his studio. Music wafted out of the open door, familiar music he had danced to many times. In fact, it was one of his signature roles. He smiled. Rio must be watching one of the many clips of his perfor-mances. Silently he looked in the door. On the wall in mid-leap the Night Bird sparkled and flew, head back, one arm raised.

But...something was off. He looked more closely, walking into the room where Rio sat on the floor, watching, his face wet with tears.

And then Triani saw it. This wasn't him, but the bastard parent he had hated for so long. The same dancer's body, long legs, slender neck, long flexible feet, and expressive hands. Shit. He was good.

Catching sight of his older sibling, Rio switched off the image quickly. "I didn't know you were up."

Triani sat down beside him. "Turn it on."

"I thought you'd be mad." Rio knew all about his sibling's abiding hatred for the parent who had given birth to them both. The one thing he didn't know was the reason.

"Just turn the damn thing back on."

They sat side by side till it was over. The lights came up in the room, illuminating the two of them in the mirrored walls. Neither of them spoke for a full minute.

"I thought it was you at first," Rio said, wiping his eyes.

"So did I."

Another pause.

"Did you ever see him dance?" Rio asked, giving Triani a sideways look.

Triani leaned back, his hands on the floor behind him. "Of course I did. I was very young, but I remember this role and several others. And I was at a lot of rehearsals before his accident."

"You have some of the same mannerisms," Rio said.

"Unconscious ones, perhaps. He was my first teacher, after all."

"Mine too."

"I know. Do you miss him? You can always visit, you know."

Rio shivered. "No thanks. I didn't see him much once I joined the Colony Dance Company anyway. I don't want to go back there."

"I don't blame you." He paused. "Look, Rio, Parla tells me you've been working with Giazin every morning, and now he has a part in the school show."

Rio nodded. "He needed some structure but mostly he needed encouragement."

Triani scowled and got to his feet. Didn't he encourage the kid? On closer examination he had to admit he didn't. The kid got into so much trouble Triani spent most of his time scolding Giazin and trying to fix things with the school so he wouldn't be expelled. "Okay. I just wanted to say thanks. Why were you crying?"

"It doesn't matter." Rio got up, too, and began packing away the image clips in a colorful basket in the corner of the studio he had claimed as his.

"Is it about last night? Nobody forced themselves on you did they?"

"No!" Rio shook his head. "Thanks for getting me out of there or they might have."

"What then? Trouble with this lover I'm just now hearing about? I'm not going away until you tell me." Triani planted himself in front of Rio, hands on hips.

"You're so annoying!" Rio wiped his eyes again. "Okay, if you must know, I can't dance like I used to. You satisfied?"

"I thought you were cleared to dance now. The stress fractures were healed."

"Yeah, well they forgot to warn me about the effects of that last growth spurt. It's thrown off my balance. Honestly, I feel as if I have no control over my own body sometimes!"

Triani reached out and took his hand. "Come on, let's go out in the garden and get something to eat."

"I'm not hungry." But he allowed his older sibling to lead the way into the garden dining courtyard and punch in the codes for *pamayo* juice, honey squares, and toasted protein buns.

"Your balance will come back soon, sweetie. You just have to keep working. I know you're a bit old for this problem, but it isn't much worse than just getting back in shape after a long absence due to injuries. You haven't grown that much."

"Yeah. That's what my dance trainer says. But it's just so... frustrating!"

Triani nodded. Rio had been a big star with his former company. In his world on the Colony Planet, his star power almost equaled Triani's. How would he feel if his body appeared to be failing him?

"There's something I want to ask you," Rio said, fiddling with a leaf. "Be honest."

"I don't lie!" exclaimed Triani hotly.

"I didn't say you do. Just listen and tell me the truth. Pom says I won't grow any taller. You realize that, right?"

Triani nodded. The Healer had explained that Merculian medicine could only do so much for a stunted growth problem like Rio's. His short stature had been a plus in his former company where some were so young but now? "What's the question?"

"Will any of the good companies hire someone as short as me? Someone only coming up to your shoulder?"

Triani looked away, thinking. He had been afraid of this question. "It depends on the company," he said at last. "The Hills company has just hired Barcelin, the kid who won the Laurel Competition Prize a few months ago. He's about your height."

"We don't have a competition system on the Colony, so I have no prizes. Maybe I should try for one?"

"Hmm. That may be a problem because technically you're a professional and a principal at that. Most of these competitions are for the youngsters coming through the schools."

"So I'm fucked."

"No, you're not. There are pro competitions, too. I've won a few."

Rio slumped back in his chair. "What if I lose?"

"You don't need to compete at all. You can audition."

"For Nevon?"

"You're sure you want to be in the same company as me?" He grinned.

"Shut up."

"There's something else you may not have thought about. It's not just about height. As far as that goes I don't think Nevon cares. But can you lift me? Everyone in the company has to be able to do the lifts with everyone else, you know. I weigh about the same as the others and that's a lot more than you were used to with that kid company."

Rio looked at him, his dark eyes wide. It was obvious he

hadn't thought of that. "I'm just about to start weight training again so I probably couldn't do it now."

"Let me know when you're ready to try. Now, I have a question for you. Who is this lover I just heard about? Why haven't I met him?"

"Because he's mine and I don't want to share!" Rio grabbed his toast and stomped off to his own suite.

Triani laughed.

FIFTEEN

Marlo sat at Eldred's tiny table on his balcony, looking at the dubious contents of his bowl. When his colleague had invited him to dinner Marlo had not realized his friend would be doing the cooking. Unfortunately, El had decided to take an active role in Marlo's new health regime. The portly investigator wished he had never mentioned such an idea when Eldred was in the vicinity. Just cutting out a few snacks here or there was what he had had in mind.

"Eat up! It'll give you energy and fill you up so you won't want anything else. Trust me." Eldred was polishing his off with gusto.

Marlo chewed, trying to avoid the small black seeds that gave out a sharp taste when crunched. Perhaps if he just swallowed each spoonful. He coughed and took a drink of the *pamayo* juice.

"You have to chew your food more," said El. "You'll get used to it."

Not if I can help it, Marlo thought morosely. He looked over the railing and watched the crowds trooping down the street on their way to the Social Dancing event at the Pleasure Gardens. He wished he was with them, walking hand in hand with Calian. He took one last spoonful and pushed the bowl away.

"I think you did the right thing posting the image of our dead body to the news outlets." Eldred set a small dish of nuts in the middle of the table.

"It was time for desperate measures," Marlo said, reaching out for the nuts without thinking, then withdrawing his hand. "I interviewed everyone still in the detention area, including Max whatshisname, Triani's friend. He seemed completely befuddled about it all, but he told me the name of the one who gave him the invitation bracelets, another Terran he said he met in a bar near the ex-pat area. I have to talk to him tomorrow. Several others said the image looked familiar, but nobody knew who she was."

"Sad, isn't it." Eldred leaned back in his chair and tossed another nut in his mouth.

Marlo nodded. "Someone somewhere knows who she is. Someone must be missing her."

This was new in Marlo's experience. Before this case, the dead person's identity had been known from the beginning and it was obvious who to interview, but with no name there was no place to start. With luck the image would bring in the necessary information.

Marlo stood up from the table and picked up his shoulder bag from the back of the chair. "Sorry to eat and run but I have to get in early tomorrow. Thanks for the meal." As he left Eldred's building, he was already planning a quick visit to the nearest Snack House. Being full is not being satisfied. By the time he got home he was both.

"Sweet cheeks! My morning is complete!" cried the after-death specialist as Marlo walked into his lab next morning.

"Mine isn't. Not until you tell me you've found how the poor child died."

"Oh, it's going to be like that is it?" Charlo turned away and reached for his PortaPad. "All right. Just the facts, then. As I suspected, it was some sort of oil-based paint she had under her nails, but not the sort we use. It's not even what Terrans use these days for their art. It's the kind used hundreds of years ago, apparently, by the famous painters of their time. I tested it against the paint used in one of those little oil paintings you found rolled up in that pipe. Anyway, that's why there are elements of poison present in her body. She must have been around a lot of it to absorb enough to kill her."

"Would it take a long time?"

Charlo shrugged. "I expect so if that really is the cause. But truthfully I have no idea. These things are hard to gauge with mixed racers. You're lucky I figured this much out already. I wouldn't have gone to so much trouble for anyone else," he added.

"Of course, you would. You live for your job. Anything else?"

"Slave driver. There's something else there but it's still to be identified. It must be quite toxic and judging by the damage to her lungs, it's something she breathed in over a period of time. I can tell you more later."

"Poor thing." Marlo shook his head. "Thanks. Let me know when you figure out the last bit."

Going up on the disk-lift, Marlo was beginning to think the flash had nothing to do with the death after all, although she certainly looked as if coming home from a party of some kind. It was well known that some Terrans were fond of mixed racers. She wasn't wearing a flash party bracelet, though, he mused, heading for the DDD unit to look for Euvi. His team was the one looking into these things.

He found Euvi in his office talking to an attractive svelte young Merculian wearing red shoes and a short semi-transparent tunic. His eye makeup was a little smudged and he looked tired.

"Hi, Marlo. Come in and meet Jarodin. He's my undercover hanging out with the Terrans who organize these flashes we were talking about. They're a prime earner for them, what with all the illegal drugs and the sex rooms. He was at a Snaker event last night."

The tired Jarodin nodded and dangled a shoe from one toe. "You think your dead mixer Euvi was telling me about was at a flash?"

"We don't know."

"I've seen him around but not at the one we raided."

"She wasn't wearing a bracelet, so I guess she wasn't there."

"She. Sorry. I'm too tired for all these pronouns."

"So Marlo," said Euvi, "was Triani there?"

"Of course, he was and so was Rio, but they left before the raid. He didn't recognize our body either."

"Maybe he wasn't in the Wallflower room."

"Yes, he was," said Jarodin. "I saw him. He was watching me dance for a few moments."

"Why didn't you tell me?"

"You didn't ask."

"Wallflower room?" Marlo asked, confused.

Jarodin stood up. "It's for the VIPs only and the bracelets sell for a high price. What they're really buying is a young Merculian or mixed racer for the night. Some bracelets, like Triani's I imagine, are gifts just to get them there to make the others feel special."

They were all silent for a moment while Marlo digested this information. "And you say these flash events are getting more numerous."

"Yeah. Look, I've got to go get some sleep. Nice to meet you Marlo. Good luck with your dead blender." He walked out, carrying his shoes in one hand.

"Flying farts," muttered Marlo.

"You can say that again." Euvi laughed. "By the way, Jarodin is a lot older than he looks, if that was bothering you."

Marlo sighed. "I guess that's good to know, anyway. Does he have to...I mean..."

"Stop worrying. He does what he has to do. He doesn't talk about it. Sorry we couldn't help you."

"Thanks, anyway." Marlo waved and made his way slowly back across the wide hall to his own unit.

Everybody thought the DDD unit had it so easy; answering calls to pick up Merculians and their friends who had partied too hard or calming down disturbances caused by overindulgences of some kind. They were always there, smiling, smoothing things over, administering antidotes in case things had gone a little too far and never a cross word. They had certainly done as much for Marlo from time to time. They always had a long list of recruits waiting to join them.

What they didn't see them dealing with were the effects of illegal off-world drugs on unsuspecting Merculians seeking a new experience, or the intensive training for the kind of raids they had to carry out. The recruits certainly had no idea of the Wallflower room where one member of the unit mingled with the lowlifes, trying to obtain the information needed to track down the evildoers who were using people as commodities to buy and sell.

As Marlo continued on to his office, he kept seeing the image of the petite Jarodin, grey with exhaustion; hearing the words, 'Triani was watching me dance.' What the ever-loving hell did that mean?

SIXTEEN

"**W**hat are you doing!" shouted Eulio from the doorway of his dressing room.

Beny jumped back, looking guilty. "I was just..." The message ribbons slipped through his fingers into their basket. "I'm worried about you."

"Well, you can stop worrying right now and stop looking through my things." Eulio strode over to his dressing table and flung the basket into a drawer, locking it with a handprint.

"You wouldn't tell me if there were any more. You always told me before."

"God's teeth, Orosin, this has got to stop. He's just a fan. A little odd, maybe, but some of them are. Triani has this one who attends every performance, no matter where he goes and just stands at the stage door every night afterwards. Never says a word. He's been doing it for years."

"This is different. The last message said, 'The curtain is coming down soon.' That's a threat!"

Eulio stamped his foot. "No, it isn't. It's just a fact. The curtain *is* coming down soon on *Prindi Nan*. You know that."

"Taken out of context, yes, it could mean that, but——"

Eulio turned on him, his blue eyes blazing with anger. "If you don't stop I'll move into the guest room tonight."

Shocked, Beny stared at his spouse. Eulio rarely lost his temper and they had never slept apart except when away from each other on business. "But Euli——"

"I mean it!"

Beny turned away, wiping at his tears. "I'm sorry. I can't help worrying." He yearned to touch Eulio's golden skin, so much of it on view at the moment, as his spouse had just come from working out in nothing but colorful briefs. At the door he paused and glanced back, wanting to say something that would smooth out the anger in the air, but Eulio had gone into the shower.

"Bloody damn," he muttered. And Pamiano wants me in the diplomatic corps, he thought in disgust.

He started towards his studio, then paused, realizing he wouldn't be able to do any work in his present emotional state. He needed some sherry. He took a short cut to the small sitting room through the fog-filled courtyard. Even the weather was depressing today, he thought, running his hand through his damp hair. He was about to pour a much-needed drink when he heard a muffled sound coming from down the hall. As he stood listening, a clatter, followed by a tinkling sound of something breaking pushed him into motion. Had one of the house 'bots run amok, causing mayhem in the food prep area?

Running down the back hall he skidded around the corner and stopped in astonishment, trying to process the scene. Dhakan stood there rigidly, a shattered glass clenched in one bloody hand. Dark oily blood dripped onto the floor.

"Dhakan! What happened?"

The man didn't answer. It was as if he hadn't heard.

Beny moved closer. The man's normally clear copper eyes were clouded, speckled with red. When Beny touched his arm, his skin felt cold, his muscles clenched.

"Dhakan? Let go of the glass. Dhakan!"

Nothing.

Frightened, Beny tried again to get his attention, but the stocky Kolari refused all efforts to communicate. Beny turned and raced to get Eulio, forgetting his spouse's recent anger.

"Eulio! I need help!"

Eulio was brushing his damp hair, turning the long strands around his finger into ringlets. He didn't turn around. "I have nothing to say to you."

"It's Dhakan. Something's happened. He's hurt and won't talk to me!"

Eulio jumped to his feet. "Where is he?"

They found Dhakan exactly where Beny had left him. Without hesitation, Eulio rushed up and flung his arms around the man.

Dhakan staggered back, dropping the remains of the jagged glass. *"Ka'xahn?"*

"Are you all right?" He was so obviously not all right the question seemed laughable, Beny thought.

"What happened?" Eulio handed the man a towel for his cut hand.

"I sorry," Dhakan said, but he sounded quite unlike his usual self. He seemed to be having trouble processing his thoughts.

"Maybe we should call a Healer," Beny whispered. He activated a house 'bot to clean up the glass and blood, all the time keeping an eye on their friend.

"I think he's coming out of it," Eulio said, watching as Dhakan washed his cut hand, accessed the medi spray, and took care of the wound.

"I am very sorry," Dhakan said again. "When I see the news flash the image of Rayana—" He swallowed. "Forgive me." He was looking at Beny, his eyes much clearer than they had been.

"Let's all sit down and have a little talk," Beny said, leading the way back to the sitting room. He poured a small amount of sherry in a shatter-proof glass, mixed it with a lot of water and handed it to Dhakan. In Beny's experience regular amounts of alcohol would reduce the man to a giggling adolescent, but a small amount might relax him enough to get some sense out of him.

"She's the one I found asleep in your rooms the night of the reception?" Eulio asked.

"She gets sick sometimes." Dhakan sipped his watered-down drink. "Her name is Rayana Chapelle." He blinked.

"When did you meet her?" Eulio asked gently.

"It was about five or six weeks ago in a coffee bar where I go often. I was by myself, and she sat down nearby and asked me where I came from. I don't like to talk about that, and she picked up on that right away. She began to talk about herself instead. Then we talked about…other things." He took another sip of his drink. "And soon she took me to her place. Later on, I bring her here because…is nicer."

Beny caught Eulio's eye and motioned to his own com-dev. Eulio nodded.

"Excuse me a minute," Beny said to Dhakan. "I have to make a call. Be right back."

He walked around the corner and stood a moment, looking out at the gloom of fog filling the courtyard. After a moment he punched in the code for Marlo.

But the regulator wanted them to bring Dhakan in to identify the body. Horrified at the very idea, Beny protested. "That is quite impossible! He's in no shape to go anywhere. He's not like others you may know. Other male off-worlders. He has no outlet for his feelings. He was brought up not to show any emotion at all or he would be severely punished. It was a terrible way to live, and it has left him… shattered."

There was silence on the other end for a moment. "I'll come and setup a virtual ID and that way he can stay where he is, and the law will be satisfied. I'll be there in half an hour."

"Oh, thank you. And one more thing, Marlo. Could you please not mention anything about the threatening messages? I would prefer to discuss it with you privately some other time."

Marlo arrived with a tech assistant who set up four poles bounding an oblong space large enough for a narrow bed in the main reception room near where the infamous painting hung on the wall. In five minutes, he activated one of the small boxes around the area and the body appeared lying on a flower-strewn bed. The beautiful strawberry blond hair had been carefully brushed around her face, artfully revealing one external ear. A touch of blush had been added to the cheeks so she appeared to be sleeping.

Marlo chatted easily with Dhakan for a few moments and then explained as gently as he could what needed to be done.

"I'm so sorry to have to ask you to do this but it's the law. This is only a holographic image, remember, but it's very real-looking, so prepare yourself."

How do you prepare yourself for something like this? Beny thought, trailing along after them. He himself would be in pieces if it were Eulio lying there.

Dhakan was made of sterner stuff. He stood for long minutes, staring at the exotic face, the first person he had found a way to connect with here in his new home on Merculian.

At last he turned away. "Her name is Rayana Chapelle," he said quietly. "If you do not need me anymore, I will go now."

"Thank you for your help. I know that was difficult."

Beny and Eulio stood watching his retreating figure as the techie and Marlo dismantled the display and quietly left.

"I'm so sorry for what I did," Beny whispered, moving closer to his spouse.

"You should be."

Beny touched his ceremonial dagger tentatively. "We could do the ceremony of atonement," he said. "That might help."

"Maybe later."

By now Dhakan was halfway across the main courtyard, a shadow in the fog.

"He's so alone," Beny said. Impulsively he reached for his spouse's hand.

Eulio let him take it, then squeezed.

He said nothing but Beny breathed a sigh of relief.

SEVENTEEN

It was late when Triani finally arrived back at his country home after going out with a group of enthusiastic fans to a dance bar near the theater. They wanted to celebrate a splendid closing night performance with him, and Triani graciously went along with them, something he hadn't done for a while. Even Eulio's foul mood earlier in the evening could not bring him down. Tomorrow was a day off, so he had enjoyed himself to the full. He had even explored the charms of the nubile young member of the group whose claim to fame might not be his face but whose young body held many charms.

Triani enjoyed this time of day, a period balanced between one day and the next. The dancer walked through a series of courtyards, avoiding the hallways and reception areas as he made his way to the gardens to smell the night flowers and relax for a few minutes in the utter stillness. He pulled off the ornamental circlet holding back his black curls and tossed it on a table as he passed through the arched doorway to the sleeping garden. For a moment he stood breathing in the fragrant air. Noticing a spikey weed growing along the side of the path, he frowned. The head gardener would hear about this.

He walked along the mossy path, its carefully maintained patterns faintly visible in the moonlight. He had no idea what the names were of most of the exotic plants that he passed, but he loved the look and smell and feel of luxury they engendered. He unbuttoned his crushed velvet emerald tunic and was about to sit down in a hidden bower swing when he paused, alert to an unfamiliar sound. Someone else was moving around out here. Parla was back in the city. Giazin was asleep or should be. Rio? One of the staff? In the distance the moonlight glimmered on the private lake, silhouetting a figure approaching from another path. For a moment Triani thought of alerting Vandari, his driver/bodyguard but the figure didn't look large or menacing. Whoever he was he had managed to get by the security probes surrounding the entire estate. Triani slipped off his shoes and silently followed. When he drew closer, he realized the figure was wearing a very short sleeping gown with thin straps.

"Hey, sweetie." Triani touched his arm.

The stranger wheeled around, one hand going to his mouth, stifling a scream.

Triani stared. "Holy shit. Well now, I don't know about you, sweetie, but I need a drink. Coming?"

"This isn't how I wanted us to meet again," the youth said, following Triani back to the house.

"I bet it isn't." He led the way to his sitting room, poured two glasses of *lim* and handed one to the youth. "What do they call you?"

"Liola Tavalino Simosin, *chai*, and––"

"How much is Rio paying you?"

"It's not like that! I swear!"

"So, what's your angle?" Triani stretched out on the inviting white sofa and crossed his ankles. From this position Liola looked more like the sexy Wallflower he remembered from the flash rather than the relatively fresh-faced kid from the Labyrinth. He watched in amusement as Liola tried to pull down his sleeping gown and wondered idly if he was naked underneath.

The kid dropped onto a cushion, tugging the material over his knees. "There is no angle," he said firmly. "The third time Rio came to the Labyrinth looking for me I gave back his credits and afterwards I took him to lunch. We've been together ever since."

"Do tell." Triani sipped his drink. "And does he know about this part-time job of yours as a Wallflower?"

Liola drew back in shock. "You were there?"

"Briefly."

"Please, don't tell Rio! I didn't realize what I was getting into when I agreed to go that night and I'm never going again. Ever."

"And you swear that, too?"

"I swear."

Triani was silent for a few moments, just looking at the youth, assessing him, trying to see behind the façade of composure. "So, what's your day job? Or is it sex all the way with you?"

Liola straightened his shoulders and raised his chin. It was hard to look offended in the skimpy outfit, but he almost pulled it off. "I'm an apprentice jewelry designer at Scando's."

Triani polished off his drink. "How would he react if he finds out about your night job?"

"Scando's my *tan*. He knows all about me."

"Maybe, but how would he feel about losing customers?"

"Are you threatening me, *chai*?"

"Just saying I know a shitload of high-profile people who love jewelry."

"And?"

Triani shrugged. "Look, sweetie, I don't care what you do at the Back Door of the Labyrinth. I used to do the same thing there when I was younger than you. But I won't have Rio pulled into that flash world you seemed quite at home in the other night."

"I was high."

"I know, but not high enough not to know what you were doing and looking like you enjoyed it, too."

"That's the job."

"Exactly, and it's illegal. I assume your employer made sure you got out some back way?"

Liola nodded.

"You know, the Regulators came around asking about who was there. I can always remember. Do you understand me?"

"Perfectly." For the first time Liola dropped his eyes.

"I don't want Rio anywhere near that shit. He has a career to get back to!"

"I know that. I wouldn't do anything to hurt Rio. And I'm not ever working another flash. I mean it."

"See that you don't."

"You can count on that. Those Terrans are wild."

Triani smiled unpleasantly. "You don't know wild until you cross me, sweetie. And you can count on *that*."

"So, are we done now?"

"Go to bed."

Liola got to his feet and bowed as if they had been having a perfectly ordinary chat. "Good night, *chai.*"

"Yeah, sure."

It *had* been a good night, Triani thought, pouring himself another drink, but discovering Liola's presence here had destroyed his pleasant high. Shit. He couldn't quite get a bead on the kid. He certainly didn't strike Triani as the sweet youth Parla had mentioned. Triani didn't believe the flash the other night was his first and only experience of such an event, either. Still, apart from that he seemed okay. His feelings for Rio appeared genuine enough and his young sibling had probably fallen hard for the kid, as one does for a first love. Triani didn't want to be the one to burst that bubble, but he had the distinct feeling Liola wasn't giving him the whole story.

EIGHTEEN

Marlo put the half-dead *flacia* plant in the sunshine streaming in his office window and carefully massaged its dried roots. He had rescued it from someone's front porch on the way to work, not caring that it might be considered stealing by some busybody neighbor. The poor thing was neglected and dying. He was just doing his duty.

"You have a right to live," he said, giving it a final pat and wiping his hands clean on the scarf hanging behind his door. He could almost hear the plant sigh in response.

"Hey, Marlo. You're late." Eldred leaned on the doorframe, a sheaf of notes in his hand. "What's that hideous thing doing here?"

"It's not hideous. At least it won't be once it gets some loving care."

"So that's why you're late."

"Why? Is Old Livid looking for me?"

"Nope. I am." El stood up and came over to Marlo's desk. "Look, we can't find any trace of that Rayana Chapelle person. We've tried every database we could think of, even passenger lists of landing shuttles from off-world ships. Nothing. The great void. Oslani thinks she didn't want to give the boyfriend her real name for some nefarious reason."

Marlo thought about that for a few moments. "Why nefarious? Maybe she just wanted to use her Terran name. She may be registered under her Merculian one."

"I thought of that but there aren't any databases for mixed-race people. There's nothing under Chapelle anywhere. Maybe that odd alien male got her family name wrong?"

"I don't think so."

"Well, there are three Rayanas as a given Terran name but

they're all alive and kicking. And we have no idea of her Merculian family name."

"So we're back where we started," said Marlo gloomily.

"It looks that way. Cheer up. Have a health bar." Eldred dropped a hard square wrapped in pale grey paper with thin blue stripes in front of Marlo and left the office.

Marlo made a face and dropped the tasteless item in his top drawer. At least things seemed to be happening on the case involving Eulio, the one Beny didn't want mentioned yesterday. Marlo shook his head and heaved himself up from his desk. Time to check in with his team.

As he crossed the Major Incident room he received a message that someone wanted to speak to him downstairs. Marlo sighed. So now Beny wanted to talk about the threatening messages. This was getting irritating.

But it was a tall white-haired Terran male who was waiting in Room 2 on the ground floor. It was really a quizzer but this one was set up as a sitting room, with pastel walls, comfortable chairs, and soft lighting.

"I came as soon as I found out," the man said. "I don't check the news much. A friend told me. I'm Frank Diaz."

"Dasha Borgardini." Marlo shook his hand in the Terran manner, picking up swells of grief. "You're the painter I saw in the *epicantare* singer's house, working on his portrait, aren't you?"

Diaz rolled his eyes. "A job is a job," he said philosophically. "What happened to my girl? How did she die?"

"I am so sorry you have to find out about your poor child like this, *Chai* Diaz," Marlo began, forgetting to use the Terran form of address in his emotional state. "Please accept my heartfelt commiseration."

"Thank you. What happened?"

"Well, we're not exactly sure yet. The initial report says she was exposed to toxic fumes over a long period of time. The poison entered her bloodstream. But tests are ongoing."

"My poor child. She loved life so. Can I see her? They told me you're the one to contact."

"Certainly. Would you mind giving me a few details first?

Her male friend said her name was Rayana Chapelle. We couldn't find any records, though."

"You wouldn't. She had a habit of changing her name on a whim when she met new people. It was like trying on a new persona for her, she said." Diaz pushed his thick white hair off his forehead and sank down on the nearest chair. "As you probably realize, my partner is Merculian. Our child was born Ryan Diaz Randarini, but she never identified as male. Later on, she had some minor surgery and changed her name to Frances Diaz Randarini. Still not satisfied, because the name Frances sounds exactly like the masculine version, she changed it again. this time to Anna Diaz, dropping the Merculian part completely. My wife was really hurt by that." He paused.

Marlo offered hot chocolate, but the man waved away the suggestion. "This must be a terrible loss, Mr. Diaz," he said, stifling an urge to reach out to the man.

"Do you have children?"

Marlo shook his head.

"We came here from Rozemar with another group of artists, Merculians and Terrans, looking for a good life for our blender families. We had heard the craze for Terran paintings was sweeping your planet and everything looked good for us. Our paintings are selling well in our market stalls and…" His voice trailed off. He stared into space for a moment, then looked at Marlo. "I don't understand."

"Was she an artist, too?" Marlo asked gently.

"She was very talented. She spent a lot of time in my studio helping out, painting in backgrounds, ornamental touches, flowers, that sort of thing. She had a series of paintings of children she did on her own that are very popular. I used her as a model often, myself. I can't believe she's gone." He wiped his eyes. "Could I see her now, please?"

"Certainly." Marlo led the way, hoping Charlo still had the poor thing as beautifully laid out as he had for Dhakan's virtual viewing. He had sent a discreet message earlier and wasn't disappointed. In the Skullery, the lights were lowered, decorative screens had been drawn, hiding all the sterile equipment, a light scent of flowers was in the air and Anna lay as if asleep in her narrow bed, surrounded by petals. A single silver candle burned at her feet. Marlo withdrew quietly and left the father alone with his child.

"Thanks, Charlo," he whispered as the after-death specialist glided in beside him in front of the tinted window. "Where did you get the grief candle?"

"My shelves are filled with treasures, sweet cheeks."

"I believe you."

They stood side by side in silence for a few moments, watching the mourning parent.

"This must be the worst, losing a child," Charlo said, his voice lacking its usual mocking tone.

"I can't begin to imagine." Marlo turned away. "Let's give him some privacy."

"He seems to be pretty composed."

"He's a Terran male, Charlo. They're not like us." Marlo pushed a button and the window beaded with opaque droplets, spreading like dark rain, obscuring the view.

NINETEEN

"**Y**ou swine!" Alesio ran across the lobby to catch up with Triani. "Did you think I wouldn't find out?"

Triani leaned against the doorway into the theater and pulled a flask from his jacket pocket. "What's your problem now, Alesio."

"I know you're behind the idea of cutting out my dusk solo!"

"You're out of your tiny mind! Why the hell would I do that? It wouldn't leave me enough time to catch my breath before I go on to do the fire routine."

"But–" Alesio paused. "You mean you didn't suggest it? What about cutting that bum lift I do with you just before our exit?"

Triani laughed. "I could do without that, but I didn't say word one to the genius. Don't trust everything he says." He offered the flask to his red-haired dance partner who now stood beside him, chewing his thumbnail.

"I don't want to be blindsided again." Alesio took a quick drink from the flask and handed it back. "What do I do?"

"Get a grip. You don't need to do anything. He won't go through with it."

The buzz of subdued conversation filled the theater as Triani made his way down to the front row where most of the principals sat in splendid isolation. He felt the rest of the company watching his progress until he dropped into a seat beside Eulio and unwound his silver scarf. Off to one side, Durina was talking earnestly to the First Soloist. Triani had a suspicion he was witnessing the beginning of an affair. In front, the stage curtain was down, the bright lights trained on the bare space in front where Evalindo would soon appear.

Durina dropped into the seat on the other side of Eulio. "Nevon's coming."

"Oh goody," muttered Triani.

Nevon walked up onto the stage, followed by the now familiar figure with the long honey-gold hair tied back with a black velvet ribbon and the ever-present scarf wrapped around his neck.

"As you know," Nevon began, "I like to think it's part of our job as one of the country's leading theaters to encourage new artists and give our audiences at least one new production as well as new versions of old classics per season. I'm pleased to say Evalindo is giving us exactly what we need in the latter department. I'm just sorry we have been scattered all over town during rehearsals, thanks to the size of the cast, but all that is about to change. Over to you." Nevon bowed to the director and left the stage.

"Thanks, Nevon." Evalindo rubbed his hands together, his bright grey-green eyes moving over the upturned faces watching him. "Hello, hello all. It's been such an honor working with so many famous dancers and you have all been so very kind to me." He paused and began to walk along the edge of the stage looking directly at first one, then another of the principals, ignoring Triani's wink.

"I know some have been a little unsettled because of the small changes in choreography and style from what you are used to, but seriously, you're all performing well beyond even my grand expectations." He grinned.

"I believe in giving opportunity to all," he went on, "which is why I have split the main roles between two or in one case three dancers, as you know; the Night Bird split between Triani and Serrin; the Day Bird between Alesio and Eulio; the Red Bird between Lumi and Durina and so on. This version of the show has a lot of solo and partner dances."

He paused and walked back along the edge of the stage, head bowed, his clasped hands under his chin. "I have also introduced a dozen young dancers to form the background for many scenes and be part of the water theme I'm using throughout. All this time they've been rehearsing at the studio beside my workshop. Could you come up here, kids? That's it. Trot, trot!"

"Shit," muttered Triani, spotting a few familiar faces, notably the kid with the amber eyes from Giazin's school who had the hots for him when he was coaching the senior circle group a few months ago. He also recognized Marlo's young *sobine* Sali who had placed second in the Laurel Hills competition where he had been a judge. This would not be a boring production.

The kids formed a line, bowed, and scampered off the stage.

"And there's one more person to introduce who's not part of the company. He'll be dancing the role of the Water Nymph."

"There is no Water Nymph," said Eulio.

"Guess there is now." Triani grinned.

"Come up and take a bow. Some of you may know him already as I understand he has danced on this stage before as a principal, and I feel lucky to have him in this production. Say hello to Rio Porvan Erlindo."

Rio bounded up on stage beaming and bowed to applause.

Startled, Triani jumped to his feet. "What the hell!"

Eulio pulled him down. "Good for Rio," he said. "I guess he's more enterprising than you thought. You should be glad."

"He's full of surprises, that one," Triani said. "I hope it's not too soon to put him under all the stress of being in a production. This dunderhead doesn't know Rio's whole background with the Colony Dancers."

"Probably not and you're not telling him."

"Shit." Triani pulled out his flask and took another swig.

"He's tough, Triani. He's come far in six months, and he wants this so badly. Look how happy he is up there."

Rio was smiling and waving as the applause grew. Most of the company knew some of his story and he was a friendly soul, who talked to everyone. Everybody liked him. Triani watched him almost skip back to his seat where he was startled to see Liola waiting with a kiss. Who let him in? Triani shook his head.

"Finally, I want to unveil the set." Evalindo was now rubbing his hands together with obvious glee. "My entire crew has been hard at work on this for months out in my workshop and a few things need a touch-up but it's near enough to start rehearsing here. Lari, curtain, please?" He ran off to the side as the curtain disappeared.

There was a gasp from the audience. Some burst into applause, some, like Triani, frowned. The set was much more substantial than they were used to, with a massive water wheel center stage at the back with what looked like actual water splashing from the top. Water also shimmered along stage right, disappearing under a long, arched bridge. An actual tree appeared to thrust its branches across the stage, hanging low enough to give room for the various birds to dance and twirl while still being able to leap easily to the ground.

"Hey, sweetie," Triani called, not bothering to stand up. "If that's real water back there I have a problem with it. Also, there's going to have to be a major change in choreo to get around all that." He waved his hand at the set. "Especially for my entrances and exits."

"And mine," Alesio put in.

Evalindo smiled ingratiatingly. "There is very little actual water I assure you. Seriously, it won't interfere with any of your choreo."

"And the Water Nymph?"

Evalindo looked confused. "The Water Nymph doesn't dance in the water. We do use special effects, which I haven't had a chance to show off, yet. Shall we continue?"

"Go ahead, sweetie. Don't mind me." Triani slouched back in his seat, but he was not happy with the set, the director or Rio. He took the tranq stick Eulio offered him and chewed it morosely.

TWENTY

"**T**his can't be right?" Marlo looked up from his screen enquiringly at Oslani. "A *Terran* is throwing message ribbons to Eulio?"

"Possibly. We've checked as many performances as we could and this female is always there with ribbons, so it could be her. But it could be this Merculian, too. He's in three out of the four consecutive nights. That's a bit excessive for even a rabid dance fan."

"Got any names?"

"We're working on it." Oslani bent over his screen.

Marlo shook his head. It wasn't impossible for a Terran to be such a fan, of course. Lots of Terrans loved Merculian dance. But this extreme sort of enthusiasm was unusual for them. And following a dancer from place to place? Going to every performance? This was odd, even for a Merculian. So there were several suspects, apparently. He glanced at his com-dev as a message came in from a blocked source.

"Dasha Bogardini here."

"I need to talk to you about Anna Diaz." The voice was dark, low and definitely not Merculian.

"You know where to find me," Marlo said.

"No! Meet me at Pantalo's Bar on the Bank Side."

Marlo frowned. This place was very close to the River District and had been raided a few times by the DDD squad for selling some kind of toxic brew that caused Corvian Bram poisoning and had landed quite a few of its patrons in the hospital. "The Circle would be better for me," he suggested, not wanting to have any part of the dive mentioned.

"I have info about Anna. Pantalo's in half an hour. Come alone."

"But–" The connection was abruptly cut off. No manners, some people. He walked through the Major Incident room to his office, frowning in concentration. It might be dangerous. On the other hand, it might be a hoax, and no one would be there. If there really was someone with information he should have, he had to go. And alone.

Marlo was glad Eldred was out on a call so he wouldn't have to deceive his old friend. He did leave a message for Eldred to find when he got back. Someone should know where he was, and he couldn't count on tags to be reliable. Then he slipped the com-dev in his pocket and checked through his shoulder bag, taking the opportunity to throw out a few crumbling stale biscuits and half a bun which was stuck to his small data pad. He looked at the dusty box at the back of the shelf behind his desk where he thought he had put his weapon, but the last time he had used it he had shot the wrong person. Luckily the victim was on the other side but still, Marlo had no confidence that things would turn out any better this time. It might even be worse. The weapon would stay where it was.

Outside, he took an old-fashioned Ring Car that swung through the old part of town in concentric circles. Marlo got off near the Bank Side. As he walked, he passed the by now familiar graffiti splashed onto the side of a building. He could smell the damp from the river, hear the zip boats plowing the water into furrows as they went by, leaving a plume of water streaming high in the air behind them. When Pantalo's came into view, the place looked even seedier than he remembered. The dusty windows were being used as a screen for garish neon advertisements for food and drink. Marlo took a deep breath and went inside.

There were few customers this time of day, but a group of Terrans sat around a game table playing Electro. They glanced at him curiously then turned back to the game. They didn't seem to recognize him. Not everyone kept up with the latest crime news. At the bar, a short Merculian in a bright green scarf and matching leggings was arguing with the Terran barkeeper.

"But I need to talk to Danino," he said, his voice tight with urgency.

"I told you, those losers are long gone. Nothing but Terrans here, pal. Now, unless you want some Lollies, get lost."

"But–"

"I mean it!" The bartender leaned over the bar and the Merculian stepped back nervously, turned and head down, hurried past Marlo and out the door.

Now Marlo was the only Merculian in the room. He sat down gingerly in a wooden booth against the wall where it was darker than he liked but he assumed this would work better for his informant, if that's what he was. He folded his hands and tried not to catch the eye of the young man behind the bar. They probably wouldn't carry *pamayo* juice here.

"You came alone?" The young man who suddenly showed up at his booth was tall and broad-shouldered, his reddish hair sticking out from under the cap pulled down over his eyes.

Marlo nodded.

"You look smaller than I expected."

Marlo shrugged. What could one say to that? "You have some information for me?"

"About my sister, yes." He slid into the booth opposite Marlo. "She didn't die by accident. She was murdered. You have to investigate."

Marlo tensed. "We did investigate, sir.'

'My name is Johnny Diaz. You investigated a suspicious death. Then my father turned up and you dropped it, calling it an accident. It wasn't, I tell you."

"You're her brother?"

"Look, we have the same father, okay? Different mothers. That doesn't matter. We were always close, the three of us kids. Yeah, we have another brother but he's too scared to talk. She was murdered!" He had raised his voice, then glanced over his shoulder. "Listen." He was almost whispering now. "She didn't die where you found her, either. Garini and me moved her, hoping you guys would find her and really investigate."

"Where did she die?"

"Outside near where we live in the District. Garini and me found her early in the morning coming back from a flash we were working. We knew they'd killed her, we just didn't know how. So we carried her to where you lot would find her."

"Who is 'they'? Who killed her?"

Diaz stared at him for few moments, then glared down at the table. "Do you people have any idea what's going on under your noses?"

It was Marlo's turn to stare at the table. Did they know what was going on? He had his theories but no real facts. Perhaps this was his chance to find out something. "We suspect someone is trying to move in on Big Stendi," he said at last.

"Trying to?" The young man laughed. "Look around! It's a done deal, man! We've been here quite a while already, really squeezing that jerk and— Never mind all that. All you need to know is that Anna was getting ideas. She was really good at what she did, painting copies of old masters and that, but she was demanding more of the action. She was getting careless, too, so when she bungled the Dégalas job...It's not a good idea to make mistakes in VO's crew. Ever."

"VO?"

Johnny shook his head in exasperation. "You have no clue, do you? Look, tell me you haven't turned Anna's body over to Frank yet?"

"Not till tomorrow. There's a lot of forms to file, that sort of thing."

"Get your coroner or whatever he's called here to go over everything again. And I mean everything! Please! It was the boss and—" He looked up as three men banged in through the front door.

Marlo looked around. They were a scruffy lot, three hairy-faced Terran males wearing heavy boots. When he looked back, his companion was gone. Hastily Marlo pushed himself out of the booth and made for the back door. He walked quickly to the path and along by the river. As he passed the graffiti-covered wall he paused and stared at it. Something made him turn around. There they were, the three large Terrans with hairy faces, watching him and laughing.

He began to walk again, trying to look at ease, not to hurry in any way. He glanced back to get one last look at the graffiti and paused in surprise. Now he was far enough away to see it! Large black letters surrounded by a neon red snake-like circle. V.O., the letters Johnny had mentioned. Out of the bottom, large claws reached out to clutch something he couldn't quite make out. But he felt eyes on him, burning the back of his head. Without turning around to look at them he began walking again towards the Ring Car stop, his head filled with questions.

TWENTY-ONE

"**Y**ou let your *tan* walk all over you, Orosin. You know how devious he is." Eulio sat in front of his dressing table, twisting his long hair up under a sparkling cap.

"Pami's been so good to me. To us. He even saved our lives once."

"I know, but that doesn't give him the right to ruin yours now."

"That's a little harsh, Eulio. This committee work isn't for long."

"Do you know when it'll be over? No. You didn't even ask, did you?"

"Don't be cross."

"God's teeth, Orosin! I'm not mad at you. I'm mad at him!" Eulio walked over to where Beny sat, held his face in both hands and kissed him. "I have to go. First rehearsal onstage. We're doing a run-through of Act I, supposedly, though I doubt we'll get far. You can tell me all about your first day later tonight."

Beny watched him leave the room and then checked his hair in the mirror. Eulio was right. Somehow he was always powerless where *Tan* Pamiano was concerned. It was as if he became a child again in his *tan's* presence. Beny stood up and straightened his tunic. He was not looking forward to his first day at the committee meeting, but he was resolved to find out just how long his servitude would be.

The address he had been given turned out to be a nondescript building almost lost among a block of similar buildings not far from the SpacePort. There were no flags flying outside, no emblems of the city or even of Merculian outside, which was odd. Inside it was bland, the only thing of note being the two National Regulators who sat watching the door as if checking whoever came in. He also felt a faint probe as he passed by the brass railing into the center hall. He might not have even noticed if his senses hadn't been on high alert.

The doors on either side of the hallway stretching out ahead of him had no names, only numbers and he clapped outside number eleven as instructed. The door opened immediately. The room inside was surprisingly small. Maybe this committee wasn't that important after all. He felt oddly relieved.

"I was told to report here," he said, as the silver-haired Merculian behind the old wooden table looked up from his work.

"Yes, yes. Come in, come in. Sit down while I look for your paperwork."

"I'm Orosin At'hali Benvolini," he said, pulling the one chair from against the wall over to the table.

The old Merculian paid no attention but just kept swiping through a long list of names in one of the screens embedded in the table. He was humming tunelessly. "Yes, yes," he said at last. A printer hummed and the oldster handed him a slip of paper. "You give this to the one outside the door. He will guide you to the signing room."

How quaint, Beny thought, looking at the paper. There was nothing written on it but his name in elaborate script and a long number.

"Thank you, *chai*." He bowed and went out into the hall where his guide waited. At once the guide wheeled around and led the way at a smart clip to a lift-disk. They stood silently side by side as the disk descended through a shaft of golden light to the floor below. They stepped out into another long hall and entered almost immediately into a large room where two Merculians in black tunics trimmed with white and silver appeared to be waiting. One stood holding a basin of scented water. The other sat on an ornate chair on a raised platform, the brocade curtain behind him rippling as if in a slight breeze. For the first time Beny felt uneasy. There was still no sign of any Merculian emblem, city or state. In Beny's experience flags and emblems were always present in any government group.

"Welcome, Orosin At'hali Benvolini," said the one in the chair. He stretched out his hand and sketched a circle in the air.

"I was asked to serve on a temporary committee," Beny said,

putting a slight stress on the word temporary.

"Anyone who joins any group in the Round Chamber must swear aloud and sign an oath to hold complete silence with all others about any and all proceedings he may witness or take part in in any way until such time as he may be released from the oath by the head of the Inner Chamber. You may not speak to anyone outside these walls about these proceedings. Do you understand?"

Beny had taken oaths before the various times he had represented Merculian and although this one seemed a little extreme and needlessly verbose he bowed in agreement. "Yes, *chai*, I do."

"You will now wash your hands, signaling the new beginning of your life with us. After that you will swear the oath, sign it and put on the white gloves and cap you will wear at all times in the Round Chamber."

At his words another Merculian emerged from behind the chair carrying the items on a silver tray. The cap was white, too, with long red braided ribbons hanging down on each side with gold tassels on the end. Beny wondered if he was expected to tie them in a bow under his chin but was soon disabused of this notion when he noticed an image on the wall of some older Merculian wearing one. He looked familiar. With a shock he realized it was one of the Praetan's acolytes who had attended at his wedding. What had Pamiano gotten him into?

"Could I ask just one question? When will my assignment be over exactly?"

"When the current difficult situation is dealt with. Raise your hand."

Beny repeated the convoluted phrases of the oath, then signed his full name with more than his usual flourish. Following the wordless instructions he put on the hat, pulled on the gloves which closed at his wrist with a pearl button. He bowed and followed his guide out the door and along the echoing corridor. At intervals above his head, sunlight filtered through a series of glass bricks, and he realized they were under some kind of courtyard.

When they arrived at another lift-disk they stopped.

"This is a far as I come," his guide said, looking solemn. "The lift will take you to the Round Chamber. The opening proceedings are over but the discussion's just beginning. They are expecting you." He bowed and backed away.

Beny shook his head. How can I be late when I arrived exactly when I was told to arrive, he wondered crossly. He stepped on the disk and without any input from him it rose through the lighted shaft, stopping at what he assumed would be the second floor.

As he stepped off, he felt another probe, more noticeable this time. The place was getting the feel of him, of his body, his DNA. It would recognize him now. As he stared at the large arched doorway in front of him, it opened, and he walked into an impressive chamber. It was perfectly round with a wide strip of tinted glass windows all around near the ceiling. At first he thought the ceiling was domed glass, showing the sky, but on closer inspection he realized it was all done with lighting and painted glass. All along the curving walls sat other white hatted Merculians wearing gloves, leaning on old-fashioned ornate desks and they were all looking at him. He straightened his shoulders and advanced into the room.

"Welcome *Chai* At'hali Benvolini. We are just about to discuss a matter of utmost importance on the subject of Rozemar, and your input on Terrans will be appreciated. Please take the empty desk."

"Thank you." Beny knew the speaker— Frandori Solinar Porferindo. Frani had been at his home on several occasions. He was there at the reception where the troublesome painting was displayed. And he had taken part in their marriage ceremony, an acolyte of the High Priest. Beny walked behind the first two members of the council, climbed up the two steps to the empty desk and sat down. Looking around the room he recognized a few more of the faces from events he had attended where diplomats, government officials, and artists mingled. Some, like Frani, had even been at his home for parties and galas. Some had probably attended his wedding. And perhaps a few, like him, had been pulled in from outside. It was the ones he didn't recognize who bothered him. It seemed that this committee was made up of members drawn from different branches of the government, municipal and national. Perhaps there were even a few of the dreaded Watchers, a secret group who kept watch on the workings of Merculian and interplanetary affairs. And if they were talking about Rozemar, this was more than just local problems. Perhaps the InterPlanetary Alliance was involved.

His wandering thoughts were interrupted when he realized someone had risen to speak. He glanced down at his desk to see the summary unscrolling in front of him.

"If you could tell us what you know about Rozemar, *Chai* At'hali Benvolini, it might give us a different slant on the problem."

Startled, Beny pulled on the red ribbons on his cap. At that moment he wished his *Tan* Pami had never been born. However, he was too well trained to mumble some excuse to get out of speaking. Perhaps his ignorance would get him excused from the committee?

He stood up. "Excellencies, you may not know this, but I am primarily a musician, so my knowledge of Rozemar is limited. All I know is that Rozemar is a large trading station about one month's journey from here, jointly administered by Terra, Merculian, and Eksaverria. I have heard that Terrans appear to have taken a major role lately in how things are run but am not sure why, or even if this is a problem. I've never been there myself but my spouse, Eulio Chazin Adelantis, visited once years ago with the dance company. He did not think much of it. Apart from that I have nothing to bring to the table about it, I'm afraid." He sat down again.

"Thank you. That was useful as it shows the problem in a nutshell. There is the general impression out there that the Terran takeover on Rozemar does not affect us. The thing is, the Terrans taking over are not the ones we originally dealt with when agreeing to take part in the governing body. They are bullies and have beaten down all opposition from right-thinking Merculians. Even the Eksaverrians who do not back down from a fight easily, have stepped away. As a consequence, crime has prospered to such an extent that the Terran criminals are now fighting each other. There is not enough room for them all to thrive so, to simplify, the Terran criminals, many of whom have intermarried with Merculians, came here, bringing their melded families with them. They have been moving in on the River District for some time now and are even extending the borders of that insalubrious area."

Beny stood up again. "But surely the Cap City Regulators are aware of this and can handle it. And what about the National Regs?"

"The city Regulators are not equipped to handle this kind of crime wave. It's like an invasion that we suspect threatens much more then theft of some jewels or even the occasional suspicious death. This is a new kind of criminal for us. We think they are after power. A lot of power."

Beny's neighbor jumped to his feet. "As I've said before, we need to close our borders."

"Shut down the SpacePort now before we are overrun with mixed race mongrels!" cried another.

Shocked, Beny shouted "No!" without thinking.

"Please abide by the rules of debate," said Frandori reprovingly. "And the rest of you, that sort of language will not be tolerated in the Round Chamber."

Apologies were mumbled and the debate carried on, but in a more orderly fashion. Most were against closing off the planet, but the very idea was so far from what Beny had been expecting that he felt deeply shaken. As the discussion went on, he realized that to know what they knew there must be a network of people sending in reports, people who had attached themselves to the criminal families, one of whom had apparently gone so far as to bear a child with a Terran villain, and they were sending in reports on a more or less regular basis about the frighteningly diverse web of crime. The leader of the renegade Terrans was named Vince Omnia, a charismatic but ruthless individual who was suspected of killing his own cousin back on Rozemar because he had betrayed him.

Beny hit the egg-shaped light on his desk which was the signal that he wished to speak. "May I ask if the Cap City Regulators know all this? And if so, do you know what they intend to do about it?"

"*Chai*, if you mean do we liase with the Regulators, the

answer is no. Our emphasis is not local. We must look at the big picture, the ramifications of what is going on go well beyond our borders. Any link with the local Regulators might tip our hand."

"How can we fix our city problem by ignoring it?"

"As you have heard, we are not ignoring it, but we need to find out what the long-term goals are. This may be about more than one city. Although so far we have no definite intel about anything beyond Cap City, we suspect Omnia will not be satisfied with a defined territory or even taking over from Big Stendi, which they seem to be doing. We think Omnia has much grander plans extending well beyond the city limits. Does this jibe with your knowledge of Terran behavior?"

Beny tugged on his red ribbons. "Some would react like that," he said slowly, "but not all."

"We are not concerned with all. We need to wait. He will go too far and then we will arraign him on far more serious crimes than drug dealing, selling sex, and forcing bar keepers to buy his noxious brew." He made a chopping gesture.

"Oh!" Beny sat down abruptly. He had a sick feeling he was about to find out a lot more extremely upsetting things that he couldn't talk about, things that would eat away at him, draining his peace and creativity and joy.

The meeting dragged on about other matters until a series of chimes sounded high above, releasing them. Just as Beny was about to get up from his desk to leave, a large, smiling Merculian planted himself in the opening, blocking his exit. He wore his white hat at a jaunty angle on top of his thick silvery curls and his white gloves were missing a pearl button on one hand.

"Hello, my friend," he said, leaning heavily against the desk. "I know your parents. Lovely people. Just lovely. I'm Aldisi, by the way. Sorry I was out of town for your wedding." He dropped his voice and leaned in closer. "Just a bit of reassurance about the Regulators. We might not liase with them directly, but Torelio over there keeps an eye on them from his roost in their very own headquarters in his hidden offices under the parking pad. Not that they know it, of course. He reports to us if he sees anything awry, as it were. So there you have it."

Beny glanced over at the ancient Aldisi waved to. He got the impression Torelio knew they were talking about him. He shivered. None of this was reassuring. He had so many questions, but before he could ask any of them, Aldisi heaved himself up and lumbered away.

TWENTY-TWO

Rehearsals for *The Night Bird* had finally moved on stage with the predictable problems. Several of the chorus had bumped into part of the tree on their entrance and a branch had to be sawn off to accommodate them. Eulio insisted on changing three of his exits to avoid the steps leading up to the water wheel. The wheel itself was causing no end of difficulties, since there had been a mistake in measurements. The structure was not as wide as it was supposed to be so the young chories were having trouble getting to the top four abreast. There was also a problem with the speed of the thing turning and eventually Evalindo agreed to have it powered by stagehands watching a monitor to keep track of whoever was on it at the time.

Triani had never managed to get back to the easy tolerance between himself and Evalindo. He wished he hadn't lost his temper and hurled his own brief sexual fling with Foraline in the director's face, since it was now obvious Evalindo was crazy about the kid. Triani still had his doubts about the safety of the water wheel especially when he found out Rio had a brief appearance on top of it at the beginning of Act I before his first dazzling solo. He wasn't completely wild about his own dramatic entrance in Act I either. At least his sib looked in control now and seemed every bit as good as he had when he was a principal with the Colony Dancers. Still, Triani was angry at the director for his casual approach to safety and went to see Nevon the day before the dress rehearsal.

Nevon looked up from his scheduling drafts and took a deep breath. "I hear one of the chories is pursuing you relentlessly."

"Yeah, Amber Eyes I call him, but I'm outmaneuvering the little shit."

"Well done. What can I do for you?"

Triani sat down on the chair opposite Nevon and stretched out his silk-clad legs. "It's that shitty water wheel, Nev. It's not safe. I've told him but he's deaf to me."

"Not surprising after— Look, the wheel is fine. You don't have to deal with it anyway."

"Rio does."

Nevon shrugged. "Rio's a pro. I haven't heard a peep out of him, by the way."

"Of course not! He's so happy to be back on stage he'd dance through fire if that egotistical bastard asked him to!"

"Stop worrying. The safety inspector got them to add a clear barrier between the wheel and the water this afternoon, so all is well."

"I hadn't noticed. Thanks, sweetie."

As he walked through the narrow corridors to the backstage area, Triani considered another problem he was having with the production; the best way to deal with the long tail feathers on his costume. They were heavier than he had expected. Catching sight of Amber Eyes lying in wait for him in the shadows, he ducked around the fountain used in Act II and decided to get to his dressing room from the other side of the stage. It would take a few minutes longer, but it was worth it not to have to deal with the kid.

He was almost there when he heard a low rumble of voices— Terran voices, followed by Evalindo's, who sounded almost in tears. Triani stopped, intrigued. Peering around one of the large props waiting to be moved into storage, he saw them near the loading dock. Curious, he edged closer. The Merculian looked frightened.

"I told you before I couldn't get all of it by opening night. I had an agreement with Stendi's people!"

"This has nothing to do with those losers. You're dealing with us, now, understand?" The Terran female reached over and slapped the smaller Merculian on the cheek so hard he staggered back with a cry.

"We get it tomorrow morning or there won't be any opening night." The male grabbed his arm and shook him.

The Merculian shrieked. "Get your hands off me!"

Triani had the urge to rush to his aid but stopped himself in time. Better not get involved. What could he do against two large rough-looking Terrans anyway? Besides he knew nothing about what was behind the situation. He flattened himself against a large crate. When he didn't hear anything more, he peeked around to see what was happening. There was no one there.

"Shit," he muttered, and decided to go back the way he had come rather than risk running into Evalindo or his thuggish pals.

He turned the corner and was relieved to see the coast was now clear to his dressing room. As he went in, his stomach reminded him that he hadn't had anything to eat since this morning. And it was now—

Holy shit! Giazin's concert!

He rushed inside and was relieved to find his dresser busily steaming his long cloak for Act II.

"Tolian you've got to help me! I'm really late for my kid's concert."

"Stand still." Tolian's capable hands undid the closing all along the side of the tight-fitting tunic. "You can leave the tights. Just pull this on over top and it'll be fine. Have you eaten?"

"No! I don't have time. Do you have any protein shots left?"

"Hold on." Tolian rushed to the cupboard behind the costume rack and came back with a needle. "Pull down the tights." As Triani peeled down the silk undergarment, Tolian skillfully injected the whole needle into one muscular buttock. Triani winced, then pulled up the tights. "Hands up." Tolian slid a red brocade tunic over his head and settled it in place. It was just long enough to work.

"Isn't this a costume?" Triani asked, catching sight of himself in the mirror.

"Looks good, that's what matters. I can clean it later. Kids are important, Triani."

"Don't scold."

"When do I ever scold?" he asked, picking out a pair of shoes that matched the tunic. "Here, put these on. And then go.

You can do your hair and make-up in the air-cab. Everything's packed."

"I don't know what I'd do without you!" Triani exclaimed, giving him a quick kiss and throwing the makeup kit into the shoulder bag.

"The cab will be there when you get to the parking pad," Tolian said, grabbing his com-dev.

Tolian had been with Triani ever since the dancer had joined the company, and today was one of many the dancer was thankful for his unquestioning loyalty. Apart from the lavish presents Triani gave him now and then, most of the time he took Tolian for granted.

The cabbie was a chatty type, but Triani ignored him and concentrated on his makeup and hair. By the time he reached the school he looked more than passable, he thought, adjusting the long necklace he had discovered in his bag. With the promise of a huge tip, the cabbie reluctantly agreed to wait. Triani would have to go back to the theater as soon as the recital was over.

A star-struck usher dressed in the school uniform showed him to his seat next to Parla, who gave him a furious look. Farther along the row he saw Rio beside Liola. On stage four youngsters were weaving and leaping to the music of a well-known song.

"I'm surprised you bothered to show up at all," Parla remarked, his green eyes dangerously dark.

"Don't start. It's been a stressful day."

"I wouldn't know. I've been here for hours."

Triani checked the program and saw that Giazin had already danced in a medley adapted from *Woodland Creatures*. Shit. He had a solo coming up after this quartet was over, which led into a partner dance. Triani was surprised he had been given so much stage time.

When Giazin made an appearance a few minutes later, Triani immediately grew tense. This was worse than is own opening night. But his child was almost letter perfect. The two minor mistakes he made he covered up like a true pro. Bless Rio for coaching him so well, Triani thought. Giazin wasn't a wonderful performer yet, but he did stand out from most of the others, including the two little blond kids he danced with in the finale. His kid had real potential. Triani felt an unexpected swell of pride.

While the theater erupted in applause, Triani turned to Parla. "Look, I can't stay. I left in the middle of a rehearsal to get here."

"You will stay until your child comes out, gets his round of applause and hears a few fucking words from his *tatsi*."

Startled by the unusual profanity coming from his lover, Triani stared at him. Only then did he notice the flowers and small bundle of message ribbons Parla carried.

"For Giaz," Parla said, thrusting the flowers at him.

Everyone was standing up now, shouting and stamping as the young pupils took their bows. Giazin stood in the middle, beaming. When he saw Triani, tears of happiness filled his eyes. As soon as the curtain came down he jumped off the stage and rushed up to leap into Triani's arms.

"You came, *tatsi*! You really came!" he cried, burying his face in his *tatsi*'s neck.

"I promised, didn't I?"

"You're coming to the garden party, too?"

Parla reached over and pinched Triani. Hard.

"Ow! Sure, sweetheart, but I can't stay long, okay?" He kissed Giazin and handed him the now somewhat crushed flowers.

"I have some ribbon messages, too," Giazin said. "See you in the garden!" He hugged the flowers, jumped down and disappeared through the backstage door.

"I really can't stay," Triani began, heading down the aisle to the arched doorway to the garden courtyard.

Parla grabbed his arm and steered him the other way out into the deserted corridor. With a sudden fierce turn, he pushed Triani against the wall. "Did it ever occur to you why Merculians in general wait so long to have children? Because they take up a lot of time!"

"What's your problem?" sputtered Triani.

"Whatever gave you the idea that it was fine to have a

child when you were so young, only to abandon him to paid minders?"

"I did not! You have no idea what abandonment means, you stuck-up aristocrat, born with a gold chain around your waist!"

"And you can't forgive me for that, can you!" Parla let him go abruptly. "What you are doing to that poor child is just a repeat of what your parent put you through, do you realize that?"

"You don't know what you're talking about!" shouted Triani, finally losing his temper.

"Really? Your selfish desire to have a child too young and the even more selfish actions after that when you went on near constant tours, never home–"

"Holy shit, Parla, I'm in demand! What can I say? And I love Giazin! He's my life!"

"Your life is on stage, and no one can reach you there, no one except Rio. Since he's been here you've spent more time with him than with Giazin, that's for damn sure!"

"Oh, for fuck's sake! He's my sibling and he's gone through hell just as I have! You know–"

"Someone's coming." Parla gripped Triani's arm hard and looked down the hall. "We'll talk later."

"Fuck off," muttered Triani and he gave a dazzling smile at the school Leaders as they passed by. "And don't bother coming home to me tonight," he added to Parla once they were gone.

"I wasn't planning to." Parla sailed off into the garden.

With a string of mumbled curses, Triani followed. He was just in time to see Giazin rush up and throw his arms around Parla.

And I wanted a family, Triani thought bitterly.

That night as the music roiled and trilled, Alesio lifted Triani smoothly onto his shoulder where he balanced gracefully, long black tail-feathers swaying. As the music rose, he was about to take flight to the branch of the tree above, when a piercing scream cut though the music, startling the musicians into silence. Triani twisted around, looking up at the wheel. Eulio rushed in from the wings and dodged behind the set.

"Get help!" he shouted. "It's Carondi and he's badly hurt."

"What happened?" Triani jumped down and rushed around

the corner. "I thought everything was fine now with the damn wheel!"

"The safety shield fell down somehow."

Triani turned in time to see Evalindo's white face. "It's my fault! All my fault!"

Yes it is, thought Triani, in more ways than one.

TWENTY-THREE

That night Beny's dreams were filled with visions of white-hatted Merculians all talking at once, crowding around him in ever-smaller circles, forcing him to his knees. In panic, he began to sink, deeper, deeper, trying to pull himself out by hanging on to the theater curtain which somehow he found in his hands. At this point he woke up, gasping for air. Eulio slept on, occasionally letting out puffs of air and shaking his head, the only sign that he, too, was not wrapped in pleasant dreams.

Eulio had kept him up late, telling him in great detail about the disastrous dress rehearsal, starting with Triani's foul mood and his own problems with his costume tassels getting tangled with his partner's so they couldn't separate when the choreography called for it. They apparently swung around and around, forcing the ever-vigilant music conductor to repeat that section of the music over and over until at last, by sheer luck, they managed to free themselves, leaving a long trail of braid behind them on the stage. Beny could see how funny this might seem to the onlookers at the time but how disastrous it would be if it happened on opening night. He made an effort not to smile at the comical image.

But the worst thing by far, and the thing that was probably the cause of Eulio's disturbed sleep was when the second soloist had fallen from the very top of the water wheel and broken his leg.

"I thought you said they put a safety shield in place?" Beny had said.

"They did, but somewhere along the way, it must have fallen down! So the water splattered onto the wheel and Carondi slipped. He'll be out for the rest of the season, poor thing."

"How could that happen?"

"I don't know! Evalindo was running around like a mad thing shouting that someone had done this on purpose."

"That's nonsense!"

"God's teeth, Orosin, this production is cursed!"

Comforting Eulio had taken his mind off his own problems for a while, but once his spouse finally drifted off, Beny had fallen into a very troubled sleep.

The next morning Beny could barely haul himself out of bed. Once he did he found that Eulio had already left for the theater. A box-note told him, in a good imitation of Eulio's voice that 'A bad dress rehearsal means a good opening night!'.

"I hope so," muttered Beny, heading out to the pool. A cool dip might wake him up. Clear the mists from his brain and clarify why the doings of the White Hats were so disturbing.

It was the secrecy, he decided, splashing his feet lazily. It reminded him too much of The Watchers, that mysterious secret society he had had run-ins with once before. The idea that some of the White Hats might actually belong to this group was more than unsettling. He even suspected Pamiano...Well, it was more than suspected, if he was being honest with himself. Bloody damn. The thought that he might now know more than Marlo about this Omnia person was like a stone on his shoulders, weighing him down. And another thing––why had his parents never mentioned Aldisi?

By now it was almost noon. He climbed out and went to get dressed.

His dear friend Thar-von Del arrived for a celebratory lunch soon after. Von had been promoted to a higher position, though Beny couldn't quite figure out what it was, the hierarchy at the Serpian Embassy being somewhat arcane. His reserved friend hadn't even told him about the promotion, leaving him to find out by accident. Beny missed their get-togethers when Von would drop in for a swim halfway through his morning run. Now he had to make an effort to see his Serpian friend.

Beny had managed to get Dhakan involved by asking him to coax the food synthesizer into producing a few Serpian delicacies. The poor man appeared the same, but Beny knew he was mourning his dead girlfriend. Beny had only to touch the man to feel the deep hurting loss. Of course, Beny could have sent him to the Serpian booths at the off-worlder market to pick something up, but Dhakan loved figuring out technology and making it do his bidding, so this was an inspired idea.

By the time Thar-von arrived, exactly on time as usual, everything was ready. They sat in the garden room, the scent of the rope trees and the *twyla* vines soft on the air. The tall pale blue Serpian was wearing the crystal figurine a lot of Serpian men wore around his neck. He was dressed in his usual long lean tunic and dark pants tucked into shiny boots. Even although they had been friends for a long time, he never touched Beny in greeting, merely smiling and bowing his head when they met. But the navy-blue eyes were warm, and the silver hair moved as if it, too, was greeting his friend.

"It takes a real celebratory event to see you these days," Beny remarked, as they sat down at the festive table. "I miss our morning visits."

"So do I, my friend, but everything must change. And there is nothing really to celebrate. Perhaps this is a celebration for you?" The navy-blue eyes held a glint of humor.

Beny looked at him across the table, his glass halfway to his lips. "Me? I have nothing to celebrate, I assure you," he said firmly, and took a sip of wine. "I'm still very worried about Eulio and those threats Marlo seems not to be taking seriously, and Dhakan is chewed up inside with his grief and I have no idea how to help. By the way, he was in charge of your meal. I hope it's edible."

"It's fine." Thar-von took a spoonful to demonstrate that it was, in fact, edible. "And your music?"

Beny reached over and pushed a branch of the rope tree back outside the window. It chirped dolefully. "I'm afraid I haven't had a chance to work on anything much lately. What with the worrying and all," he added.

"Perhaps Councilor Pamiano is not much of an inspiration."

Beny laughed. "You know me too well." He poured more wine. "By the way, do you know much about Rozemar?"

Von put down his spoon and sat back. "That is not usually

a topic that comes up in casual conversation," he remarked. He reached for his tall glass of the orange *siva* all Serpians seemed to love. "My planet doesn't have anything to do with it, but I would advise you not to choose it as a vacation spot. Two colleagues at the embassy just got back from a visit there. One was robbed and beaten and the other one bought a very expensive red statue, the kind the Evenki are famous for, and discovered it's a fake. It's a lawless place, Ben, by all accounts."

"Hmm. Sounds like it."

Thar-von looked at him for a moment, then nodded.

They talked of other less contentious things as they finished their meal. It turned out that Von had seen a production staged by Evalindo and admired it greatly. "I did wonder whether much of what we saw on stage and around it really had anything to do with the story, but it was an interesting experience."

Beny sighed. "I'm usually not on edge about going to opening night but this time... Everything is different. There was a bad accident on stage last night, too. And Eulio's not dancing with Triani, this time. I know Alesio's wonderful and all that, but it's a big change."

"Change itself is not inherently dangerous," Thar-von began, and his voice took on the almost sing-song quality it had as he shifted into a Serpian proverb. "When in motion, the wheel must turn in the dark as well as in the light and will always arrive no matter the illumination."

"Maybe, but I prefer the light!" Beny said.

TWENTY-FOUR

Opening nights on Merculian were always celebrated with much sparkle and dash. But nowhere was this more apparent than in Cap City for the première of the Evalindo production of *The Night Bird*. The impressively wide arched entrance to the Merculian National Dance Company teemed with fashionably dressed crowds of dance fans, all excited by the idea of what spectacle lay ahead. Light from the floating crystal globes in the lobby glanced off jeweled hair combs and glittering bracelets and daggers. Colorful belts and sashes and elegant dress shoes all blended in to add their note of finery to the scene.

Unlike most of his compatriots, Marlo was not mad about dance, his passion being singing in all its forms, but he was determined to be here tonight for the first professional appearance on stage of his only sibling's beloved child, Sali. Even though the youngster was onstage a mere few times and always in the background, it was a big step towards the career he had worked for most of his young life.

Marlo had rarely seen such a fine display of elegance and style. Even though he was wearing his best tunic and silver bangles, he felt distinctly underdressed, especially as the tunic felt tighter than it had the last time he had worn it. Calian was dressed in the traditional formal robe of the *Meshdravi*, of quilted pale blue satin with bows down the front, trimmed with seed pearls. He even had matching shoes and pale silk stockings.

"You do look lovely," Marlo said for the third time, admiring his lover in the mirror they passed on the way up the wide moving stairway to their seats.

Calian just smiled.

The moment they were inside the auditorium it was clear this was no ordinary performance. The air was filled with birdsong and the faint scent of the rope trees visible along the walls. The sound of water led their eyes to the side aisle where a faint stream trickled along to form a small waterfall in front of the stage. One enthusiastic dance fan dipped his foot in the stream and shrieked with joy. "It's real!" he cried, waving his damp shoe in the air to prove it.

Once in their seats, Marlo leaned over the velvet railing and watched the crowd down below. Not surprisingly, he spied several people he knew: Parla of course, Beny with a few friends who looked vaguely familiar, the Terran dancer Max, and—*Liola*? In one of the best seats in the house, too. And there was Cushna, more than usually dapper, on the arm of an older Merculian whose face Marlo couldn't see. Then he caught sight of a big Terran male with a beard. Where had he seen him before? He sat back and closed his eyes to think.

"See anyone interesting?" asked Calian.

Marlo opened his eyes. "Just a few crims I wasn't expecting to see here."

"Why not? They can be dance fans and crims, too, no?"

Marlo laughed, but the presence of the hairy-faced male he now remembered from that seedy bar bothered him. The man did not strike Marlo as a dance fan.

At last the lights dimmed, the birdsong rose in volume then faded into the opening notes of the prelude. The audience settled into their seats as the well-known music swelled around them. Even Marlo was familiar with the prelude, as it was played often before concerts of all sorts, even by groups of amateurs in the Pleasure Gardens. But he was startled when the long rising trills near the end were joined by a deep thrumming sound and suddenly he felt a rush of air and looked up just in time to see the Night Bird himself sail by, long tail feathers streaming out behind him, his black eyes glittering as he hit the spotlight. There was a gasp from the audience as Triani swooped above them to alight gracefully on the highest branch of the tree on stage. He paused for a moment and then reached down to preen his feathers, his long fingers held under his chin serving as his bill. The stage came to life around him as the water wheel turned, sending a sparkling stream under the ornamental bridge in the corner and along to the front of the stage where it flowed across the apron and out of sight. The audience burst into prolonged applause.

"What an entrance!" exclaimed Calian.

"And he hasn't even danced yet," murmured Marlo, who had seen Triani on stage only once before and ended up a complete emotional wreck afterwards. But this dance was not a tragedy, he reminded himself. As Sali had explained it to him, the Night Bird spent most of his time pining after the Day Bird, while courting the other birds he could meet in the darkness, his realm. But none of them satisfied his hunger. He knew he could not survive in the light of day so he could not approach his loved one directly. But they could meet for a short time twice a day, at dawn and dusk, the times when day meets night. And at the end, they were together. But this part was a bit vague. Sali said he would have to wait to see it.

Of course, the Day Bird was doing more or less the same thing in his realm, so there were lots of solos and partner dances and of course the chorus of colorful birds and the raindrops dancing on the wheel in the background. And then the Water Nymph appeared, to a ripple of applause as the audience recognized Rio. He only had three solos, but he made sure he would not be forgotten when it was all over. Breathtaking, murmured Marlo's neighbors. And the redhaired Day Bird was charming, casting a spell over everyone when he was dancing solo. When Triani joined him, it was magic! The two were so different in looks and character that it worked perfectly. And Eulio as the Yellow Bird brought down the house as he tried in vain to court the Day Bird, by turns cocky, submissive, and then throwing it all into a brilliant display of technique and bravura as he danced one last courting dance. Finally, realizing he was doomed to failure, he grabbed the smaller Red-wing and swept them both up onto a higher branch and leapt off stage in perfect unison.

The second act sped by in no time, by turns thrilling, sensuous, charming, and achingly sweet. Marlo marveled at the stamina of the two main characters who spent so much time on stage, either dancing or perched aloft on the tree, watching and reacting to everything that went on around them and down below. The only criticism Marlo could think of was that there was almost too much happening on stage, as the Water Drops danced about, sometimes even splashing in the water stream or just hanging around on the little bridge. But by the end, when the Day Bird and the Night Bight bird refused to part as day began to flood the stage with light, and their feathers began to change colors, Marlo clutched Calian. The Night Bird twirled his love up and under the low hanging branches of the tree, and then up, and up in graceful leaps, and then they both just—disappeared in a flash of thunder.

"Are they dead?" whispered Marlo, his eyes moist.

Calian just squeezed his hand. "Wait."

And the light flooded the stage again and there they were in a triumphal crash of music, at the top of the tree, their feathers now both black *and* white, matching the great black and white plumes on their heads. They swayed together, locked in an embrace as the spotlight slowly shrank around them, and then the stage went dark, and the air was filled with birdsong.

Thunderous applause crashed out from the audience who stamped and shouted and flung masses of flowers as the cast took their bows. And there was Sali in his diaphanous costume as a water drop. And Rio taking a solo bow. Then Eulio, the Yellow Bird, his arms full of flowers. And at last, Alesio and Triani, hand in hand, each deferring to the other in a masterly display of modesty.

By now Marlo was thinking about the reception, to which he was invited, thanks to Sali. He knew it would be grand with lots of wonderful treats he didn't often get a chance to sample. He was almost licking his lips in anticipation. They made their way to the Grand Salon, holding hands as they discussed the production. As soon as they entered the large, gilded room, someone handed them each an edible party bowl filled with delectable nibblies. Then the serve-bots glided by with tall glasses of Crushed Emeralds.

Marlo looked up from his bowl when applause broke out to see the director, Evalindo, making his way into the room, wearing a bright silk scarf wrapped around his neck, and matching fingerless gloves. He was all smiles, but his eyes looked tired, and no amount of careful makeup could hide the greyness of exhaustion in his face. It must be a great relief to him to be finished with his part in the production and have it such a success, Marlo thought. Ripples of applause kept erupting as members of the cast began arriving, getting stronger as the principal dancers began to appear. The redhead Alesio got a rousing ovation as did several others whose names Marlo had forgotten.

"Hello, *com* Bogardini."

Marlo turned to see the handsome face of the singer Orelin Travesi Canilor, dressed in the blue velvet outfit he had been wearing for his portrait, heading towards him. He saw him notice Calian, and almost stumble. But to his credit he kept coming.

"*Chai* Orelin. May I present my lover, Calian Drushki Sindrav."

"I enjoyed your rendition of Simitan last week," Calian said with a bow.

Orelin looked surprised. "It was a very minor role. Next week…" He looked away.

"It's a small but pivotal role," Calian said gravely.

Orelin smiled and looked directly at Calian for the first time. "Thank you. I always thought so, too." He turned back to Marlo. "I wanted to invite you to a public showing of my portrait, the one that was being painted when you came to my house, remember?"

"Of course." He made it sound as if Marlo had dropped in for a glass of mint wine and biscuits. "I'd love to see the completed portrait."

The singer launched into the details of place, time, and detailed instructions about how to get there and was almost finished when applause broke out again, but this time it kept getting louder and louder.

Triani had arrived. Wearing a large turquoise ruff and low-cut turquoise and black silk top, he advanced into the room with stately grace, smiling right and left, reaching out to touch first one then another as he passed by. Marlo glanced around looking for Parla and found him standing by the window, stunningly elegant in black satin. He was making no move to join his famous lover. Perhaps he didn't want to get in the way of all the adulation, Marlo thought, but he wondered.

Marlo was finishing off his bowl when he saw Liola again with Rio. That was a surprise. How long had that been going on, he wondered. Discovering that he had munched the last of his bowl, he looked around for another one. Calian had wandered out into the gallery and was deep in conversation with a group of dancers from the chorus, so Marlo went in search of sustenance by himself. He had just spied some bowls on a long floating table near the wine fountain when he became aware of a flutter of unease in the air.

"Where's Eulio?" someone asked.

"Yes, he usually gets here before Triani, who always likes to make a solo entrance." Affectionate laughter followed this remark.

Marlo picked up his new bowl and another glass of wine. Hearing Beny's raised voice, he turned around quickly, spilling wine all down his front. "Flying farts," he muttered. Beny was talking to Triani in the middle of the room. He looked worried. Parla had noticed the commotion and was making his way to join the group.

Marlo wandered over in time to hear Beny begging Triani to go back and check for Eulio.

"Why me?" Triani asked irritably.

"Because you're the only one who can get into his dressing room," Beny said.

"Go yourself, Benvolini!"

"I can't! Because of the size of the cast and all the new stuff backstage no one is allowed back there but the cast. You know that!"

"I forgot. Why are you so worried, anyway?" Triani was looking distinctly annoyed by now.

Marlo couldn't help being intrigued as he lingered close enough to hear the outcome of this little battle of wills. Suddenly he noticed Sali heading towards him with a handful of message ribbons on his hands and he remembered the odd messages Eulio had been receiving lately. Perhaps there was something to worry about after all.

He hugged his *sobine* and congratulated him warmly.

"You're wet, *Tan* Marlo!" exclaimed the youngster, drawing away.

Marlo smiled, dabbing at his front vaguely. "Just a little wine, dear," he said, before letting the youth run off and join his friends. He looked so happy! When Marlo glanced back at the group in the middle of the room, he was just in time to see Triani and Parla walking quickly to the door that led to the stage entrance. They appeared to be arguing.

Marlo shrugged and went in search of Calian. He was no longer out in the gallery, and it took a while, pushing through the crowds before Marlo found him at last, pouring wine for a singer friend of his.

Before he could say anything, Triani was back, cutting a swarth through the crowds to Beny, arms waving.

"Eulio's not there!" he shouted. "I looked everywhere. He's just...disappeared!"

A high-pitched voice cut through the babble.

"No!" Evalindo fainted.

TWENTY-FIVE

In the chaos that followed Evalindo's dramatic collapse, Triani searched out Marlo and drew him aside.

"I see you've been enjoying yourself, sweetie," he remarked, looking at the wet greenish stain down the other's tunic.

"Life is for enjoyment." Marlo wiped a few crumbs off one cheek.

"Listen, all is not sweetness and light back there in Eulio's dressing room. Come with me. There's something you should see." He turned, not waiting to see if Marlo would follow. Because of the crowd of adoring fans, it took a while to get to the door but once through it, Triani started to walk quickly.

"At last we're alone!"

Triani froze. Almost at once he felt a wet tongue pressing against the bare back where his silk top plunged almost to his waist. He spun around and nearly knocked over the young kid Amber Eyes.

"What the hell do you think you're doing!" he shouted, pushing the kid away.

Amber Eyes scrambled to his feet. "I'll do whatever you want," he whispered, stretching out a hand to touch Triani's chest.

The dancer batted his hand away. "I want you to get the fuck out of here! And we're not alone," he added, glancing over to see that Marlo had caught his sash in the closed door and was endeavoring to get himself free.

"Later?" the kid pleaded.

"Never!"

The kid turned away and nearly ran back to the gala, releasing Marlo as he rushed through the door.

"Hormones," muttered Triani. "That kid is worse than I ever was."

He could hear Marlo padding along behind him as he turned into the carpeted hallway and laid his hand against the gold star on Eulio's dressing room door. It opened silently.

Marlo followed him in, slightly out of breath. "What do you want to show me?" he asked, looking around.

"Those." Triani pointed to a large bouquet of black flowers tied with a huge white satin bow.

Marlo peered more closely at the flowers and reached out a hand to touch them.

"Careful," warned Triani. "They have thorns."

"What are they?"

"Roses." Triani paused and laid one hand on the dark curled petals. "They're a Terran flower."

Marlo leaned closer but didn't touch.

"I had a Terran boyfriend long ago," Triani went on. "He used to send me red roses every opening night, whenever I was close enough. He said red was the color of passion." Triani paused again and turned away for a moment to collect his thoughts. Images of Lucius rushed into his mind, and he felt a stab of loss so strong it made him dizzy. He blinked hard. Now was not the time for memories. "Anyway, he told me about the different colors of this flower and what they meant. Black was not good."

"What does black mean?"

"If I remember rightly, it has to do with death."

Marlo sat down abruptly. He looked again more closely at the flowers. "Technically they aren't really black," he said slowly. "I'd say more a very dark purple, don't you think? So maybe you're wrong?"

"I'm not fucking wrong!" shouted Triani, anger pushing out all other feelings. "Something bad has happened to Eulio and you have to find him!"

"This room looks tidy to me. There's no signs of a struggle of any kind. Can you tell me if anything's missing?" Marlo looked up at him, his brown eyes searching.

Triani walked around, checking the costumes hanging neatly in one end of the room, the rows of dance shoes, head dresses, and wigs. Then he checked the box of jewelry, mostly paste, for the stage. He looked through the cosmetics and hair combs. "It looks as if he got changed into his gala outfit. None of that's here, not even his dagger."

"Perhaps we should talk to his dresser. Wouldn't he be the last person to see him?"

"Usually, yes, but this production has a very large cast and Eulio released his dresser to help with the kids upstairs on the nights he's not dancing Day Bird."

"Where else did you look?"

"I checked the landing pad on the roof, but there's no sign of any air-cabs having landed. I asked the guard who keeps an eye out up there."

"Where else could he get out unnoticed?"

"Holy shit, Marlo! He wouldn't! He and Benvolini stick to each other like glue! Always!"

"No need to shout." Marlo stood up. "Show me where the exits are from here. Just humor me."

Triani went out and began to gesture as he spoke. "There's one entrance into the theater on the right. The way we came in on the second level goes to the grand salon and there's another way out the back by the stage door, which is also locked and Urvino is usually back there, though not tonight," he added.

"Anywhere else?"

Triani paused. "The loading dock. It's probably the only one not locked down. The crew likes to keep it open so they can sneak out for breaks and a quick hit of smoke."

"How do you get there?"

Triani turned at once and led him out of the luxury of the star dressing rooms through a dim labyrinth of passages, past huge sound boxes, neatly tied ropes and cables, banks of lighting equipment some disappearing into the shadows high above their heads. At last, they saw a bright light and a figure hurrying by.

"Hey, Garlin, have you seen Eulio?" Triani called out, recognizing the assistant stage manager.

"Not since the last curtain call. I just came back for my comdev. I left it in my office. Then I'm getting the hell out of here!"

Triani waved and headed to the lighted doorway. He pushed

the door up higher and jumped out into the brightly lit yard back of the theater. There was a huge hover flatbed parked all along one end of the yard with the name of Evalindo's Workshop studio on the side. But nothing else.

Marlo was taking his time looking around just inside the loading dock. "There are recent scrape marks here," he said.

"It's a fucking loading dock!" shouted Triani, beginning to pace. "What did you expect?" He headed to Evalindo's vehicle and climbed up on the narrow edge that ran all around it. But he couldn't manage to get inside no matter what he tried. He jumped down again, frustrated.

Marlo was sitting on the edge of the dock swinging his legs, apparently contemplating how to get to the ground. "Jump!" Triani shouted. "Holy shit! It's just a few feet."

"To you maybe," Marlo said, but he pushed himself off the ledge and landed without incident. "Where does that go?" He pointed to the right.

"The alley that runs past the stage door. The other way is where the loaded float beds come in to deliver supplies, scenery and shit. It leads out to the main commercial transport pads where they can take off. Nobody walks that way."

Marlo turned around and looked back at the theater. He walked closer and peered at some graffiti on the wall as if Eulio might be hiding inside. Then he paced back and forth, looking at it from different angles.

"For fuck's sake!" Triani burst out. "What are you going to do? It's been close to two hours already!"

"Was this here yesterday?" Marlo asked, pointing at the white square with the black and red squiggles.

"What difference does that make?"

"Just answer the question." Marlo's voice was suddenly firm, sounding more like an actual regulator than an absent-minded *tan*. Not that Triani had a *tan*, to his knowledge.

"Look, I don't make it a habit to leap into the theater through the loading entrance," the dancer said acidly. "You'll have to ask one of the stage crew."

At that moment Garlin arrived at the entrance. "Did you open this door?" he asked Triani accusingly.

"It was open already, sweetie, so don't blame me."

"Could you tell me if this graffiti was here yesterday?" Marlo asked, pointing to the offending paint on the wall.

Triani sighed.

Garlin craned his neck to look down at the wall. "I meant to get that painted over," he said, straightening up. "We've been pretty busy."

"When did it appear?" Marlo repeated.

Garlin scratched his head. "Lessee. I noticed it yesterday after the dress rehearsal. The ambulance that came to pick up the injured kid was parked out here, you see, so I noticed it then."

"Thanks."

"Now what?" demanded Triani.

"We need to find Eulio and fast."

"That's what I've been saying all along!"

"And I need to talk to that Evalindo person."

"He should be finished fainting by now. I'll get him. And I'll get Nevon, too. He's in charge of this madhouse after all."

"Thanks, but please, try to be discreet about it. I don't want hordes of people down here trampling all over possible evidence."

"Sure, sweetie. Discretion is my middle name."

"You don't have a middle name," Marlo pointed out.

Triani laughed. "Meanwhile, what are you going to do?"

Marlo pulled out his com-dev and punched in a code. "I'm calling in my team."

"Finally!" Triani leapt up on the loading dock and hurried off.

TWENTY-SIX

Marlo kept staring at the graffiti, walking back and forth, trying to find the sweet spot where the letters and shapes stood out and at last he did. He saw the VO surrounded by the vicious-looking serpent, dripping fangs open right under the V. What could it mean in this particular spot? It had to mean something or it wouldn't be here. Most of the graffiti seemed to be on the edge, or even lately inside, of Big Stendi's territory. That at least made some kind of sense. A warning, or a challenge, or possibly a boast. But here? What did the serpent people want with the theater? He wished he could talk to Johnny Diaz again, but he had no way of contacting the man since he had blocked his contact codes when calling Marlo.

For the first time Marlo wondered if a Terran would be able to decode the graffiti. He thought of his Terran friend Boothby whom he hadn't seen for a while. She had a Merculian lover last he'd heard and a new job so probably both were taking up most of her time these days. He reminded himself to give her a call to test her out on this idea.

To his surprise, Oslani arrived first. He and his lover had crashed the reception after the performance, and he was dressed to impress.

"Have to get out for a night of freedom from the BB," he said, seemingly energized by this new turn of events.

"You still calling the poor child the Boring Baby?" Marlo said, unbelievingly.

"Well, we've shortened it," said Oslani, hopping down to look at the graffiti. "Well, well."

Ferdalin had been at the performance, too, and was halfway home when he got the summons. He arrived soon after Oslani. Finally, Eldred and three of the others, plus Euvi who happened to be at work late and got the call there.

"Nice to be doing something other than drugs and sex," he remarked cheerfully, pushing up his sleeves. "You organizing a search for Adelantis? He's my fave, you know so I'm all over it!"

"Good, good." Marlo saw a smartly dressed Merculian heading his way from the lane. This must be Nevon, the one in charge of the theater whom Triani had mentioned. "Eldred, take over for me, and see they search the place inside and out. Just avoid the reception. Obviously he's not there."

He turned towards Nevon and began to ask questions about Eulio, the production, who may have threatened him lately, but the director seemed at a loss.

"Everyone adores Eulio," he protested, waving his hands about expressively. "And he wouldn't just leave like this. Obviously he must have been either lured outside on some pretext or been incapacitated in some way and taken out. But why?"

Why indeed.

When the search team hadn't turned up any clues, Marlo called for backup, extended the search area, and organized a clap and chat in the neighborhood. No one would mind being brought to their door this late if it helped locate one of the brightest stars of the Merculian National Dance Company.

All night teams of Cap City Regulators searched for Eulio Chazin Adelantis around the theater and its environs. They clapped at doors, chatted to people in the streets going home from Dance bars or parties, as well as some who had been at the Reception. Marlo never did get a chance to talk to Evalindo, who appeared to have left the theater with Foraline before anyone could stop him and now couldn't be found. Beny had pointed out with great ire that he had told Marlo about the threats on the message ribbons and he had been ignored! Marlo suggested Beny join the search party, thinking it would at least keep him occupied and out of the way. The obsessed fan idea was way down the list of things for him to worry about when black Terran flowers and the ominous Terran graffiti were part of the toxic mix. But there was still the vexing question of why the serpent people would be after Eulio.

Later that morning, when Marlo was once more sifting

through the security images from the cams aimed at the loading dock, he got a message that Triani was downstairs and wanted to see him. There was a group gathered around the dancer when Marlo arrived, raving about the *Night Bird*. Triani looked tired but he was always charming with his fans.

"You got anything to drink, sweetie?" he asked when they were seated in Room 1. "I'm parched."

Marlo handed over a tall glass of wake water.

Triani scowled but drank it anyway. "Okay, I just wanted to tell you something. It's not about Eulio and I've no idea if this has anything to do with anything, but it's odd." He paused and leaned forward, fixing Marlo with his intense black eyes. "This was a few nights ago backstage when I was…let's just say I was trying to avoid someone, so I took the long way to get to my dressing room. That's why I ended up walking near the loading dock where we were last night. Evalindo was there with two tough-looking Terrans, and they were threatening him. I think it might have been about credits, but I don't know for sure. They were pretty rough with him. One of them even hit him. Evalindo looked terrified. But as I said, this has nothing to do with Eulio. I just thought you should know." He tossed a tranq stick into his mouth.

"Thanks. Every little bit could help."

Triani stood up in one smooth, sinuous move. "Eulio is my best friend," he said, his voice husky. "If there is anything, and I mean *anything* I can do to help, just let me know."

Marlo struggled out of the chair which seemed slow to release him. By the time he was on his feet, Triani was gone. "Flying farts," he muttered. The more he thought about it, the more he saw this bit of news as an important piece of the puzzle. What if all this was really about Evalindo? What better way to get back at him for whatever reason than to take away one of the biggest stars of his new production? Eulio would certainly be easier to grab than Triani, say, and his good nature was well known. Marlo decided that he would have to do some research on the reclusive Evalindo. He hurried back to the team room and filled them in.

"We need a deep scoop into Evalindo, especially his finances.

Where does he come from? How did he get started? Is there any blot on his character anywhere? That sort of thing."

"What about the weird ribbon messages?" Oslani asked. "You want me to keep on that?"

Marlo hesitated. Could there be anything there? "Put it aside for now. I need everyone on the Evalindo background."

"I've found something on the security cams, I think." Capane, the youngest member of the team, was observant but lacked confidence. "I've been going over the security stuff for the back of the theater for the hour leading up to the arrival of Triani and you, boss."

"Good. I haven't had a chance to get that far. What did you find?"

Capane clicked on the images, so they were now projected on the wall. Oslani twisted around to see. "This is about twenty minutes or so after the last curtain call. Here are a few of the backstage crew jumping out and they hike away over to the alley that leads to the street, see? Then, about ten minutes later, this hover car arrives and backs up to the dock."

"Slow it down. Is that a logo or maybe writing on the side?"

"It's hard to make out clearly. The car sweeps in fast, as if the driver knows the way or maybe just, you know, practiced, see? No one gets out so I guess they must climb through the back directly into the building, clandestine, like." He said the long word as if it was rehearsed. Then he blushed.

Ferdalin laughed. "Clandestine?"

"It sure looks that way," Marlo said quickly. "That logo looks a bit like what's on Evalindo's big flatbed hover that's parked out there. Get the techs to enhance the thing. What happens next?"

The images sped up. Nothing seemed to be happening until all of a sudden, the car pulled away as suddenly and smoothly as it had come.

"You can't see anyone getting in so they must have crawled in through the back," Oslani remarked.

"Why would Eulio do that?" Ferdalin said.

"Maybe he was drugged, or knocked out or something," Capane suggested, his eyes shining.

Marlo shuddered. "Possibly. Or it was someone he knows."

He wished Eldred was here, but he was still leading the search teams. He also wished the security lights over the dock were angled so he could see into the doorway, not just the space in front.

"How did that person know the loading doors would be open?" Oslani asked. "Are they always left like that?"

"Triani said the crew usually leaves them open so they can nip out during a break, but why they were still open once the performance is done I have no idea," Marlo said. "I do know the Assistant Stage Manager was cross about it, so I suspect they aren't usually open that late. Does our kidnapper have an accomplice?"

"I'll check into that," Ferdalin volunteered.

Marlo chewed on a honey square while squinting at what he could make out of the writing on the side of the hover car. It could be anything, he decided disgustedly. It was almost as if it had been painted over.

"Marlo, I think I've got something!" Oslani was grinning from ear to ear. "It's not the answer but it's certainly a great place to start. Evalindo is from the River District."

Marlo smiled with satisfaction. At last! Something solid to investigate!

TWENTY-SEVEN

Beny was exhausted. He had stumbled home early that morning after a night of fruitless searching with the Regulators and crashed into his empty bed, clutching a pillow on Eulio's side. He was asleep instantly, but his sleep was plagued by wild dreams in vivid color. It was the same thing, over and over: Eulio in the distance, his figure getting farther and farther away while Beny ran and ran, panting hard but getting no closer. Then, the ground gave away beneath his feet just as he seemed to be getting somewhere. He screamed, jerking awake, short of breath and sweating time after time. Even strong sleep lozenges had little effect.

At last, he rolled out of bed and went for a swim. That didn't help. When Thar-von arrived unexpectedly to offer his support, Beny was glad to throw himself against his old friend, appreciating how the Serpian endured this close contact because he knew his Merculian friend would derive some comfort from the embrace. But Thar-von couldn't stay long.

Alone again, Beny wandered through the house, thinking he saw Eulio everywhere: wrapped in lacy shawls snoozing on the long couch near the pool, sitting in his favorite chair rubbing special paste on his dance shoes to make them more supple, reaching out to grab his hand as he passed by. Each time his eyes filled with tears. He kept going to Eulio's studio, hoping he would surprise him there, hear his laughing explanation that he had been there all along just working.

He contacted Marlo four times before receiving the recorded message that he would be informed if there was any news at all. He knew Marlo was doing his best and appreciated that the investigator had allowed him to join the search party last night but now he was asking him to wait. That was impossible.

Instead, he stepped outside into the crowd of vidsters who had been milling around for hours and made an impassioned appeal. He knew it would be instantly viewed by anyone checking for news and hoped it would remind them to call the hot line Marlo had set up if they had seen or heard anything. To make this more appealing, he offered a substantial reward for any information that proved useful. This was mostly to arouse the interest of any Elutians who might have noticed something but not bothered to tell anyone. To his surprise, soon afterwards Triani announced he would match the reward, this raising it to a truly princely sum.

Half an hour later, Beny was standing in the main reception room gazing at an early image of Eulio in pale diaphanous robes poised on one foot, his long blond hair blowing in the breeze when Dhakan came in and quietly announced the arrival of Parla.

"I'm sorry I couldn't get here earlier," Parla said at once, holding Beny in a tight embrace. "His parents are distraught, as you can imagine. Now they're calling on anyone they can think of who might help so I thought I could safely leave them to it and come here."

"I did that, too," cried Beny distractedly. "I called everyone!" He was clutching a pair of Eulio's dance shoes he had picked up somewhere. "I'm going mad with worry!"

"Have you had anything to eat?"

"I'm not hungry."

Parla walked over to the wall and punched in a number of codes. "You need to keep up your strength. Come over here and sit down."

"Marlo doesn't pay any attention to me," Beny said angrily, sitting down at the table across from Parla. "I told him about the threats ages ago. Several times."

"You mean those ribbon messages? Eulio said they were just weird fan stuff. He gets them all the time."

"Not like this."

Juice and food appeared beside them and Beny began to crumble a slice of protein bun absently as he told Parla his theories about the messages.

"Let me see them," Parla said, and finished off his juice. "Where are they?"

"Well, I'm not sure. Eulio stopped telling me about them and we had an awful fight when he found me raiding his message basket to get the latest ones. He locked them away after that and I nearly spent the night barred from our sleeping chamber."

Parla smiled ruefully. "I might be able to break that lock. We're cousins so our DNA is similar. Come on."

Beny got up and led him to the chamber. "This doesn't seem quite right," he murmured, but he pointed out the locked drawer where the basket was.

It only took a few minutes for Parla to break the seal and he pulled out the basket triumphantly. "Let's get them all spread out on your banquet table and see if there really is some pattern to this."

Beny trailed after him, trying not to feel too hopeful about this project. But Parla was an architect. He was an organized thinker. He might actually be on to something with his method.

An hour later the surface of the huge banquet table in the ceremonial reception salon was filled with tidy rows of disks, their ribbons cut off to save space. Parla had insisted they be arranged by date, which was clearly marked on the back of each one, along with the name of the production. Then they began to read each one and decide which to save for consideration and which were too frothy or standard issue to keep on the table. The basket began to fill up again as they read things like "Thanks for the great performance tonight, Eulio!" and "I never tire of seeing you in this role." Or just *"Toori! Toori!"*

"Keep the ones which look as if the person made up the tribute himself," Parla suggested. "Then we can consider if there is anything underneath the words."

This took a little longer but once they knew what to look for they picked up speed. When the table was less than a quarter full, they paused to consider what they had.

"Where are the latest ones?" Parla asked.

"I guess they're still in his dressing room. Can you call Triani to pick them up and send them over?"

Parla sat back in his chair and fiddled with his copper

medallion. "I'm not sure Triani will answer any call from me just now," he said at last. "We've had quite a serious blow-up. I said some terrible things to him, and I doubt he will forgive me anytime soon. The worst part is that I haven't had a chance to apologize, and I need to. For some of it, anyway."

"Try, Parla! We may be on to something here."

Parla pulled out his com-dev and punched in Triani's private code. To his obvious surprise, the dancer answered right away and in such a loud voice Beny could hear him from the other side of the table.

"You call to apologize, you shit?"

Parla pulled the device away from his head and looked at the arresting face of his lover. "I will but not here. I'm with Orosin. We want to know if you could please get Eulio's message basket from his dressing room and send it over. We're trying to piece something together."

"You think this might help?"

"It's a possibility, yes."

There was a pause.

"Please!" called Beny.

"Yeah, yeah, sweetie. Keep your panties on." And he was gone.

Beny and Parla looked at each other.

"I need a drink," said Parla.

Twenty minutes later Beny was into the sherry and Parla was finishing off a glass of *lim* when Triani appeared, carrying the basket. Dhakan was right behind him trying to catch up so he could introduce him properly.

"I need no introduction, sweetie. Buzz off." The dancer strode into the room and dumped the messages on the empty end of the table. "Looking for threats?" he asked conversationally. He sat down.

"Thanks, Triani," Beny said. "And that's exactly what we're looking for."

Triani began to cut the ribbons off the messages with his flashy dagger and shove them into a pile near Parla, who began to organize them in rows.

"This one's speckled," Triani remarked, setting it aside. "What do you suppose that is?"

"So are some of the others." Beny began studying the speckly ones. They were unusual and seemed to be all original.

"Only a few, though," Parla pointed out. He reached over for a handful and began to help Triani in the ribbon cutting.

Beny began to read the speckled ones. After a moment, he looked up, his face bright. "Listen, if you read these in a row, they make some sort of sense," he said excitedly. "And it's … weird. Listen:

'I come to see you every night, Eulio
And I love you more each time, my dear one
And as I get to know your grace, my joy only builds
And as music crashes, the finale approaches
The curtain will come down soon,
I saw that look for me alone tonight
You will soon dance, your face beside mine!
You will come because I need you to complete my life's
    masterpiece.
We need no one else, you and me—my wonderful muse.
Your beautiful face will soon shine here for me alone!'"

There was a pause.

"Holy shit," said Triani. "Call Marlo."

"I think I better go in person," Beny said.

TWENTY-EIGHT

"Old Livid wants to see you." Eldred gave Marlo a sympathetic look and rushed back to his desk.

Marlo had been expecting The Summons but that didn't mean he was prepared. Having spent most of the night searching for Adelantis meant there hadn't been enough time to get far in the investigation of Evalindo or anyone else. He knew pointing that out would be seen as an excuse, which he supposed it was. He swallowed a stim and took a deep breath. Walking into his boss's office, he noticed at once that the bottle of pink liquid had made an appearance on the huge desk. That was not a good sign. The pressure must be getting to Old Livid.

"Have you been doing anything at all useful anywhere to find Adelantis? You certainly never seem to be doing anything here." Liviano ran a hand over his sweating forehead.

"That's because I've been doing interviews," Marlo said. "I've just come from his spouse who gave me a good strong lead, one of several we're following."

"Which are?"

Marlo paused. When stated out loud the graffiti situation might sound thin, but he was convinced it was important, so he led with that. "We're working on decoding all the graffiti I've collected, starting with the one left at the theater the night before the dancer disappeared."

"That smacks of real desperation."

"We're also looking at a group of odd message ribbons which *chai* Benvolini just brought in now. I took them down to Charlo who has his lab techs analyzing the odd speckles that appear on most of them And I have someone working on figuring out if those alien black or purple rose flowers might mean something. Triani seems to think they do."

"None of this is going to satisfy all the powerful types who are breathing down my neck constantly. Surely you have something better?"

"Well, we have the questionable background of the director, Evalindo. He's from the River District."

"Everyone in the River District is not a criminal, Marlo!"

"I know, but—"

"And why in the name of all that's holy would he kidnap his own star?"

"Not him, *com.* The people he borrowed credits from to back his business."

Old Livid paused, about to take a swig of the pink liquid. "That sounds promising, but still not something I can give the family."

"Not yet, no," Marlo agreed.

There was a pause.

"Has it ever occurred to you that he may have gone off with a new lover?" Old Livid raised one eyebrow.

"But he's married!"

"Exactly. So the only way he can be with someone else he might want sex with is to run off."

"But it's illegal! Besides, he's been married all of six months and he adores his spouse!"

"Maybe, but it's not unheard of."

"I *know* him!" Marlo objected.

"You've *worked* for him, there's a difference. Now, go do some work for me! Why are you sitting around here? Get out and work!"

Marlo jumped up with alacrity and hurried back to the team room. His chief was getting more cynical by the day. Besides, they had only been working on this for about twenty-four hours. He was just in time to meet Charlo, coming in the door.

"You could have just called," Marlo objected.

"And miss the look on your luscious face? Never. Listen to this. Those speckles on the ribbon messages you sent down an hour ago are from the same paint that was on the dead blender."

Marlo sat down at the table. "But she couldn't have sent the last few. She was already dead. And by the way, have you found out anything to support the theory she was murdered?"

"I wish you'd never talked to that sibling of hers. I was just about to send her off to her father, telling him she died of cardiac arrest when you called in that latest info. I didn't mention anything about the poor condition of her lungs caused by the paint fumes combined with the toxic varnish smell. That didn't kill her anyway and he's upset enough. He keeps dropping by the outer office and pleading with me to release the body. I'd love to! But no, you said—"

"Charlo!"

The post-death specialist grinned. "Anything for you, sweet cheeks. Yes, I finally found an injection site under her external ear. This would be nigh impossible to do to oneself."

"Like this?" Marlo demonstrated, turning his head to one side and miming a needle injector high up into his own neck in approximately the place an external ear would be if he had such things.

"Sure, doing it like that is possible, but you wouldn't hit the sweet spot that way. If you want to kill someone you have to hit a vein, which in this Terran/Merculian blender is a little further back."

"I see." Marlo brought his arm down. "What was in the needle?"

Charlo shrugged. "No idea. It may just have been air. That would cause an air embolism that could stop the heart. No way to prove it, though."

"Flying farts!"

"Exactly. So, can I release the body now?"

Marlo sighed. He wished he could contact Johnny Diaz for more information, but as things stood, there was no reason to hold on to the poor thing. "Let her go."

"Thanks, sweet cheeks." Charlo grinned and saluted before sweeping out of the room.

"Don't you ever get tired of him?" Eldred asked, looking up from his screen.

"He's harmless." Marlo clasped his hands together and noticed the thread on one sleeve was coming out. He broke it off with a frown. "Anything on Evalindo yet? I need more background before I go and interview him."

"Well, his finances look...odd." Tabor flashed several complicated graphics onto the wall. "There's a lot more going out than coming in. Early on there are a few large deposits but I haven't been able to trace the source yet. I'm working on it. There has to be money from somewhere to fund all that property he has at the edge of town where his Wonder Workshop is. And he has a lot of people working there who have to be paid. Not to mention he has a house in the Eduan district."

"Okay. I've been digging, too." Oslani leaned back and steepled his fingers. "From what I've gathered, his kind of business has huge expenses setting up and it runs for a while without big returns. Later on the returns start rolling in when dance companies all over the planet rent his production to perform everywhere."

"But things haven't got to that stage yet?" Marlo asked, trying to understand.

"Not yet," Tabor broke in. "There's some income but *Night Bird* is the biggest production he's done so far and it's potentially the biggest earner."

"Maybe he couldn't hold on," murmured Oslani. "Maybe they want him to pay back the latest loan."

"That's what it sounds like." Marlo got up. "Keep working on this. And Oslani, could you go back to the ribbon messages for a while? There may be something there we missed."

"Sure. What are you going to do?"

"Find Evalindo and ask him a few questions." Marlo noticed the colored thread was now dangling about two inches from his sleeve and he ripped it out in annoyance. The sleeve promptly dropped to almost cover his hand. Fabulous.

TWENTY-NINE

Nevon's large but cluttered office was crowded and stuffy. Someone cracked open a window, letting in a much-needed breath of fresh air. Half the soloists of the company were there, perched on the edge of tables, cross-legged on the floor, a couple, like Triani, sprawled on the few chairs. Alesio chewed his thumb.

"I know Eulio's disappearance is difficult for all of us, and it means there's a lot to take into consideration here."

Triani snorted.

"Wait a minute!" Lumasine jumped to his feet as he usually did when he had something important to say. "Just so you know, my ankle is fine, and as long as it's taped I can dance the Day Bird as well as anyone. I did last night, didn't I? You got any complaints? Is that what you're going to tell me?"

"Not at all!" Nevon held out both hands in a conciliatory gesture. "I called you all here to see how you felt about closing the show until Eulio is found, not to critique performances."

There was a pause while they looked at each other.

"I think we should keep going, dedicating each night to Eulio," Alesio said at last. He was applauded loudly. "Let Carlini dance Eulio's role. He's up for it, right Carlini?"

The slight blond soloist perched on a stool in one corner smiled shyly and nodded, his pale face flushed with pleasure.

"For once Alesio said something sensible," remarked Triani.

"So be it. Eulio's understudy will take over the role." Nevon dusted off his hands as if that settled the question. "Let's hope it won't be for much longer. Thank you for coming."

The dancers left the room, muttering amongst themselves.

Triani made his way out the stage door, down the alley and across the street to his small but luxurious apartment on the top floor. He was so wrapped up in thoughts about his missing partner that he didn't notice the elegant figure waiting outside his door until he almost bumped into him.

"What are you doing here?" He waved the door open. "Finally come to apologize, you shit?"

"You not answering my calls made setting a time impossible." Parla followed him in and sat down, crossing his legs.

"Blame me, as usual." Triani threw his dance bag in the corner and poured himself some wine. He didn't offer any to Parla. "So?"

"Look Triani, I don't retract the essence of what I said, only the way I said it."

"What the fuck does that mean?"

"I had no right to throw some things you told me in deepest confidence in your face like that, especially in a public place. For that I sincerely apologize. I wish I could take back those words."

Triani perched tensely on the edge of a table. He reached up to the shelf behind him, took down a jeweled casket, grabbed out a pill and swallowed it. He closed the casket but kept it on his lap, his long fingers caressing the jewels absently. He felt so emotionally stirred by Parla's words, his very presence, he was afraid to speak for a moment.

"You think it's that easy? That I'll hear your voice and just melt?"

"Nothing is easy with you, dear. I've learned that much. I'm so sorry I hurt you."

"Isn't that what you wanted to do?" Triani spat.

"I wanted to wake you up to what was happening to Giazin. His little face was so bitterly disappointed when you didn't show up for the beginning of the recital I couldn't bear it. He kept saying: 'But he promised!' over and over."

"I fucking did come!" shouted Triani, jumping up and spilling the casket to the floor. "I saw his solo!"

"Not the first one."

"He should know how busy I am!"

"He's seven."

"Anyway, that's my business."

"Which means you're shoving me out of your life again, doesn't it?"

"Holy shit, Parla! What do you want from me? Giazin is well taken care of! I make sure of that!"

Parla got up and gathered up the casket and a few spilled pills. He handed it to Triani. "He has the best of everything. Just not you."

"So you're leaving me because I don't spend more of my time with my kid?" said Triani incredulously.

"I'm not leaving you. I'm just trying to explain."

"Shit." Triani put the casket back on the shelf and poured wine for Parla. "I'm not a perfect parent but I'm doing my best." He handed the wine to his lover. "And don't you *ever* throw my private past into my face like that again!"

Parla took the wine glass and touched Triani's cheek. "I swear," he said.

Triani pulled him closer. "You better keep that promise."

An hour later, Parla dropped the dancer off outside the Jewel Building. All this talk of family had reminded Triani that he hadn't seen his own young sibling lately and Parla had had to tell him the kid had moved in with his lover Liola. Triani hadn't had time to go home much lately so he hadn't noticed the youngster wasn't there. This bothered him, especially as he was not enamored with the kid Rio had fallen for so hard.

"Seems a bit pricey for a so-called apprentice jewelry designer," he remarked, but Parla just shrugged and took off.

Triani made his way inside, past the obsequious door manager who just stared before admitting that *Chai* Rio Porvan Erlindo did indeed live on the fifth floor. "May I say I just loved your performance as the Night Bird opening night, *chai!*'

'Thanks." Triani forced himself to linger a few moments before jumping on the lift-disk to be whisked out of sight.

Rio opened the door, and his mouth formed an O in surprise. "Why didn't you tell me you were coming?" he exclaimed, stepping back to let him in. "I'm just waiting for Liola. He should be here soon."

"Oh goody." Triani walked in, looking around at the spacious entry, the huge mural sweeping up to the high, colored glass ceiling, the mossy carpet with its complicated pattern.

Flowers perfumed the space and there was a walk out balcony through one floor to ceiling window.

"Holy shit, Rio! I hope you aren't paying for all this."

Rio shook his head and laughed. "Honestly, Triani, do you ever think of anything but credits? Anyway, this is Liola's place."

"The apprentice jewelry designer." Triani was still examining the room, noting the exotic statue in one corner, the expensive gems scattered carelessly in a bowl on one shelf. "Brings his work home does he?" He picked up an enormous *mantino* stone and held it up to the light. "Holy shit." It was genuine.

Rio was putting the final touches on a small table set for two. A sprig of flowers was at one place. As Rio bent over to light the candles, a large red egg-shaped jewel swung from a crystal chain around his neck.

"He give you that?"

Rio smiled and looked down at the necklace. "It's rare. It's from Rozemar."

The name rang a distant bell. Perhaps he had been there on tour. He didn't remember. Liola must be bringing in a lot more being a Wallflower than Triani had thought. He certainly hadn't given up that life if it supported all this. Or maybe something else was going on.

"Does Liola have another job?" he asked, idly picking up a jeweled dagger.

"Of course not. Why would he?" Rio glanced at the door then at the delicate timepiece on the wall. "He should be home by now," he said worriedly.

"Oh, for fuck's sake!" Triani burst out. "Liola is perfectly capable of looking after himself, believe me, which is more than I can say for you!"

"Just leave if you're going to be like that!"

"Rio, I'm trying to protect you!"

"Oh sure! I bet you didn't even notice I was gone!"

The truth of this stung. "Fine, then I'm out of here. Don't be late for the curtain!" Triani swept to the door. As he went through he heard Rio shout:

"Don't bother coming back!"

And that stung, too.

THIRTY

Newshounds still buzzed and swarmed annoyingly around the door of the Adelantis-Benvolini home. They had been there now for days as Beny sank deeper and deeper into gloom. Eulio's image was everywhere on the news channels, speculations about his whereabouts getting wilder and wilder. To distract himself, Beny had gone to several more meetings of the White Hats, leaving his home by the side door and sneaking back the same way. He had hoped they might have some information about Eulio's whereabouts, but they were as much in the dark as everyone else. Each time he returned filled with an increasing anxiety. He looked around his familiar city with new eyes, seeing the signs of an increased Terran and mixed-race population everywhere. The off-worlder market now had a much larger section dedicated to Terrans, selling everything from dried meat to oil paintings and earrings. He had also noticed a few odd paintings on walls around the riverbank. Graffiti, the Terrans called it, but its purpose was lost on most Merculians. The Round Chamber had asked him about the Terran use of such painting. Was it art? Or were they just defacing Merculian property?

"It can be art," Beny had told them, "or it can be an angry protest. Or just a territorial thing." He was thinking back to his time at the IPA Academy, with its preponderance of Terran students and teachers. There had been graffiti there, but it was mostly to piss off the authorities, as far as he remembered.

"Ah. Just as we suspected. Here it must be a territorial thing. The criminal element staking a claim to its territory. This is the work of Vince Omnia."

The others had nodded and Beny wished, for the hundredth time that the group was not such a top secret organization so they could tell the Regulators what they knew. But he couldn't worry about the Round Chamber and the strange habitués in their odd regalia. He had let them know today he would not be back until Eulio came home. All he could concentrate on now was his beloved. Was he lying somewhere, sick and disoriented? Had he lost his com-dev and couldn't communicate with anyone or call for help? Had someone taken him? But why? Nothing useful was coming in on the tip-line Marlo had set up and no one had tried to communicate about paying a ransom. It occurred to him that that idea was very Terran.

"Don't hurt him!" he prayed now. "Please, just don't hurt him!"

Dhakan entered the room quietly and cleared his throat. "There is someone called Evalindo to see you, if you are willing." The Kolari male had been hovering close by ever since Eulio disappeared, trying to submerge his own loss in Beny's. It was wearing.

"Show him in," Beny said.

Dhakan handed him a cool damp cloth to wipe away his tears and left.

"My dear *Chai* At'hali Benvolini, I am so, so sorry to disturb you at this anxious time." Evalindo was clasping his mittened hands in the folds of the deep red scarf around his neck. "The thing of it is, you see, I feel …somewhat…responsible for this…this…. May I sit down? I feel a little poorly."

Beny stared at him uneasily. He had beautiful eyes but there were dark circles under them, and his face was deathly pale. "Please, sit down. Would you like a glass of…something?" He glanced at Dhakan, who hovered near the door.

"Thank you, yes. Water. I need to take my medicine. I have health problems, you see." He took a purple envelope out of his pocket and when the glass arrived, tipped its contents into the water. At once small blue bubbles began to rise to the top, breaking into a froth and gradually turning the water blue. When the bubbles stopped fizzing, Evalindo drank the whole thing at one go.

Beny watched, fascinated by the whole performance. Once the drink was gone, he said, "You were saying something about feeling responsible? Do you mean about Eulio?"

Evalindo wiped his mouth with one finger. "Yes. Forgive me, my dear *Chai* At'hali Benvolini. I need to fill you in on something very...personal, so you will understand what I mean." He paused and traced a circle on the table in the ring of water left by the sweating glass. "This *Night Bird* production at the National is the biggest and best production I have ever done. And it was very, very expensive. In my business, it takes a lot of credits up front to mount a production. The payoff comes much later and is usually very profitable, but meanwhile...Well, there is a time when one is quite...living on air." He wiped the wetness of the table completely with his hand and cleared his throat.

Beny held back his impatience, wondering how he could prod the director along to the part concerning Eulio.

"Do forgive me for going into all this. It is hard for me to admit I have mismanaged my finances somewhat." He paused again.

"And Eulio?" Beny couldn't help blurting out.

"Yes. Dear Eulio. He is such a wonderful performer as well as a delightful person. I am so sorry he has been taken because of me!" Evalindo sniffed and wiped his eyes.

Bloody damn, Beny thought. He glanced at Dhakan, who was still standing near the door biting his lip.

"You see, I had to borrow heavily to get this job done. I have a large number of people working for me who need to be paid and many different kinds of materials to buy and...well, that doesn't matter to you. Suffice it to say, I overextended myself and had to borrow from the wrong group...and then my debt was taken over by...a much worse group, you see, and... Well, my dear *chai*, these people will stop at nothing to get the debt paid off. They... They threatened me." He paused again.

"Bloody damn! Just tell me!" Beny exploded.

The director seemed to shrink into himself. "I couldn't pay the whole thing so they gave me 24 hours to get the rest but then, when I still couldn't scrape it all together...Eulio was taken to hurt *me*! *My* production! You understand?"

Beny sat back in his chair, trying to digest all this. "Are you telling me that if you pay off the rest of the debt, they'll let Euli go?" he said at last.

Evalindo nodded.

"How much?"

Evalindo looked away. "I didn't know who else to go to," he said, and told him the amount he still owed.

"Bloody damn." Beny stared at the director. Why did you wait for days to tell me, he wanted to scream, but what good would that do? "All right, just give me an hour to set this up. I'll have to move some credits around and get a special transfer to my ring for that amount. Do you know where they are, these people? Where we should go to pay them?"

"Yes. I've been there before."

"Wait here. If you want anything, ask Dhakan."

It took a lot of talking to get things set up and Beny didn't have access to all their combined assets yet, but he managed in just over an hour. He hadn't wanted to involve anyone else, certainly not Eulio's family. There was a chance this scheme might not work out well. He wasn't sure how much to trust Evalindo but at least it was something to try that made some sort of sense. He couldn't stay here doing nothing any more.

"I will come with you," Dhakan announced as he started back to rejoin Evalindo.

"No, you will not," Beny said firmly.

"But I must help. You cannot go alone with this person," Dhakan said, clenching his hands. "I cannot lose you."

"Dhakan, you won't lose me," Beny said gently. "Thank you for your offer of help, but I need you to stay here in case Eulio comes home. I don't want him to find an empty house. Please. Stay."

Dhakan stared at Beny for a long moment. "I will stay," he said at last.

Beny and Evalindo crept out the back way and set out for the River District in an air-cab, which let them out near the Dragon Bridge. Evalindo became more and more nervous as they walked along the river bank and they passed fewer and fewer people strolling in the afternoon sun. They passed one of those walls covered with the graffiti the Round Chamber people had been discussing. Beny could make no sense of it as he went by. Then a rundown bar came into sight and Evalindo slowed down. The flickering sign had some of the letters of the name missing but Beny guessed it said Pantalo's.

"I have to check here to make sure where Crystal and Leo are now," he said.

"But you said you knew," Beny objected, glancing at the dubious bar with distaste.

"I know how to find them. There's a difference." The director coughed. He pulled out a small bottle and took a swig. "I'll go in and ask."

"I'll come, too."

Evalindo shrugged and slipped the bottle back in his pocket. He hesitated. "They're not very nice in here, my dear *Chai* Benvolini. I'm sorry."

Beny had already decided the manners in this sort of place would not be salon ready. Once inside, he almost held his breath. It was crowded with large hulking Terrans whose hygiene was not top quality. They seemed very hairy to the Merculian, used to his own species' smooth hairless faces. The men and women surrounded some sort of game table and were cheering on their player with hoots and cheers. Beny winced.

The two Merculians made their way to the back. Evalindo held his scarf over his nose and Beny took short breaths. The tall lanky youth behind the bar leaned over and glared at the director.

"What the fuck you want now, hermie?"

"I need to talk to Crystal."

"So? Why not give her a call?"

"I need to talk to her face to face. This is important!"

"Oh yeah? Who's your cute friend?"

"If you mean me," Beny said, trying to stand as tall as possible, "I am someone who also needs to talk to this Crystal person."

A tall Terran female shoved Evalindo out of the way as she pushed up to the bar. "Give me a Shtolli, Len," she said.

The director caught hold of Beny's arm to keep from falling.

"Where can we find Crystal?" Beny raised his voice to be heard over the din of cheering behind him and hung on to the edge of the bar to keep from being pushed aside.

"Oh, for God's sake!" exclaimed the female. "Crys is probably over at Bixie's across the river. You know it?"

"Yes." Evalindo looked even more pale than he had before, Beny thought as they made their way back outside.

"Is it far away?" Beny asked, straightening his tunic.

"It's in the old section of the River District," the director said. "I'm so sorry!" He was almost sobbing.

Bloody damn, thought Beny. If he says he's sorry one more time I am going to push him over and trample on him! He slipped his large cred-ring into his inside pocket and followed Evalindo across the narrow footbridge into the alleys and byways of the River District, a place where he had never been. He hoped Evalindo really did know this place. He had heard it was easy to get hopelessly lost here and he had to find Eulio.

THIRTY-ONE

Marlo spent fruitless hours trying to track down Evalindo. His house was deserted but a helpful neighbor told him the director hadn't been home for days.

"That cute little dancer he seems to be with now dropped by a few days ago and left about half an hour later with two bags. Maybe they're going away for a while?"

That seemed unlikely but one never knew. Perhaps he just wanted to avoid an interview. "Did he leave in an air-cab?" Marlo asked.

"Yes, but I'm afraid I don't know which one. Sorry. I'm usually more observant but just then my com-dev buzzed and… Anyway…" He shrugged.

"You've been a great help. Thank you."

But Marlo was now at a loss. There was a slim chance the 'cute little dancer' the neighbor spoke of could be with the Merculian National, but there were many dance companies in the city. He could be in any of them. Anyway, Marlo didn't know his name. He checked with the theater, but the director hadn't been seen there since Eulio's disappearance four days ago.

Marlo headed for a Snack House to pick up a sweet layer bowl and do some heavy thinking. It was possible Evalindo had nothing to do with this mess, he mused, chewing thoughtfully. Triani may have misinterpreted what he saw, though it would be difficult to misinterpret a big Terran hitting a much smaller Merculian. And then there was the graffiti. And the black flowers.

He put down the bowl and stared out at the park across the wide street. He licked his fingers absently as his com-dev emitted the familiar coded buzz for the secured channel.

"Dasha Bogardini here."

"Marlo, get over to the Paseral Footbridge fast." Old Livid was shouting. "Eldred is on his way there now with Charlo and a few of your team. Be as quick as you can. This is bad. Real bad."

"Another body?" Marlo quavered, but Liviano had gone.

Marlo left the Snack House at once, waving goodbye to the owner, who knew him well. What was going on in Cap City? The Paseral Footbridge led to the River District but only the outskirts of the infamous neighborhood. Marlo climbed up to the old Ring Car station nearby and swung himself onto the colorful car that had just arrived. There was a station near the footbridge, and it would be faster than finding an air-cab. He arrived in ten minutes and walked quickly along the bank. A small crowd was gathering on the bridge, leaning over, trying to see what was going on underneath. He spotted a group of his team near the water on the other side under the bridge. One of them was throwing up.

Marlo paused, his stomach lurching unpleasantly. Then he started across the bridge, ignoring the newshounds who tried to ask him questions and struggled down the bank, slipping and skidding until he landed on his bottom, sliding the last few feet.

Eldred helped him up. "I've never seen anything like this," Eldred said, tears in his eyes. "Prepare yourself."

Marlo stepped over the vomit and walked carefully to the statue of the winged beast who helped support the bridge above. Between the paws sprawled a naked body, almost as if the large animal was holding it out as a trophy. Marlo paused. There was something familiar about the body. He forced himself to go closer.

Charlo reared up from his examination and shouted, "Someone get up there and extend the canopy! Those news buggers are sending float cams!"

Eldred and the young one who had probably done the vomiting sprang to action and soon the scene was completely shielded. For now.

Charlo's face was grey. He glanced at the investigator and shook his head. "He's been here a few hours," he said at last, "but he wasn't killed here. The bastards who did this went to a lot of trouble to display him this way."

"Why?"

"That's your job!" He moved aside, letting Marlo see the body up close for the first time.

"Oh, my gods of the universe!" exclaimed Marlo, clapping a hand over his mouth. "I *know* him." He turned away for a moment. This was the worst murder he had ever seen. It was especially bad since he recognized the dimples and usually sparkling blue eyes of Liola Tavalino Simosin. They weren't sparkling now. He reached out and closed the staring empty eyes, not caring about evidence. Someone had drawn red tears down one cheek. "He worked for Big Stendi."

"A Merculian couldn't have done this," Charlo said.

The body was obviously on display, making a cruel statement. They had carved a circle in the middle of his narrow chest, congealed blood making it stand out grotesquely against his pale skin. His legs had been forced far apart and a large carved, painted flower had been shoved deep inside. Incongruously, his fingernails and toes were painted a deep blue to match his eyes. It was the luminous sort of paint used by the young party set. His pubic hair was trimmed into a heart shape. Had he done that himself?

Marlo swallowed. "Did he die quickly?"

"I don't think so. I can't tell you a whole lot yet, but I know this was done while he was still alive." He pointed to the carved circle. "He must have done something that pissed someone off big time."

Marlo looked more closely at the circle. Was it a crude representation of the O of the serpent people? Did they kill poor Liola as a sign to Stendi to back off? But the youth wasn't that important to the Stendi crew, as far as he knew. But then again, he rarely could get much out of the kid. Maybe Marlo had completely misjudged him.

The after-death team had arrived and were now tenderly wrapping the body, ready for transport.

"Someone must be missing this one," one of them said.

And Marlo suddenly remembered the last time he had seen

the youth, his arm around Rio Porvan Erlindo at the *Night Bird* Gala. He turned away and climbed wearily up the bank to sit in the shade of the bridge out of sight of all the prying eyes above.

"Are you okay?" Eldred sat down beside him and reached over to touch him just long enough to let him feel the sympathy.

"There's no record of any parents for Liola back at HQ is there?"

Eldred shook his head. "He said his *tatsi* wasn't in the picture and his *mertsi* is dead, as I recall. I think he has a *tan*, though.'

Marlo grunted. "Scando, that dealer in stolen gems. I'm not sure he's actually related. They don't share any names."

Eldred nodded. "He may have lied about all of it."

"I have to go." Marlo let Eldred help him up. "Clear those gawkers off the bridge before they take the kid away. You're in charge."

There was a regulator car and driver waiting for him at the top of the bank. Liviano must have sent it. Marlo climbed in with relief. "Just take me home," he said. His hands were unsteady as he contacted his boss and gave him a quick report. "I need to go home now before I contact his people."

There was a pause. "If you need some time off..."

"I'll be in tomorrow," Marlo said quickly. "This evil person has to be found."

Once home, Marlo took off all his clothes and had a long, long shower, as if trying to wash away the evil he had been so close to under the bridge. Liola was no angel, but no one deserved this desecration!

He dressed in clean clothes and made sure all buttons were present and nothing was fraying. He went so far as to dig out his best shoes, even though they pinched his toes a little. By now, Rio would be on stage. The afternoon performance of *The Night Bird* would be drawing to a close. He called an air-cab, still not feeling up to driving, and arrived at the theater soon after.

This was the worst part of his job, and he was thankful he had not had to do it very often. But this time... He decided he should tell Triani first. Rio would need support and the volatile super star had better be prepared to give it. As he descended from the parking pad on the roof, he tried to find the words he would need to get the bad news across. There was no good way.

"What the hell are you doing back here!" Triani greeted him as he walked into the dressing room. The dancer was sprawled half naked in the chair in front of his dressing table. He sat up straighter when he saw Marlo's expression. "What's the matter? What happened? Is Giazin okay? Tell me!"

"He's fine. This doesn't concern you directly, but I need your help with something."

The dancer ran his fingers through his hair "This is bad, isn't it?"

"Yes. There's no easy way to say this. Liola is dead. I know he's close to Rio, so I thought——"

"Holy shit! What happened?" The dancer stared at him, shocked.

"He was killed, but I'm not at liberty to give out any details."

"Fuck! I wasn't keen on the little shit but...murder?" He grabbed a pair of leggings and pulled them on. "Pass me that shirt and we'll go to Rio. We can't let him get out of here first."

Marlo reached over and handed him the shirt. Two minutes later he was puffing along after Triani out of the luxury of the Principals' section and upstairs to the lesser ranks. He barreled into the door at the end with Rio's name on it. It was the only one sporting a gold star.

Rio was already dressed. He was just adjusting a long glittering hair ornament into his black curls where it dangled almost to his shoulder.

"Triani, I meant what I said——" Seeing Marlo he stopped. "Excuse me, I didn't see you there, *Com* Marlo. Did you enjoy the show?"

"I need to talk to you," Marlo managed.

"I don't have much time. Liola and I are going dancing at Balio's." He picked up a bunch of message ribbons and dropped them in a basket.

"Rio, I'm very, very sorry, but he won't be coming." Marlo swallowed. "I'm afraid he's dead. I'm so sorry."

The smile faded from Rio's face. Confusion clouded his dark eyes. "No. No. You must be mistaken. He'll be here any minute."

"No, he won't," said Triani softy.

"You just shut the fuck up!" Rio shouted. "You're *wrong*."

"Rio, dear, I'm afraid he's right. Liola is dead."

Rio sat down suddenly. "But...how? He can't be. He's younger than me! He won't even have his *cimbola* ceremony for another few months."

"I'm sorry," Marlo repeated.

Rio began to cry.

Triani pushed Marlo out of the way and bent down to put his arms around the sobbing youth. His sibling began beating his hands against Triani, trying to push him away. "Get away! You hate him! You don't know anything about real love."

"Maybe not, sweetie, but I know about loss and I'm not going anywhere." Triani knelt down and hung on until Rio stopped struggling.

Marlo left quietly, his eyes damp.

THIRTY-TWO

Beny scraped something green and smelly off his shoe and ran through the covered alley to catch up with Evalindo. They had been walking steadily along narrow streets, the broken pavement littered with decomposing drug boxes and discarded bits and pieces of unrecognizable junk. The damp smell of neglect was everywhere, mixed with some acrid odor Beny didn't recognize.

"It's home brew," Evalindo said noticing his expression. "We're near one of the main *brams*, as they call them." He promptly covered his nose again.

Beny hoped Eulio wasn't being held too close to one of those places. "How much farther?" he asked, noticing a gaggle of mixed racers and young Terrans lounging against a crumbling wall doing smoke. Beny moved a little faster. He had a good sense of direction, honed by his years in the IPA Academy, but he was now hopelessly lost with no idea of the way out of this place.

"Up here," Evalindo said suddenly, pointing to a long narrow flight of stone steps that took a turn to the right where a red arrow had been painted on the wall. Once they got there, Beny was relieved to see there was a door right at the landing with a small V carved in the wood above. It looked as if it had been done recently.

About to clap at the door, Beny stopped as Evalindo pulled him back.

"It's a bar," he whispered.

"There's no sign," Beny pointed out.

"That's the point."

Beny felt the fear and desperation leaking from the director's touch. "If you say so. You go in first."

"But—"

"They know you. I'll be right behind you," he added encouragingly as he stepped back.

Evalindo hesitated. At last, he touched the door at the left side, and it opened. He stepped through into the dimness beyond and Beny forced himself to follow. It smelled strange in the long narrow room. Beny took in as much as he could with one swift glance. One wall was decorated with images of all kinds of weapons, not at all reassuring. At the back to the right of the bar, several large Terrans were throwing an axe at a target to shouts of approval. Bloody damn, he thought, feeling sweat break out between his shoulder blades. The air was heaving with smoke, and not the good kind to Merculian nostrils. Loud Terran voices laughed and boomed, the low registers strange to Merculian hearing.

"Look who's here!" shouted a deep voice. "And Evi's brought a little friend, too. How sweet." A bearded male strolled up, looming over the pale Evalindo. "Glad you came to your senses. It's always better to pay. Hand it over."

"So now we're even and you won't threaten my productions or performers anymore?"

"Why would we do that, doll?" It was the female who had been throwing axes. "Who's your friend?"

"I am Orosin At'hali Benvolini," he said, as calmly as he could, "and I have the credits. But first I want to see Eulio."

"You can see anyone you want, doll, *after* you turn over the money."

"Business first, know what I mean?" the male added. He was looking far too closely at Beny for him to feel comfortable. He realized someone had moved between him and the door. There was no exit that way. That left the window to the left of the door or the one high up on the gallery above, if he could get that far.

The woman reached out and grabbed both his hands in her large one. He forced himself to remain still although every fiber of his being cried out to pull away. He knew what she was looking for.

"Where's your cred ring?"

Beny could feel her anger. "Where is Eulio?"

She released his hands and slapped him hard on the face.

Beny ground his teeth in rage as he staggered to keep from falling.

"Don't play games with me," she growled.

"You want me to turn him upside down and shake it out of him?" asked the male with a broad grin.

"That won't be necessary," Beny replied with dignity. His face burned on one side, but he held himself erect and slid the ring out of his inner pocket. "First the credits, then––"

"Yeah, yeah." She held out her hand, grabbed his wrist and touched her own ring to his, extracting the whole amount Beny had transferred earlier. "Okay. Nice doin' business with you." She dropped his hand.

"We'll be here when you need another infusion of cash, Evi," added the bearded male, grinning at Evalindo.

"Wait! Where's Eulio?" cried Beny.

"Don't ask me, doll." She laughed.

"No, no. I paid, now where is he?"

"You accusing me of something?" The female had turned away but now she paused and looked down at him, scowling. Her eyes were hard as stone.

"I'm just asking you to keep your end of the bargain."

"What bargain? I loaned your pal money, you paid it back. End of story. Now clear off."

Beny jumped forward and grabbed her arm, trying to feel if she was hiding anything, but all he felt was anger. And the others were rushing towards him.

"Come on!" Evalindo made for the door, now that the male had moved away from it and slipped outside, leaving Beny to fend for himself.

Beny acted on pure instinct, and the aggression training he had learned years ago at the Academy. Pressing forward, he thrust his leg behind her knee. As expected, she tumbled back with a cry of rage, giving Beny a moment to jump though the opening in the ring of people. He drew his dagger and stabbed one of the males in the arm as the man reached out to stop him, then leapt, feet first, out the window. The thunk of an axe rang out as it hit the wall, missing his head by inches as he slipped a moment on the broken glass, tearing a long cut on his arm, then scrambled to his feet. At that moment a tall gaunt male wearing a black vest over his sparkling white shirt paused on the steps, blocking his way. Beny was aware of cold grey eyes before he slashed out with his dagger, slicing the man's hairy wrist before he leaped past him and slid onto the sloping roof and down onto the ground. He didn't pause to see if he was being followed. He just ran back the way he had come, then turned to his left. At every step he feared another axe would tear into his shoulder or worse, the man he had wounded would shoot him with something lethal, but he couldn't hear any pursuers.

From up above someone called his name. Evalindo was crouching on the upper level, gasping for air. He gestured for Beny to turn right along an alley. When he did, he saw a flight of narrow rickety steps leading up, and up till he arrived on the third level outside a row of cube houses, set at odd angles to each other. Bridges led from one to another here and there but without an intimate knowledge of the place it would be impossible to guess which ones were public throughways and which private. He was glad he had kept in shape with his daily workouts.

"They're not following us, but they might put the word out for others to be on the lookout," Evalindo said. "Follow me."

Beny wondered how the director knew this malodorous place so well but now was not the time to ask. He plunged after the thin figure whose scarlet scarf now flew out behind him like a beacon, as he leapt with surprising agility from one uneven platform and bridge to another. Occasionally people of various races or mixed blood would open a door to shout at them and once someone from a higher level flung garbage down on them but at last Beny caught sight of the river and the Pasarel Footbridge. By now the light was fading fast but in another few minutes they would be safe. He still didn't know where Eulio was. All he knew for certain was that his spouse wasn't with the gang he had just escaped from. Oh Eulio! Where are you?

THIRTY-THREE

Marlo couldn't sleep in spite of several dream lozenges of different colors and strengths. At last, he gave up and went to sit on his garden shelf. Absently he massaged the roots of the big *trafel* plant he had rescued from almost certain death on a neighbor's front porch weeks ago. It had grown too big for the desk in his office, so he had lugged it home. Now it was repaying his loving care with beautiful spikey orange blossoms. As he watched the flowers slowly waking up around him, he was thinking of Beny's unexpected appearance last night, catching him just as he was leaving work. Beny, looking quite the worse for wear, had told him what had happened with Evalindo in the River District and demanded to know what progress had been made in Eulio's case. There was nothing much to tell the poor soul. Marlo just wished Evalindo had come with him. But no, apparently the director had dropped out of sight again.

A clapping outside his door startled him. A moment later, Eldred appeared.

"Don't get up," he said. "I've brought you some hot chocolate."

This was a big concession from Eldred, who rarely touched the stuff himself. Even though Marlo had given up on the healthy diet regime El had tried to convince his corpulent colleague to follow, it was still out of character to indulge him like this.

"What's the matter?" Marlo took the chocolate and sipped warily.

"I couldn't sleep either."

That didn't answer the question, but he drank his chocolate anyway. Eldred would get to the point when he was ready.

They sat side by side for a while in silence. At last Eldred spoke.

"I always get up early," he began, "and I do my exercise regime and then read the news flashes while I eat breakfast." He paused. "I'm sorry, Marlo, but I have to show you something truly dreadful."

"I knew there was something," he murmured uneasily. His new-found calm was fast disappearing. "Show me."

Eldred activated an image and projected it on the wall of the small house.

Marlo gasped in shock. "The bastards! The evil pieces of excrement!"

Liola's desecrated body filled the area, everything they had done to him clearly visible. Marlo forced himself to study it.

"That isn't from a regular news source," he said. "Not even the dubious ones would publish something like that."

"There's no tag," Eldred added.

"Look at the angle," Marlo went on slowly. "That wasn't taken from the bridge or even the top of the bank. The shadows are wrong, too. It was taken earlier. And look at the poor child's legs. That right leg was not hanging over that much when we got there. The bastards who killed him took this image because they wanted everyone to see what they'd done!"

"I knew there was something odd about the angle."

"Turn it off." Marlo climbed to his feet. "This was all for Big Stendi," he said. "This is war."

"In the River District?"

"I doubt it will stay there. We've got to get that image taken down."

"No one in tech will be in yet," Eldred said. "I'll send a request marked urgent."

"Keep on them. I'm going to get dressed. See you later."

All the time he was getting ready that horrible image stayed with him. His anger and grief steadily mounted as he imagined Rio seeing this. Did he ever read anything but *Dance News*? Marlo had to get it down and traced. He contacted Oslani who said Eldred had already sent him the image.

"I'm working on it," Oslani said. A baby cried out in the background. Someone began to sing, and the crying stopped. "Look, Marlo, someone very smart has done this piece of crap.

The origin trail seems to go around in circles, and I can't get anywhere with the damn thing!"

"Keep trying."

"I'm going in to HQ now. The techie unit might be able to help."

This was unlikely. If Oslani was stymied, there wasn't much hope anyone there could help. But there was someone who might. Without stopping to give it any more thought, Marlo punched in the contact for his Terran friend Boothby. She was legit now but years ago she had been a cracker. Now she was using her amazing technical abilities to help keep the InterPlanetary Alliance cyber system invulnerable.

"Marlo!" she exclaimed at once. "Sorry I haven't been around much lately." Then her expression changed to a concerned frown. "What's up?"

"Boothby dear, I need your help with something...terrible. I need to trace who took a certain vile image and is now broadcasting it everywhere. Do you have time to–"

"If it's important to you, sure."

"Oslani can't seem to make much headway."

"He's good but I'm better." She grinned up at him.

"I'm sending it now, for your eyes only." He pushed a button.

"Jesus!" She looked shocked.

"I'm sorry."

There was a pause. "Look, I can't do this here. We're coming over."

"We?"

But she was gone. Perhaps the new lover worked at the same place. That hadn't occurred to him before.

In no time Boothby burst in the door with a striking Merculian in tow. "This is Rosian. He's almost as good as I am." She grinned down at him fondly.

"She means every bit as good." Rosian smiled a gap-toothed winning smile that was all that was needed to show his appeal to Boothby. That and the sprinkle of freckles on his nose, his muscular build, the long straight reddish-brown hair down his back and the sexy swing to his narrow hips when he walked. Marlo wondered if she realized how old Rosian was. Not that it mattered. Merculians looked about the same age for a long time, only their compatriots noticing the tiny signals of passing time.

They both began pulling small silver rolls from their bags and spreading them out on the table Marlo had cleared for them. Without another word, they activated their lightboards and logged into the news channel. The cruel image came up almost at once.

"That is unforgiveable. No Merculian would do this."

"Shut up, Rosi."

"It's true," he said, sitting back and looking at her, his head on one side.

"Could you two just find who did it and argue later?" Marlo pleaded.

"Sure, boss. This is just how we roll."

At that moment the com-dev buzzed on his private line. Triani. "How's Rio?" Marlo asked at once.

"Under sedation. The healer is with him. But if he wakes up and sees that abomination in the news he'll go stark raving mad! It's even on *Dance News* for fuck's sake! Get it down, Marlo!"

"I have my best people on it and we're moving as fast as we can."

"Move faster!" Triani broke the connection.

"What does Triani have to do with this?" Boothby asked, her hands still flying over the keys, her eyes glued to the screen, tracking along the hidden byways through cyber space.

"The poor thing was his sibling's lover."

Rosian's fingers stumbled for a moment, then went on. "I'll try the Breen Loop algorithm, Boo. You keep doing what you're doing."

Boothby nodded. "You can go, boss. We'll contact you as soon as we crack this thing."

"And we will," Rosian added. His long rusty hair gleamed in the sun from the open door as Marlo left.

When he walked into the Major Incident room, it was still early and even Old Livid hadn't arrived. Marlo's team, however, was all hard at work. This case was so vicious no one wanted to be absent when a breakthrough happened.

Oslani glanced up. "Those IPA people have better equipment than we do," he said resentfully.

"How do you know?"

"Oh, come on. Boothby's my occasional babysitter and I called to find out if she could come over this evening."

"It's not a competition. Just do what you can," Marlo said. "I have to see Charlo. I'll be back for reports."

None of the usual insinuations or comments followed him as he made his way down to the Skullery. The post-death specialist was sitting in his office, drinking something dark. He didn't get up when Marlo came in.

"Cause of death was strangulation." He took another drink and got up to rinse out his glass. "The one doing it had large hands. Terran, I would say, though it could have been a blender, I suppose."

Marlo nodded. This fit with his own way of thinking.

Charlo sat down again and began to fiddle with the few items on his shiny white desk. "Before they got around to that, they raped him. Two males, several times, front and back. Then they carved the circle on his chest. Someone had trimmed his pubic hair into the shape of a heart, although that could have been done before the kid fell into their hands. Then they... shoved the stick with the flower..."

"Yes. When we find these people, we can identify them from traces left on the child?"

"The bastards who did the rape, yes. I've started building a 3D ident-image using the DNA they left behind. You'll have their faces as soon as I finish, but it takes time, especially with Terrans."

"I know you'll do your best," Marlo soothed.

"If there were others involved, females for instance, I don't know. I haven't quite finished. There may be skin drift and that would do it."

"Let's hope so." Marlo looked at his old colleague. Charlo could be annoying sometimes but he was good at his job, and he took a lot to heart, hiding behind his sly humor and supposed overactive libido. Right now, there was nothing jocular to be seen in his drawn face.

Marlo got to his feet and leaned over the desk, reaching out to take the specialist's hands in both of his. The shock of pain hit him more strongly than he was expecting but he didn't break the link until Charlo withdrew.

"We'll get the bastards," Marlo said and left the room. But he wondered.

Upstairs rang with jubilant cries. "It's gone!" they chorused as he entered.

"The image?"

"Yes! No trace of it."

Marlo glanced at his com-dev as it buzzed. "Boothby?"

"It's gone, boss, but we didn't trace it. They took it down themselves, which makes me think we were getting close. These people don't want to be found. Rosi says it was a warning."

"I expect Rosian's right," Marlo said.

Any hopes of further good news were dashed as he was sifting through reports from the tech crew who had been working on cleaning up the image partially visible on the van used to abduct Eulio. In spite of all their expertise, they had managed to discover only that whatever had been there had been painted over just enough to make it indecipherable. Depression settled over Marlo like a heavy fog. Flying farts! Who was this person?

Just at this point, a young regulator he didn't recognize appeared in the doorway, shifting nervously from foot to foot. Marlo waved him in and waited. And waited. The youngster seemed tongue-tied.

"You have something to tell me?" Marlo prodded gently.

The youngster clutched his message cube and turned red. "I h-h-have it! We f-f-found him, *Com!*" He waved the cube in front of Marlo.

"Who did you find, dear?" Marlo asked patiently. "Perhaps it would be easier to stream the message?"

The young Regulator looked relieved and shone the image of a tall Terran female on the wall. At once Marlo recognized Eulio's stalker, only now there was a name and address attached.

The excitement, however, was short-lived as once more they were led down another blind alley. The address turned out to be a public building near the SpacePort. Still, it was progress of a sort.

That night the wind had risen and was whipping around the corners of Marlo's small house, creating a sort of moaning noise that went along with his thoughts. Marlo was just finishing his stale leftover hot pot when there was a noise outside on his garden shelf. He grasped Helly's arm, which had come off while the rickety 'bot was trying to clean the sleeping chamber, and advanced as quietly as he could. He flung the door open and found Cushna outside, clutching his jacket together against the wind and hauling a brown bag behind him.

"Marlo, ya gotta help, nah?"

"Why?" asked Marlo, holding more tightly to the door.

"I was on ta same crew as Liola, wasn't I? I don't wanna die!"

While Marlo stared at him dumfounded, Cushna stepped nimbly through the still-open entry and closed the door.

"You're snaps, Marlo," he said. "For a razzer," he added. "Got anything to eat?"

THIRTY-FOUR

Right on time, Beny marched up to the Round Chamber, his white hat and gloves in place, carrying the large glowing egg that showed he had made an official request to speak to the assembly. He sat down at his desk and set the orb down where it seemed to glow brighter. The others took their seats around him, each one nodding a greeting as they arrived. Beny had not tried to cover the long scar on his arm, made by the shattered glass as he slid to his escape yesterday. Instead, he had chosen to wear a short-sleeved tunic to make it all the more visible. He also had a bruise on his cheek and had not treated that either. He needed his statement to be as strong as possible. Everyone who greeted him noticed, though they tried not to react.

Beny was barely aware of the opening rituals, standing and sitting when the others did, going over the arguments he would use in his head. When his egg emitted a trilling series of chords, Beny stood up.

"Excellencies. Any government agency, no matter what its stated purpose, has as its underlying though often unspoken duty to act only for the good of Merculian citizens. This is a fundamental tenet of our society, taught in schools, chiseled on walls, depicted in statues. It is so basic it is rarely talked about. And yet, here am I questioning its truth. Here am I saying no. This is not true. We have been taught a lie!

"If it were true, Liola Tavalino Simosin would not be dead, displayed so cruelly to all by the very thugs you have been monitoring.

"If it were true, the *Conte* Eulio Chazin Adelantis, member of a First Order family, celebrated star of the dance world here and in other parts of the InterPlanetary Alliance and my beloved spouse for a scant six months would not be missing for over a week.

"When I arrived in this august and secret chamber, I was told of your role, of all the knowledge you had, all the bits of the puzzle you gathered so you could see 'the big picture.' But what good does this do if you cannot carry out the role of any government agency and help one of its most famous and beloved citizens? Of what good are all the rituals and pomp if a child dies needlessly? What good is served by seeing the 'big picture'? Nothing but cant and childish games!

"Did you do anything to prevent the horrifying murder of that young Merculian citizen? Was his cruel death only a footnote to the 'big picture' you are all drawing for your own amusement? And will my spouse have to meet the same fate before there is any action against this alien invasion you discuss at such length?

"I give you notice now that I will not stand idly by while this happens. I swear before you all that I will act—alone if need be—but I will…" His voice broke and he paused to get his emotions under check. "All I ask for is a little help!" he burst out at last and sat down abruptly.

He wiped his eyes. This was not the way he had meant to end his speech, but he couldn't help that now. Let the bridges burn. He didn't care anymore.

There was a long pause, during which he could feel the shock and swirl of emotions of the people around him.

At last, the leader, Frandori Solinar Porferindo, rose to speak. "Usually, after a new member makes a speech in the Chamber, there is applause, but this would not be appropriate in your case. Please let me assure you that everyone here feels your pain. We, too, often chafe under the restraints of this office, but in order to handle this 'invasion,' as you call it, with the least number of casualties, we have to look at it from all sides. I can tell you that it is very unlikely that *chai* Chazin Adelantis's disappearance has anything to do with the Omnia mob. They would demand a large ransom. If it doesn't earn them credits or give them power of some kind, they don't do it. We would know, since we have a number of operatives embedded with that crew. And by the way, there are several members of Eulio's family in this assembly," he added with a faint smile.

Beny looked around in surprise. No one he recognized, but Eulio's family was large.

"The crew from Rozemar has irons in many fires: money lending, which I think you know about, dangerous designer drugs mixing Merculian and alien powders, a type of sex slavery which we don't understand, illegal and dangerous alcoholic drinks to mention just a few. Now, to assure you that our information is accurate, let me tell you about the story of your Dégalas painting. One of the things this mob does is steal valuable oil paintings to order for wealthy collectors near and far. When you received your painting as a wedding gift, news spread, and an order went out from a collector. These Terran villains are very patient and started to set up the robbery by getting one of their people, a mixed-race female from the Artision Compound, to get friendly with your alien male friend Dhakan, so when you two finally went away, she moved in with him, stole the painting, and then left. She was also one of their best counterfeiters but somewhere along the way, she screwed up her assignment. Perhaps she fell ill, we aren't sure, but she didn't get the replacement painting done in time. Somehow, the Regulators found a stash of other paintings and returned the one they thought was yours. It wasn't. Soon afterwards, she was killed. She had made too many mistakes."

"You know all that and still did nothing?"

"We know all that and still don't know where Vince Omnia is or even what he looks like. We need that information. We need to get a clearer idea of what he's planning in order to prevent far worse things from happening."

"In short, you won't help me."

"We can't help you," he said.

Beny stood up. "I don't believe you." He reached up and pulled off his white hat, tugged off his gloves, flung them on the desk and stalked out.

THIRTY-FIVE

The wind had died down by the time Marlo struggled awake late next day. His first thought was that last night's visit by Cushna was just a bad dream. Then he heard a tuneless humming coming from the other side of his locked chamber door, followed by a delicious smell that made him salivate. Slowly he got up, took a few stims, dressed and tidied things up before at last opening the door to the wonderful fragrance of the kind of breakfast food he only ever had at Calian's house. In the prep corner, Cushna was ladling out red noodles drizzled with clear sauce. He was fully dressed, a towel tucked under his chin for an apron, and he was using one of Calian's three-footed pots. Marlo sat down, deciding to wait till after eating before telling the dapper thief that he had to leave. Somehow the villain had managed to make toasted *fiolis* and now presented them with a flourish as he sat down opposite Marlo.

"You don't cook much, nah?"

"Not if I can help it. Where did you get the noodles?"

"At the market two lanes over."

"You went *out*? After giving me that whole performance last night?"

"Swirl it off, Marlo! I slide under the garden shelf, over the fence and through the back gardens. No snuff."

"Oh well then!" Marlo threw his hands up in the air. "Flying farts, Cushna!"

"The Snakers ain't watching *here*, ya know! That's why I come."

Snakers. That must be Riverspeak for the rival mob of off-worlders crowding in aggressively on the home grown crims, like Big Stendi and Cushna, one of his top street-leaders with a group of very active thieves and fences under him. These had included Liola, Marlo had discovered last night, who had been so devoted he had joined the Snakers to get info on this new sex-for-sale thing for his leader. But the Snakers appeared better organized, more tightly knit and completely ruthless. No wonder Cushna, with his high profile in the district, was worried. His chief could barely protect himself any more, it seemed.

Marlo chewed the toasted *fioli*. "I could put you in protective custody," he suggested.

Cushna jumped up angrily. "Nah! Off me now, razzer!"

Marlo shook his head. "Sit down. No one is going to kill you in Regulator HQ."

"Unless you catch a snake and toss him in the cold hole with. I stay here. I cook good, nah?" He looked at Marlo, his expression sly. "You took Loro in and he was a thief. Not a very good one, but still, on the run."

Shocked by the casual mention of his dead lover, Marlo pounded the table with his fist. "Get out!" He pointed to the door. "Go. And don't come back."

"Nah! I'm sorry, but it's true!"

There was a clapping at the door. Marlo froze.

Cushna leapt up again, grabbed his brown bag and fled into the sleeping chamber, closing himself inside.

Marlo flung Cushna's plate into the regenerator and went to the door. Boothby and Rosian walked in, carrying drinks in brightly colored warmer circles.

"Smells good in here." Rosian sniffed the air appreciatively.

Boothby glanced at the closed door and paused. "Is Calian here?"

About to make up some story about having to leave, Marlo caught a whiff of what they were carrying. "Is that coffee?"

"Sure thing, boss. We didn't have time to pick up any coffee last time, so we thought we'd catch you now." She sat down on what had come to be known as 'her' chair. "We have a few days off and thought maybe we could help. Be like old times, right?"

Marlo didn't answer. He was busy savoring the heady taste and feel of the rich whipped cream on his tongue as it slowly swirled into the dark coffee below.

"Oh yum," said Rosian, equally lost in pleasure.

Boothby laughed. "You Merculians and your coffee! Anyway,

boss, when we were here before you mentioned something about graffiti. You said you'd send me some images, but I guess you've been so busy you forgot."

Marlo swallowed the last of the coffee and reached for his com-dev. He projected a few of the graffiti images on the wall. "Since this is done by Terrans, I thought you might see something we missed. I suspect it's saying something, but we can't decipher it."

Boothby leaned forward in concentration. "It's words in the Terran alphabet, but the writer can't spell worth a damn." She laughed. "Anyway, it looks like a list of times and places for the latest flash events." She pointed to the big image Marlo had snapped of the graffiti near the bar.

"So it's advertising?" Marlo felt a stab of disappointment.

"That one is. There might be a few drugs listed there, too, if those words are code. Otherwise, they don't make any sense. The other one from the theater is more interesting. The words around the snake thing say: 'Beware! King Serpent eats all in his path.' And this line is messy, but I think it says something about losing everything if you mess with us. It's almost as if this person has just learned how to write."

"That's a threat."

"Looks like it."

Rosian pointed. "Isn't that the universal sign for credits? See? Right there."

All three sat staring at the images. Now that it had been pointed out, even Marlo could see the writing, though he couldn't read it.

They were so concentrated on the images nobody heard the sounds of someone coming down the steps from the parking pad on the roof and pausing at the open back door.

"Forgive me for interrupting."

Marlo turned, startled. "Beny!"

Rosian got to his feet and bowed. "My sincere sympathies, *chai.*"

"He's not dead!" snapped Beny.

Rosian stepped backward as if stung.

Eulio's spouse seemed to have faded, somehow, Marlo thought.

Even his bright reddish-gold hair had lost its luster. And the bruise on one side of his face was worse.

"I wanted to catch you before you went to work," Beny said, moving inside and sitting down. "Hello, Ms. Boothby."

"We're here to help," she said.

"Thank you." He looked at Rosian. "And you are?"

"My name is Rosian Labari Goliano, Boothby's colleague at the IPA. I have top A level clearance."

Marlo was relieved to hear this. He knew the InterPlanetary Alliance had stringent standards and did deep background checks on anyone working for them. "I was going to contact you once I got to the office, Beny. We've identified the female Terran who's been stalking *Chai* Eulio. Her name is Gloria Thompson. She gave a false address, but we'll find her."

"Does she work with paint?" Beny asked.

"That's the theory."

Beny leaned forward. "Do you know where the Artision Compound is? I have it on the best authority that it's an area in the River District where these new artist people live but I haven't been able to find it on any map. It makes sense that this Gloria female would take Eulio there since she's an artist."

"I've never heard of it." Marlo looked at Boothby but she and Rosian shook their heads. "Artision, you said?"

Suddenly the sleeping chamber door burst open and Cushna appeared. "Nah! It's Arshan Camp, ya razzers! Ya got it wrong. If ya need a map to get there, Marlo, it's on yer wall!"

"Who are you?" Rosian grinned at the thief.

"Oh, you're a tasty snack!" Cushna grinned back, his head on one side. He slunk down the three steps into the room and reached out to touch Rosian's long reddish locks.

Boothby bridled and looked at Marlo sharply.

"Cushna, stop it! Explain what you mean about the map."

"It's on yer wall, nah! Loro done it with the flowers."

Marlo frowned. "How do you know it was Loro?"

Cushna laughed. "A slow razzer, you! He was showing you where he lived, in case he had to bolt there, like, to lie low a days. Didn't you know that?"

"He would have told me," Marlo mumbled.

"Nah! He wasn't straight ahead. He liked games"

I'm not going to cry, Marlo told himself sternly. He blinked. How could this thief know his dead lover better than he did?

Beny stood up. "Could I see this…map?"

Marlo hesitated. It was bad enough that Cushna had invaded his space. No one had been allowed in there except Calian since Loro died three years ago. After all this time it seemed almost sacrilegious. But then he remembered Eulio, who might be close to dying if not dead already. He got to his feet. He tried not looking at the smug face of Cushna who was grinning as if he had just scored some major points.

Marlo led the way up the few steps into his chamber, knowing there was no polite way to stop the others from following. The primitive colors blazed all around him, the walls glowing with the flowers Loro had painted just for him. The others said nothing, standing there staring at his private painted garden. Marlo hugged himself, feeling alone and curiously exposed.

"Could you explain this?" Beny said, looking at Cushna, who had maneuvered himself next to Rosian.

"Look." The thief began tracing lines with his finger, following certain types of bright blue flowers.

Boothby stepped up and handed him a memory light pen. "Use this so we'll have a record."

"If I hadn't been just lyin' around with nothin' else ta do I woudn'a jigged to it. I grew up there, nah."

Marlo watched in amazement. A map began to form as he followed the route traced by the pen. Once it was pointed out, he could see the path made by the flowers clearly.

"He didn't finish." Cushna had arrived at the part on the last wall where the painting petered out.

Marlo stood up abruptly, emotions threatening to spill over if he didn't get them all out right away. "Shall we go into the other room?" he suggested, leading the way.

Boothby took back her pen and activated the memory. The map flashed onto the floor of the sitting room, every twist and turn clearly visible. "Wow. That's amazing."

Cushna leaned against the wall and smoothed back his hair. "Yahner. This route starts where the Path comes out, see. That there is the Arch." He pointed to a spot on the floor. "You'll see it as soon as you leg it off ter level one. It leads strict to the Camp, up the next level, like I said."

Boothby switched off her memory pen and handed it to Marlo who slipped it in his pocket.

"So how do we find this Path?" Beny said.

"Nah, that there not razzer stash."

Marlo looked up sharply. "Consider the consequences."

Cushna shook his head.

"This is a matter of life and death," Marlo said quietly.

"So right! Mine, nah?"

Marlo swallowed hard. The flower map was one thing, but the Path probably belonged to Big Stendi.

"Who is this person?" Beny asked softly.

Marlo ignored him. "Remember why you're here, Cushna?" he asked almost conversationally. "What I can do with the push of a button?" He held up his com-dev, his finger on the Regulator call button.

"Ya wouldna."

"I would." Marlo took a step forward. "And there's our unfinished business about that powder, back in the quizzer. That report can still be written."

"Nah!" Cushna backed up looking cornered. "Hard stone, you." He sniffed and glanced around the room as if looking for a way out. "This never flow from me, nah?" he said at last.

"Agreed. Now talk."

After another long pause, Cushna finally began to explain how to access this secret route leading under the river and into the heart of the District.

Flying farts, Marlo thought, as he listened. No wonder the miscreants got away with so much, able to disappear suddenly and evade the Regulators. But why had no one ever found out about this 'Path' before? He looked at Cushna's resentful face and felt a wave of anxiety. Now he owed the vilain, which was not good. How could he get rid of him after this?

THIRTY-SIX

Giazin held on to his *tatsi's* hand as they walked through the garden at the side of the sprawling house. Triani concentrated on keeping his anxiety and frustration from leaking through to his child, since he was trying to reassure him that everything was alright. It wasn't. The sudden reappearance of Rio in a hysterical state and then in a sedated near coma without any explanation had thrown the child into his own form of high anxiety, which resulted in tantrums the like of which had not been seen for some time.

And then Giazin asked about Liola.

"He won't be back, sweetheart." Triani began to walk faster, hoping they could get to the front gate where he could release the kid into Govsy's waiting arms before he had to answer the question he knew was coming next.

"Why? Because Rio's sick?"

"Rio will be better soon, you'll see. Now it's time for school." He gently pushed the child to the gate.

But he wondered if his young sibling would be better any time soon. He had now been cut out of the production of the *Night Bird*, which had been easy since the solos had been add-ons anyway. He would hardly be missed. Unlike Eulio. "Shit," Triani muttered. He couldn't think of anything more he could do for Eulio, but he was trying to be there for Rio. At the moment, his young sibling was under the care of one of the Healer's assistants who stayed with him day and night. The one practical thing Triani could do was to go to Rio's apartment and gather his things together. There was no way Rio could go back there to live. For one thing, he couldn't afford it.

Triani walked out to the park pad and looked around for the sporty new two-seater with the bright silver fins, sporting his call

sign and the new logo of black dance shoes hanging from a large
T with purple ribbons. Vandari, his trusted driver, stepped out
of the shadows. "*Chai*, the Sportster is in the shop. Both booster
boxes had to be realigned. I put a top priority on it, and it'll back
this afternoon."

"I just bought that thing last week! Make sure the dealer pays
for it." Triani looked at the two remaining air-cars consideringly.

"If you are going downtown, the Luxor would be faster,
chai. I will drive."

"Fine." Triani slid into the spacious back area of the car
where the seats sensed his presence and conformed at once to
the shape he liked. A shelf opened, presenting several bottles of
wine, water, and jars of his favored recreational drugs. He lay
back for a moment, then popped a buzzer in his mouth. How
was he going to explain Liola's murder to Giazin? He should
have done it already. He had hoped Parla might step in, but he
had refused. Anyway, his lover hadn't been around that much
lately since he was working on his presentation plans for the
next architectural project he was bidding on. He was up against
heavy competition, apparently. Triani sighed. When he was
faced with tragedy, as he had been several times in the past,
he had flung himself into his work. Why couldn't Rio do that,
instead of seeking oblivion. Soon he would have to insist that
Rio get back to the studio and start working. That's what a
dancer does. Especially one with his genes.

When they arrived at the Jewel Tower Building, the obsequious Door Guardian let him in with smiles and bows. On the fifth
floor, Rio's door opened to his touch, recognizing him. Inside, he
was startled to see three Merculians. They looked just as startled
as he was.

"What are you doing here?" Triani demanded.

"Who's arskin'?" the one with the short fluffy hair said.

"Look, you shits, this place is Liola's."

Fluffy head shrugged. "We got orders to clean it out, nah,
and take everything back to his *tan*."

"Not so fast, sweetie. Some of this belongs to my sibling Rio.
We're here to collect his things."

"Nah? Says who?" Fluffy hair stared at him. With a shock,

Triani realized the cretin had no idea who he was. He felt Vandari moving up behind him.

"Don't give no mind to Lemis, *chai*. We're all a tickle knocked on ter edges after what happened.'" This was the dark-haired one Triani sensed was the leader. "Bust on, do. Dressing room's through that door. The boss don't care about clothes and that, nah."

"Thank you." Vandari touched Triani's arm lightly, stopping the stream of anger about to erupt from his employer.

"You're all heart, sweetie," muttered Triani, following Vandari to the dressing room. He shut the door and leaned back against it. "Who the hell are those people?"

"It's better not to ask. They have distinct River District accents."

"Shit." Even after death Liola was a puzzle. Triani reached out to touch the closest filmy tunic. The mingled scents of perfumes wafted out from the rows of clothes hanging on either side of him. On one side he recognized some of the things he had seen Rio wearing, but he suspected Rio and Liola often wore each other's clothes, since they were both on the small side.

"I brought two floating boxes," Vandari announced, flipping one open. "Which side is his?"

Triani pointed, feeling suddenly overcome with emotion. He looked at a shelf running along the back and spied a familiar perfume bottle. "So that's where that went!" he exclaimed, scooping it up. "The little rotter."

And then he saw the two bangles he had paid Liola with the first time he saw him outside the Back Door of the Labyrinth. The first time Rio had met him. The first time the kid had sex. "Ah shit!" Triani grabbed the bangles and slipped them on. Rio might want them.

Vandari was as efficient as ever, packing up Rio's clothes, hair ornaments, shoes and ribbons and leggings, jackets, a few hats and a pile of scarves.

"That's probably not all his," Triani remarked, looking at the overflowing box.

"*Chai*, I suggest we leave as soon as possible. There are three of them and only two of us."

"I'm sure you could handle all three."

"Thanks for your faith in me but I would prefer not to test it."

Triani looked around the dressing room one last time and felt the sadness of the place close around his heart. He blinked back the pain.

"Come on. Let's get the hell out of here."

THIRTY-SEVEN

Marlo leaned against his office window, pushing the pliable glass farther out so he could see around the corner where groups of Merculians streamed by carrying black ribbons and the occasional grief candle. Where were they going?

"I hear there's a growing crowd down by the Pasarel Bridge," Eldred said, joining him at the window. "I doubt this is what those murdering bastards were expecting."

"News just came in about some kind of small explosion in the River District." Marlo pulled himself back to a standing position. "Rubadani's team is on it."

"Could be Big Stendi. He must be pissed off."

Marlo shrugged. "It's possible, I suppose. He does like to create distractions."

Since there had never been this kind of vicious brutality in any murders before on Merculian that Marlo had ever heard of, there really was no telling what to expect. The shock of that horrifying image had spread through the city and at first there had been no reaction, almost as if that picture had paralyzed everyone. Now they were waking up and expressing their grief in the best way they knew how, an emotional outward display.

"A couple of Elutians have set up a stall in the main square selling the ribbons," Eldred said.

"Of course, they have." Marlo began looking around for his belt. He had to report to his superior about his plan to rescue Adelantis and he had just noticed his blue sash was stained with dark yellow berry juice.

"It's under the desk." Eldred pointed. "What are you going to tell him?"

"As little as possible." Marlo retrieved the belt. It seemed to have shrunken. He held his breath for a moment to get it buckled.

"Can you trust Cushna?"

"I'm trusting my Loro." And Beny, he thought. "Look, Eldred, I want your help, but this is very…iffy. I need to take as few people as possible and Beny insists on going. Boothby has military training, too, and of course I want you. But Old Livid might veto this whole scheme. Wish me luck."

"We'll proceed as if it's a go," Eldred said. "I'll leave once I've finished my report on the last interviews and meet you at your place. I'll let the other two know."

"Thanks." Marlo touched Eldred's arm for a moment, then squared his shoulders and set off for Liviano's office.

As soon as he walked in he saw Euvi from DDD and Donera from the Undercover Ops Team. This was unexpected. Marlo nodded to them and took the remaining seat.

"Whatever we decide on here is going to be part of a combined operation against Omnia," Old Livid began, "so I've invited these two to sit in on our discussion. A rep from the National Regulators is present remotely." He waved at the wall where presumably this august being was listening and watching unseen.

Flying farts, thought Marlo uneasily. He had never worked well with the quasi-military Nat Regs.

"As I said, this is to be a joint operation," Old Livid began at once. "Donera and the Nat Regs have been working on this plan for a while, but when I told them of your idea, Donera suggested they move everything up so it all happens at once—your rescue and their raid against the Serpents. So, explain your plan." His chief sat back and crossed his arms.

All of a sudden, Marlo's sketchy idea seemed very thin indeed. The presence of Donera made him nervous. He had far more experience in this sort of thing than Marlo, but he didn't know the people involved. However, if anyone even got a sniff of the origin of his so called 'map' the whole thing would be vetoed. Marlo had to take the initiative.

"Let me make something clear from the beginning," he began. "My only aim here is to get Eulio Chazin Adelantis out of there in one piece. My plan is not an action against the

Serpents or Snakers or whatever they call themselves. That's not my mission."

There was a pause. They all looked at him.

"Gotcha," said Euvi, smiling encouragingly.

"Going into their territory *is* an act against the Serpents," Liviano pointed out.

"Only if they realize what I'm doing," Marlo replied. "So, acting on intel I've received from very reliable sources, I'm taking a group of three handpicked people through an underground passage and exiting near where Adelantis is being held. Surprise is our best weapon and the fact I have a map."

"Underground passage?" Old Livid exclaimed. "Where?"

"The entrance is under the Dragon Bridge."

"Any chance you could share that map?" Euvi asked.

"Of course. Once I'm back," he added.

"Just who are these 'reliable sources'?" asked Donera, leaning forward menacingly.

Marlo drew back and stared at his colleague. He glanced at Liviano and noted his face was getting dangerously red. "You, especially, should know I cannot name my sources."

"At least tell us who are these 'handpicked' people you're taking?" Donera's voice was cool.

"As leader I have the right to pick the ones I'm trusting with my life," Marlo replied, equally coolly.

"This is a joint operation," Liviano pointed out.

"I realize that, *com*, but I don't see how it changes the rule about a leader picking his own team."

"It's hardly a rule." But Old Livid's face was back to its normal hue.

There was more arguing about this but eventually Old Livid backed him up, as did Euvi. It was decided that Donera and his team would wait to start their part of the operation until Marlo was back at the Dragon Bridge, with or without the star dancer they hoped to rescue.

"Our success depends on you getting back unnoticed. Understood?" Donera glared at him.

"Perfectly." Marlo glared back. "Our exit will be underground, remember. Anything else?"

"My team is gathering now."

"So is mine," Marlo said, hoping that was true.

"We move this afternoon. I need to know exactly when you enter and leave the District. What's your ETA?"

Marlo glanced at the large chronometer above Old Livid's desk. Timing was something he hadn't figured out since he hadn't known about Donera's part in it all. He made a quick estimate of how long it would take him to get home, rally his troops, and get down to the river. He still had no clear idea. "I'll let you know once we get started."

Donera grunted. He didn't look pleased.

"Meanwhile there's the matter of weapons," Liviano said.

Reluctantly, Marlo agreed to his people being armed. He thought of Beny and mentally shrugged. He noted there had been no comment from the Nat Reg who was supposedly listening in to all this. What did that mean?

Much to his relief, Marlo discovered his handpicked group was all waiting in his house when he contacted Eldred after the long tense meeting. Marlo himself was late, caught up by the crowds surging in a steady stream towards the river. As he passed the Pasarel Bridge he heard the high clarion sounds of trained singers soaring over the heads of the crowd. Peering around the people in front of him, he caught a glimpse of a group of Meshdravi, dressed in their pale blue robes, standing in the middle of the bridge, singing the opening chants from the Memory Service. Marlo would have loved to pause and listen, but time was clicking off the minutes in his head. He wiped tears out of his eyes and pushed his way past the bridge. An image of the young Liola on his narrow bed in the cool impersonal after-death lab sprang into his mind. Charlo had done his best, even resorting to light make-up to hide the bruises, but still no family member came forward, only the dubious Scando, fence, jeweler, and patron of the young crim-in-training. The crowd of mourners didn't care about who he was or who he might have become. They mourned the loss of youth, the brutality of his death, the cruel alienness of it all.

When Marlo walked into his house, he almost fell over a box lying on the floor. It had the seal of the National Regulators on it, so this answered the question of how they felt about his small raiding party. They might not agree wholeheartedly but they wouldn't let them go unarmed.

"It just arrived, boss," Boothby announced, staring at the box. "What have they got to do with this?"

"Nah!" shouted Cushna in disgust. "Swelled toppers, them."

Privately Marlo agreed but he ordered Cushna back to the sleeping chamber anyway so he could explain to his small team about the weapons. Marlo was not a fan of carrying arms, but it was part of the bargain. Boothby was no problem of course, although she had brought her own super-stun, which was fine with him. Beny appeared to draw on his old training as an IPA junior officer and seemed unconcerned, checking the weapon out expertly before slipping it in the small of his back under his jacket. He knew Eldred actually kept up to date by frequent practice in the firing range under the HQ building. Marlo was beginning to think everyone was better prepared for trouble than he was himself.

They had all been studying the map provided by Cushna from Marlo's painted garden and as they made their way through the crowds to the bridge farther up the river, Marlo prayed he could trust what the thief had sworn he had seen. This far west there were few people of any description about, so they slipped down the river bank and began to look for the opening to the Path under the Dragon Bridge. But without success.

Marlo sat down and studied the water. Had it risen? Was that the problem? Or was it lower than usual? This was something he hadn't thought about before. Would it even matter?

Eldred sat down beside him. "People are coming," he said urgently. "Any ideas?"

Marlo stared ahead of him. "Other side of the river," he said. "We assumed it would be on the River District side, but Cushna never said that. He just said under the bridge."

"He could have been lying."

"Possibly." Marlo had been worrying about this, but he had nothing else to go on.

They climbed back up to the bridge, crossed over and slipped down the bank on the other side. Sure enough, they found the opening, well hidden by vines and long grasses right under the bridge work. Boothby helped Marlo clamber through into the cool dimness. Narrow steps led down, and down, carved into the earth and packed hard by use. How long had this been here, Marlo wondered. Soon they were under the river and Marlo felt queasy, imagining all that water over their heads, separated by mud and silt and shifting sand, held back by a thin layer of wood above their heads. He swallowed hard but kept going. When the ground began to rise he heaved a sigh of relief. But the Path on the other side was very narrow, the timbered roof so low Boothby had to stoop. What happens if we meet a group coming the other way? Marlo wondered. He winced as he felt his weapon sticking into his side. How could he fire at someone he knew nothing about? Who may not have anything to do with this evil they were fighting? He stopped abruptly and turned around.

"You okay, boss?" Boothby was right behind him, almost looming over him since she couldn't straighten up.

He nodded. He saw Eldred behind Beny give a hand signal he was sure wasn't in any manual and he smiled appreciatively.

"Let's take one last look at the map." He flashed the memory pen onto the ground, and they all studied it intently for a few moments. "Remember why we're here," Marlo went on quietly. "We find *Chai* Adelantis and bring him home. And that is it. Other than that, we try to blend in." Which might be difficult now that he noticed Beny was wearing a scarlet velvet jacket with tassels on one shoulder. Oh well.

Time was passing.

He switched off the map, turned around and trudged off determinedly into the underground heart of the River District.

THIRTY-EIGHT

Triani was tired of thinking about Eulio's possible fate, so he threw himself into the minutiae of his own life. This morning he was feeling more relaxed than he had for a long time after a massage session with his dance therapist. The muscular Merculian might not be sexually attractive, but he was very good at his job. Showered and dressed Triani decided to go to town and pick up the new outfits he had ordered from his favorite designer and then a quick visit with his manager before having a late lunch with Parla. Triani sensed his lover needed to be treated with more care than usual if he expected him to warm his bed any time soon.

He stopped in the parking pad outside his main gate and looked around perplexed. There was no sign of his beloved new two-seater.

"Holy shit! Vandari!" Before he had finished punching in the code, his driver appeared around the corner. "Where the hell is my new car? I thought it was fixed?"

"Young Rio took off in it earlier this morning," Vandari said. "There were no instructions he was not to do so."

"Shit! I never should have taught him how to drive! Where did he go?"

"I suspect to the apartment he shared with Liola. I checked the tracking trail before he got out of range."

"For fuck's sake!" Triani stamped his foot in frustration. His day was planned. He didn't have time for his young sibling's erratic behavior. The only air-car available at the moment was too big for him to drive with ease and he hated air-cabs.

"I will drive, *chai*."

"But the place is empty! There's nothing there!"

"No things, perhaps..."

And that's what changed his mind. A few words from an employee. But one who had been with him for a long time, which was in itself unusual. He trusted Vandari, in spite of his somewhat questionable background. How was it that while it seemed there was a choice, in reality there wasn't. Damn! Family came first, apparently, even family he hadn't known about until six months ago.

Grumbling, he settled down on the comfortable interior, snapped open a bottle of mint wine and began to cancel meetings.

"You're doing the right thing," Parla told him, and Triani made a face at his lover's image. Parla smiled. "He's hurting, you know."

"I'll see you tonight and we'll make up for it," Triani said, trying not to sound as if he was hopeful.

"We'll see."

"We better," muttered Triani, disconnecting.

It was only the sharp memories of his own tragic loss of a lover years ago that made him understand something of what Rio must be going through. Liola was his sibling's first love. In his case? Triani shrugged. This question always made him feel uncomfortable.

He was relieved to see his bright two-seater parked at the Jewel Building, even if it was taking up two spaces. The apartment door was open and the sound of wailing grief filled the empty space inside. Triani rushed in and found Rio in the dressing room, on the floor, his face buried in a filmy tunic of Liola's, one of the few things still left.

After a moment's hesitation, he knelt down beside him and put an arm over his shoulders.

"Go away! You hated him!"

"I didn't. And even if I did, it's how you feel that matters."

After a few moments, Rio leaned against him. "You feel just like *mertsi*,' he said, his voice choked with tears.

Triani opened his mouth to say something caustic about why that was but stopped, catching sight of Vandari's frown. Instead, he put his arms around Rio and braced for the pain. He didn't say anything when the wave hit.

Rio sat up and blew his nose on his handkerchief. He folded

up the tunic and put it in his shoulder bag. "It smells like him," he said softly, glancing sideways at Triani.

"I know."

"I want to go see Liola's *tan* Scando. He knows me. I need to…to talk to him."

"The jeweler? Okay. I'll take you." Triani jumped to his feet, glad to have something practical to do. "Go wash your face. I'll meet you in the two-seater."

Five minutes later they were on their way to Scando's while Vandari took the big Cloud car home. Rio's pale face was without make-up, his dark eyes held a lost look, but he was more composed.

When they arrived, Rio ran straight into Scando's outstretched arms.

"My poor dear child," the old Merculian murmured. "I've been trying to contact you about the Memory Circle." Over Rio's head he nodded at Triani. "Liola never talked about anyone the way he talked about you, dear."

Rio drew away. "His Memory Circle? Is it too late?"

Scando shook his head, his colorful round hat shifting slightly. "I was just about to close up now. Are you ready?"

Rio nodded.

"I can take him," Triani said, stepping forward.

"Thank you, *chai*, but this is a private family affair. Rio will be fine with me."

Invitation only Memory Circles were not that unusual, but Triani didn't like Rio going off with this person he barely knew. "I could just drop him off, then," Triani persisted. "He's my sibling."

"I know, *chai*, but there are no public parking pads there and it's just easier for me to take him. I'll bring him back here in about two hours." He stood up and waved to the door, which snapped open.

Triani hesitated. "Where is it being held?" he asked, still not moving.

Scando smiled, and walked out the door ahead of Triani, forcing him to follow. "It's not a venue you would be familiar with, *chai*.'

'I bet it's the Palion Hall, right?" Rio said. "Liola mentioned it a few times as a special event place."

Scando smiled. "Shall we go?"

"Wait." Triani took off his long necklace of jet beads marbled with gold and handed it to Rio. "Wear these. It just happens they're the correct mourning colors. Black and gold, you know?"

"Thanks." Rio slipped the costly beads over his head.

Triani stood watching as the old Merculian shepherded Rio into his equally old air-car and they took off in a slow spiral. At last, he hopped into his own car and began to think about rescuing his day. Although it was too late (and too risky) to ask Parla to change plans yet again, Triani was pleased to find out he could still meet his manager and after that there would be plenty of time to visit his favorite designer.

He was in the showroom giving his final approval to the latest elegant and daring outfit he would wear to the IPA Ball when he heard the news. At first it didn't register, he was so busy leaning into the pliant young body of the designer's new assistant, letting his fingers secretly stray down the youngster's bare back, feeling the kid's hot skin respond to his touch. Triani enjoyed the power he had to arouse the other so quickly, to play him so skillfully with just his touch, to make it so hard for the kid to concentrate on what he was supposed to be saying, all the while feeling the interest flame hot into pulsing desire. The assistant began to tremble. Triani smiled. He was withdrawing his hand when he heard the news blast again.

"This is an official warning. There have been several unexplained explosions in the west end of the River District. No one is to go into the area until the all-clear is sounded. All bridges to the District are closed to nonessential traffic."

Triani pushed the trembling youth away from his side and stared at the satin-draped wall as if expecting to see more details written there. But his mind had suddenly made a frightening connection. Palion Hall was in the River District, right near the spot Rio's lover had been murdered. The west end.

"I'll pick it up later," Triani said abruptly, already moving to the disc-lift that took him smoothly to his air-car. He swung into the car and set the controls, pulling back on the throttle so hard it made the little runabout buck as it took off in the wrong direction. Rattled, Triani swung it around sharply into a U turn and dropped down one lane into traffic heading north. A warning blast sounded on his dashboard, setting the lights to flashing at this flagrant violation of the rules. There would be a major fine now, but he didn't care. Rio was in danger.

THIRTY-NINE

It was getting hot inside the tunnel. In the silence, Marlo could hear their muffled footsteps against the hard-packed mud. He grimaced in pain as the toes on his left foot throbbed, reminding him of another mission months ago where things had turned deadly. That time he had been lucky to escape with nothing worse than almost losing his toes. He trudged on, trying not to think about it. He wished he knew how near they were to the opening to the surface, but Cushna had warned him that the map was not to scale and his digital long-range calipers didn't work under ground. The minutes clicked by in his mind, throbbing in his brain—click, click, click—as he tried to figure out how long it would take before Donera got impatient and charged across the bridges with his unit. The ETA Marlo had finally given him was just a guess, after all. He took a deep breath. There was nothing for it but to keep on trudging.

He called a halt when they began to hear voices. Boothby hadn't heard anything, but the Merculians had. Marlo sank to the floor to catch his breath. Giving a hand signal, Eldred crept ahead to scout and was back just as Marlo was getting anxious.

"It comes up inside a sort of closet in a building," Eldred whispered. "There's an area to see into the room beyond while completely hidden. I saw a few mixed-race people and a bunch of Terrans in the place but they didn't stay long. I think it's a storehouse or something like that. They're all carrying bundles."

The presence of so many Terrans sounded as if they were no longer in Big Stendi's territory, something else Cushna had failed to mention. What side was the thief really on? Were they being led into a trap? Giving up two Regulators, a member of the diplomatic corps and a female Terran working for IPA cyber security would be quite a coup and would be well rewarded.

Then he thought of the real fear in Cushna's face when he had arrived at his door so unexpectedly, fleeing for his life.

"What's the plan, boss?" Boothby was getting restless.

"Same as it was before. We emerge one at a time and try to blend in. Try to look as if you know where you're going. That's important. Remember the map. After we get out of the building, we all head left along the first turn, then immediately right through a sort of tunnel, then take the stairs that should be straight ahead to the upper level. The entrance to the compound is supposed to be through a wide stone archway Cushna pointed out. In case we get separated we'll meet up there. Boothby, put that weapon away."

She scowled but slid her powerful blaster out of sight.

Beny got to his feet, peeled the braid and tassel off his left sleeve and slid it in his shoulder bag. "I didn't realize I'd be going on maneuvers today," he said with a weak smile. "My weapon's in the small of my back," he added.

Eldred waved his in the air then pushed it into his pocket.

Marlo motioned to Boothby to go first. If they were in Snaker territory, she would fit in better than they would. A few moments later he followed and caught up to her. Soon they were all out in the narrow streets and alleys deep inside the River District. The buildings here were very old, many of them with ornamental stone fronts that must have been impressive at one time. Now they were neglected, moss growing in the cracks where the mortar had fallen out. Since the District was bounded on nearly all sides by water, the only way to expand was up and the inhabitants had been very ingenious at doing just that. Wooden cubes and odd towers now rose in jumbled splendor above their heads. Rickety galleries and bridges joined them, and the occasional ladder clung to the side of an old building. It was confusing to an outsider.

Marlo glanced around before heading left. There were a lot more people milling about then he had expected, Merculian, Terran, and mixed race. Other times he had ventured this far on Regulator business the narrow streets had been almost alarmingly empty except for the odd gang of young people, watching resentfully from behind their glasses of smoke. Today there was anxiety in the air. Perhaps ramped up by the small explosions that had been in the news? He never did receive Rubadani's report about them. Quite a few people were carrying bundles as if they were about to leave for a short trip. Maybe, like Cushna, they no longer felt safe here. The crowds were new, but the smells were the same, only now mixed with the sweat of fear from all these people.

They shouldered their way through the throng and were going up the uneven stone steps when several loud bangs split the air like a series of thunder cracks. Marlo pushed himself against the side of the stairs and grabbed the grimy railing. Above their heads he glimpsed a plume of almost lavender smoke twisting up into the air just before a group of large Terrans rushed past, shoving everyone out of their way. They all had black and white bandanas around their necks. A few were brandishing odd weapons Marlo didn't recognize. He slipped and lost his grip on the railing, saved from falling by Boothby's strong arms. From the contact he picked up nothing but energy.

"You okay, boss?"

"I'm fine. How's everyone?"

Eldred stood up and Beny started moving up the steps towards the archway just visible up above. "Stink bombs," he said, wrinkling his nose. "Let's keep going. The archway is just up here, I think."

Marlo moved in front of him quickly and rounded the corner in time to see a couple of Terrans trying to close the gate leading into what must be the compound beyond. They were having a difficult time. The gate was old and probably seldom used. Marlo pointed to Eldred who rushed up to talk to them. He looked small beside the Terrans but determined, as he tried to get their attention.

Boothby moved up on the opposite side. "Hey, guys, need some help?" he heard her say as he drew closer, He knew she was trying to provide a distraction and as expected, they stopped their struggle long enough to look at her. Beny seized the opportunity to slip though the archway into the compound, followed by Marlo and Eldred. They waited in the shadows while Boothby had a few more exchanges with the Terrans before joining them.

"They're artists," she said. "They claim not to know anything about Eulio. They're scared, boss."

"I don't doubt it." Marlo kept moving along in the shadow of the arch until they emerged on the other side. But instead of the large open area they expected, they came to a kind of irregular space with several alleys leading off in all directions. The map had not prepared him for this. Perhaps it was new. Where to start?

Marlo went up to a mixed-race couple who were putting shutters up over their windows and asked for the artist Gloria Thompson.

"What do you want her for," the female asked. She wore a long dangly earring in her one ear and her round Merculian eyes were an unusual grey-green color.

"We think she knows where our Merculian friend Eulio is." Marlo could feel Beny's tension even though they weren't touching.

"She's raving mad, that one. I doubt you'll get much sense out of her. She sure can paint, though," she added enviously.

Her male friend leaned against the wall of the yellow house. "We haven't seen her for quite a while, come to think of it," he said. "You can try down that way. She's right at the end, number 12C, top level. That's her studio but who knows where she is."

"Thanks. What's going on here, anyway?" Marlo went on, not able to help himself since they seemed friendly enough.

"Who knows." She shrugged. "Our great and glorious leader doesn't tell us humble artists anything anymore, even though we were the ones who suggested coming here in the first place."

"Come on, Mags. We need to get this done."

Marlo thanked them and turned away. Eldred and Beny were already moving down the alley to the left. Boothby strode along slightly in front of Marlo as they followed. The wooden houses here were painted vivid colors. They looked newer, with a lot of large windows, many extending up to the roof. Number 12 was just like the others, distinguished only by being up a flight of wooden stairs painted bright blue. The paint was worn away in the middle.

Beny rushed ahead and took the stairs two at a time. Marlo followed more slowly, wincing as is left foot hit an uneven step. He saw the open door and Beny standing there just inside, staring at the walls, tears running down his cheeks.

"Bloody damn!"

Marlo stepped inside. "Oh, my gods of the universe," he murmured, turning around and staring. Every inch of the walls was covered with portraits of Eulio, his beautiful face calm, smiling, pensive. One was full length, almost life-size, showing Eulio in a graceful dance pose that must have been difficult to maintain, long ribbons in his hair. All were beautifully painted, every stoke and detail perfect. She was very good, whoever she was.

"Oh Euli!" cried Beny, reaching out for one of the smaller paintings and ripping it off the wall. "Where *are* you?"

FORTY

As Triani circled low over the area around Palion Hall, he noticed a pall of blue smoke drifting over the area to the east. Down below, the narrow streets were crowded, and he could see no place to land near the building. Farther to the west there was a small circle of open space that might work. For a moment, he thought of his dance partner Eulio, whose careless approach to parking would never allow him to make such a pinpoint landing; then, with consummate skill, he managed the tricky maneuver and stepped out with relief. A few Merculian youths were lounging around watching him as he walked back towards the Hall.

"Keep an eye on that for me, will you? I'll make it worth your while."

He didn't bother to look back at them but kept on going, cutting through an alley he was sure would bring him out near the building he wanted. He was just in time to catch a crowd of people streaming out of the Memory Circle. He was surprised at how many of them there were, many wearing the full long black ribbons as well as the black and gold shoulder rosette of mourning. Maybe he had been wrong about Liola.

"Triani!" Rio had spotted him and came rushing over, his face wet with tears. Long black mourning ribbons hung from one shoulder, attached by a black and gold rosette. "It was such a wonderful service," he gushed. "Everyone loved Liola. I finally met his family, well his *tatsi* anyway. And his *Tan* Stendi. They're both so nice! I wish you could have come."

"I'm here now, sweetie. Come on. We've got to go." He pulled his sibling back towards the alley.

"Why?"

"There's a city alert about this place. Some kind of bomb or something. We have to get off the island."

"It isn't quite an island," Rio objected, "and anyway—" He paused. Apparently realizing nobody was standing around being social as was the custom after a Memory Circle, he followed Triani through the alley.

"Holy shit!" Triani stared in disbelief as he emerged to see about five Terrans and the Merculian youths he had entrusted with his car now busily taking it apart. "Get away from there!"

Rio yanked his arm. "No, Triani! They're Snakers! Let's just walk back across the bridge."

"That's my property!"

Rio held on with a surprisingly strong grip. Apparently all that weight training was having an effect.

"They'll kill us, like they killed Liola." Rio was whispering now and that did more to stop Triani then any amount of pulling.

"How do you know that?"

"*Tan* Stendi told me to be careful around anyone wearing a black and white scarf or handkerchief or anything like that."

Triani pulled back into the alley. He was remembering the tall Terrans at the flash, many of whom wore those colors. His idea of Liola shifted again. "Holy shit," he muttered. "That car cost a fortune."

"We can get another one."

"*We*? Hah! You couldn't even pay for the stabilizers!"

"Oh, shut up about the credits and let's get out of here."

Triani took one last look at his fast-disappearing car and sighed. "Go right, not left," he shouted as Rio turned in the wrong direction coming out of the alley.

"I can't. It's too crowded."

Triani grabbed his hand and began to push into the crowd. He was surprised to see people glance at Rio and part to let him through. Must be the mourning ribbons, he thought, taking advantage of the brief opening. Somehow Liola had become some sort of martyr around here. But this didn't last for long. Another sharp crackle of noise and clouds of colored dust rose in a tall funnel behind them. Everyone began to push in the other direction, panic in the air. Triani clutched Rio's hand tighter and headed for the stairs leading to the upper bridges. He thought he remembered the way but soon discovered that much had changed since he had been a frequent visitor here, many years ago, evading the kindly Regulators who insisted on taking him out of town to the Children's Village where there was no theater. He ran away every time and found refuge here. But today this place was no refuge.

He paused to get his bearings, pushing up against the wall as a group rushed by, calling to each other to hurry.

"They're closing the bridges!" one of them shouted.

Triani wasn't worried. He assumed that whoever 'they' were, they would let him through. He was a celebrity. Everyone loved him. However, it wasn't lost on him that it was Rio who was recognized here, given preference because of his mourning ribbons. If all else failed, that could work to his advantage.

The crowd shifted, surging in the other direction now, and Triani edged along the wall until a sudden rough shoving match pushed him through a half-open door into a bright interior. Someone came over and slammed the door shut behind them.

"Sorry, sweetie, we didn't mean to barge in like this."

"It's a madhouse out there, I know," his host said, his voice friendly. "Just wait till things settle—–*You*! You piece of shit! Get out!"

Triani stared at the red-faced Merculian in the fuzzy green slippers. "What have I done to you?"

"You ruined my cousin's life!"

"Oh, come on!"

"He met you at a theater gala and fell hard for you. And you led him on! And on! And then you just walked away leaving him broken!"

"Wait a minute." Rio stepped forward, hands on hips. "You're telling me your cousin is a big dance fan, goes to galas even, and yet he doesn't know about Triani?"

"That shit broke his heart!" shouted their angry host.

"And your cousin has no responsibility here? Your cousin the great dance fan, who probably reads *Dance News* and all the dance gossip but doesn't know about Triani's gorgeous lover, Parla Serlini Adelantis, First Order family, prize winning artist in his own right. Have you *seen* him? There are stunning images of them together everywhere. And yet your cousin kept pursuing Triani in some demented hope he would leave this paragon for *him*? Really? Is he delusional?"

"How dare you!" Their host's face was now apoplectic.

"We don't stay where we're not wanted." Rio slipped his hand in Triani's and marched out the door, head high.

"Holy shit, Rio! Where did that come from?" Triani drew in a breath and then coughed. The air was getting thick with something unpleasant that caught at the back of his throat.

"That doesn't mean you aren't a shit, you know. Keep moving." Rio pushed past him and looked around for a way out of the crush.

"We could get around this if we could just get over there." Triani pointed to the left. "There's more room and we could get back to the main bridge that way. But this crowd–"

"Take off your shoes." Rio was taking his off as he spoke. *"Night Bird* scene 12, Act I."

"Scene 11," Triani corrected, getting the idea at once. Why hadn't he thought of that? The angry tirade of Green Slippers had rattled him more than he wanted to admit. He didn't even remember that kid! And then coming out to all this noise. He tucked his shoes into his shoulder bag.

"Better if we go up on this side, then head over that way," he pointed out, shouting to be heard. "Follow me."

The steeply sloping roof felt rough under his feet and by the time he arrived safely on the platform on the lower level, his silk stockings were shredded. Grimly he put his shoes back on. He watched Rio do the same and then looked around, getting his bearings again. "I don't remember that bunch of brightly colored places with all those windows, but there's the stone archway. We can get out to the main street that way."

Triani jumped quickly down the next flight of stairs ignoring the pain and was making his way through the lighter crowd when a Merculian stepped in front of him.

"Chai Triani, isn't it? You've come to get your dance partner?"

This sudden change of subject was jarring. "Ah, sure, sweetie," he said, after a moment's hesitation. "Is he nearby?"

"I'll take you."

Rio moved up beside him. "You trust him?"

"No scarf," Triani murmured.

"But maybe it's a trap and they want you, too."

Triani shrugged. "It's worth a shot," he said, and followed their guide into a bright orange house full of people.

"It took you long enough," a familiar voice greeted them. Eulio was lying on a many-cushioned couch, being tended to by a Terran male.

"You could have helped, for fuck's sake!" retorted Triani.

"No, I couldn't!" As Eulio struggled to sit up, the one mixed-race person in the crowded room reached out to help him.

"What have you done to him?" Triani demanded, looking around accusingly at the Terrans.

"Nothing. It's just…well, the fumes from the paint were getting to him so we bought him here from Gloria's studio so our doctor could take a look at him. It's not Gloria's fault. She didn't know he was allergic to the varnish."

"We just found out he was there," explained a female.

"You look like shit, Eulio."

"So would you if you'd been wearing the same outfit for over a week and kept in a hot stuffy place, forced to pose for hours and fed weird food!"

"Can you walk?"

"Anything to get out of here."

Rio rushed to his side. "Lean on me. We'll get you out."

"Follow me." As Triani turned to leave, he stopped as another group appeared in the doorway. "Well, if it isn't the Rotund Regulator and his Excellency the Spouse. Be my guest." He stepped aside and Beny rushed over to take Eulio in his arms.

"*Chaleen*! My own love! I found you!"

"*I* found him," Triani corrected.

"It doesn't matter who found him," Marlo pointed out irritably. "Now we have to get him and everyone else out of here. Fast!"

As he spoke, the whole place began to shake. Seconds later a deafening explosion made everyone clap their hands over their heads. Several people fell to the floor including Triani as the building shook. At the same time, the large windows shattered, shards of glass pouring down like glittering rain.

"That fucking Stendi's blown up the Warehouse!" shouted a Terran voice. "Cover your mouth and nose! God knows what mixture of drugs will be in the air now!"

From his place on the floor, Triani heard Marlo say, "Fabulous."

FORTY-ONE

Marlo was beyond being surprised at anything by the time they found Eulio, but the explosion and the resultant chaos frightened him. As he struggled to his feet, he stared around at the desolation, the shimmer of broken glass on the floor, the dazed people, the remains of a wall outside the broken window. Glancing out the door he noted that the stairway to the ground was gone. He touched his face and realized he must have cuts from the shattered glass. He wiped his bloody hand on his tunic.

"Boothby, you okay?"

"Sure, boss, but this building's probably no longer stable. I can help Eulio and the kid."

"'The kid' is fine." Rio cautiously shook glass out of his dark curls. "You know the way?"

"We need to go back to the Path."

"No can do, boss," Boothby said. "It looks like the way back is blocked by the remains of that pile of cube houses." Boothby pointed back the way they had come.

"The main bridge is over there, anyway." Triani pointed in the other direction. "Let's go."

"Wait!" Marlo forced himself to concentrate. If they were to get out of here, they all had to follow the same plan, but now that they couldn't get back to the Path, there *was* no plan. No one had expected such a serious explosion, especially from Big Stendi, but everyone had been shocked by the brutal murder and Liola had been one of Stendi's people. He motioned to Eldred and they both went out the door to stand on the shaky platform, looking down on the confusion of collapsed walls, debris, and stunned people, trying to find their way among the rubble.

"Why don't our people send fly-overs?" Eldred looked up in the murky air.

"See those Terrans way over their on the roofs? Their sole object is to shoot down float-cams, drones, anything coming from outside. We tried that a few months ago." Marlo pulled a crumpled bag of *chaico* chips out of his pocket and took a handful. They tasted like sand in his mouth, but he didn't care.

"Dasha Bogardini."

The Terran male Marlo remembered meeting at the bar weeks ago, who told him his sister had been murdered, was standing behind him.

"Johnny Diaz, isn't it?"

The man nodded. "I can lead you out."

"Why?" Eldred asked at once.

Diaz looked around before answering. "Because I've had enough." He paused again. "I'm on your side." His voice was so low Marlo barely heard the words.

Beny, apparently, did. "Would you happen to own a white hat?"

Marlo frowned. What was he talking about?

"I don't own one, but I know some who do," Johnny replied.

"Sometimes an oath is not strong enough to hold in times of personal danger," Beny remarked.

"You got that right." Diaz looked down at the reddish-haired Merculian intently. "No one acted, no matter what they were told."

"What are you talking about?" Marlo shifted his aching feet nervously.

"We can trust him." Beny turned away to put his arm around Eulio.

"But he's wearing one of those bandanas I was warned about!" Rio said accusingly.

"Camoflage, right?" Boothby asked. "Have you got any more, Johnny?"

Diaz pulled one out of his pocket and handed it over. "You're in Omnia territory now and it helps to blend in."

"What's the hold up?" shouted Triani. He pushed Beny aside and stepped on the platform. "Holy shit."

"Exactly." Marlo moved cautiously to the edge, peering down at the tangle of steps. He had tied his own pink handkerchief over his mouth but the warning tingle in his throat made it clear this was not enough to avoid the drug-saturated air. He took a breath, shivered, and lost his balance. Pain scraped his backside and the hand he reached out to try to stop himself. Slivers of glass and grit etched small painful cuts along his arm. He dug in his heels as the air swirled into colors and he felt his muscles soften. No!

"Hey, boss!" Somehow Boothby was beside him, apparently unaffected by the drugged air from the Warehouse. "As chief, you're supposed to lead *from* the rear, not *on* your rear." She laughed and pulled him to his feet. Then her face softened with concern. "Hey, you're bleeding."

Marlo winced. "Don't worry about it." He looked around, trying to figure out which way to go.

"The main bridge is that way." Triani was beside him, his bright yellow collar pulled up over his nose and mouth.

Marlo shook his head, concentrating. He had a sudden urge to sing but he suppressed it. Somewhere above him, someone else burst into song, a high Merculian voice, quite good actually, he decided. Damn those Snakers and their alien drugs!

"Triani, have you got a Lula, by any chance?"

"Well, listen to you!" Triani laughed and produced a deep blue capsule from the pouch at his waist. After a moment's hesitation he took one himself. "Can't trust these Terran drugs."

Marlo noticed Triani's hand was scraped raw. He swallowed the pill and looked up to see Eulio, Beny, and Eldred, sliding down the pile of debris. Eulio was the one singing. "Better give him one, too," Marlo said.

"What do you think I am?" Triani drew his dark eyebrows together in a frown. "You're lucky I had two."

"Yes, of course. Thank you." Marlo watched Johnny Diaz catch Eulio in his strong arms just as the Merculian was about to topple over and set him down on the ground. Eulio kissed him.

"Shit," said Triani.

"He won't wear the handkerchief over his face," said Beny worriedly.

"He'll survive." Triani adjusted his own make-shift mask. "He's done more drugs than I have."

"If we go this way we'll be above the Warehouse," Johnny said, ignoring the dancers. "Omnia will probably be down there with his muscle by now. He'll want to assess the damage to his precious product. We'll go around the other way on the upper level. Follow me." Johnny began to push his way through to an alleyway, then opened a door halfway along and led them inside. "This is my place. The back door opens on the street leading to a bridge."

Marlo paused and glanced at the large oil painting of three people, one of them Johnny, the other two mixed race. His siblings? He leaned against the wall of the cozy room. "Give me a minute." Keying in the code for the top priority channel, he gave a brief report to Old Livid. "We found Eulio, but we can't get back the way we came in. You've got to hold off Donera!"

"I can't! You're taking too long! Get out of there now! That's an order!"

The channel went dead.

"Fabulous." Marlo realized his chief couldn't get much info from the live feed he had turned on once out of the Path because of the crowds, but Old Livid must realize how chaotic things were here. It would show that much.

Johnny Diaz was waiting for him. "We have to leave before things get worse," he urged. "Out this way. It leads to the second level and an exit to one of the bridges."

The bedraggled party made their way through two other luxuriously furnished rooms and then out the back door into dusty sunshine and shouts and more chaos. Eulio was still singing, but much softer now. He was obviously getting tired. Beny and Boothby half carried him through the dusty streets, no one paying them the slightest attention. By this time, they all looked like refugees, covered in dust, their clothes ripped, still glittering here and there with shards of the broken window, and trickles of blood betraying their encounters with the shattered glass.

Marlo felt the steadying effects of the Lula pill dispelling a bit of the fog. On a balcony up above them, he noticed a blond mixed racer dancing, ripping off his clothes in apparent ecstasy until he was completely naked, revealing interesting anatomy. Marlo forced himself to look away and kept going, following the tall muscular figure of Johnny Diaz. The crowd had thinned out considerably now that they were on the second level and those left seemed stunned, often just standing still, laughing uncontrollably or in a few cases, crying as if broken hearted, fat tears running down their dusty cheeks.

"This is surreal," muttered Beny. He was pale with dark circles under his sherry-brown eyes, his red velvet tunic filthy, one sleeve yanked off and ripped in two to provide masks for himself and Eulio, who kept tearing his off in annoyance.

They were making their way close beside one of the more solid houses when Eulio grabbed Beny's hand. "Dance with me!" Pulling his startled spouse around the corner, he leapt up narrow steps leading to a platform jutting out from the second story, apparently into midair. Marlo shouted a warning. The blast had shattered most of the railings around the platform as well as the wooden steps that had led down to the square just visible in the haze below.

"Come down here!" Marlo shouted. "After them, Eldred. That's not safe!"

But Eldred was too slow. Eulio was leaping gracefully from side to side, a wide smile on his face and then, suddenly, he leaned backwards, breaking through the remains of the railing and pulling Beny with him over the side and out of sight. Eldred disappeared right afterwards.

"Holy shit!" Triani leapt up the stairs, followed by the others.

Marlo panted after him, his heart thumping. To his immense relief, he saw the gleam of water down below. Three figures splashed about; Eulio swimming in a circle on his back, his eyes closed, Beny trying to pull him to the opposite shore, with Eldred making an effort to help. Marlo sagged against the wall of the house in relief, trying to get his breath under control.

"That's the tributary of the Uvi River," Johnny said. "We're on the other side of the District now."

Marlo just nodded.

"It's as good a way as any to get across, right?" Boothby said. "See you."

"Wait!" Too late. Marlo sighed and took another look at the swiftly flowing water below. All four swimmers were already a way downstream. Fabulous.

"Let me see." Rio pushed through to look at the water. Then he moved to the other side of the platform and looked down to the ground two levels below, where the flight of wooden steps had been. "What's that place?" Rio pointed to a large square building. Clouds of smoke hung heavy around it. "Is that what blew up?"

Johnny Diaz moved up beside him. "Right. That's the Warehouse." He paused, watching several tall men, two with beards, moving about. The smooth-shaven one, obviously the leader, was gesticulating wildly while the others tried to pull out large packages from the corner of the still smoldering building. One whole wall had collapsed, exposing large bales of brightly wrapped packages. Some had burst open, allowing the colored dust inside to escape on the air. The group was trying to plug the rips and cover it all. Surprisingly, the rest of the building was still more or less intact except for the roof.

"The one without a beard is Omnia, the sick bastard who set this whole thing off with his latest murdering sadistic rage." Johnny scowled. "It never occurred to him that that youngster's cruel death would set all this off and turn so many of his own people against him, never mind Big Stendi."

Rio stared up at Diaz, his dark eyes wide. Without a word he began leaping down to the ground, using the tumbled beams that remained from the stairway, sure-footed as only a dancer could be who had been trained all his life to dance on a steeply raked stage and jump from disks at differing levels.

"No!" shouted Marlo but Rio paid no attention.

"Holy shit!" Triani watched his sibling in horror. "Go after him!"

"I can't," Johnny said. "Vince would shoot me on sight after what I did."

The little group watched as the small figure leapt across the rubble straight at Omnia, shouting at the top of his lungs: "You killed my lover! You putrefied piece of rotting excrement!"

The Terran group burst out laughing as Omnia batted the

small figure aside as if he was nothing more than an annoying insect. Then, as Rio leapt back with surprising strength, he
shouted something at his henchman who grabbed the dancer
and flung him with a casual show of strength into the river
behind the building.

"Can he swim?" Marlo asked anxiously.

Triani nodded. "Not very well," he added. He sighed heavily,
checked that his shoulder bag was closed and dove in himself.

"I have to find my brother," Johnny Diaz said quietly. "You
go, Marlo. We'll get out over one of the bridges somehow."

"I'll let the Nat Regs know you'll be coming." Left alone on
the platform, Marlo watched the Terran run back the way they
had come. A dash of color and movement caught his eye as a
woman rushed out of the house to his right, clutching a baby.
She ran straight for the place where the wooden stairway had
been a few minutes ago. Marlo shouted a warning, but she kept
going. As she rushed by, he instinctively reached for the child.
Its mother screamed as she fell to the jagged tangle of wood and
stone two stories below. Marlo winced.

A glint of sunlight made him look up as a marksman on
the roof across from the Warehouse aimed for his chest. Panic
pushed him to action. Clasping the surprisingly heavy baby
tightly against him, Marlo turned and leapt into the river.

FORTY-TWO

"**T**RIANI RESCUES KIDNAPPED DANCE PARTNER!" screamed the headlines. Underneath in brilliant color was the image of the celebrated dance star, one hand held out behind him for balance on the steep river bank, the other clutching Eulio's wrist as he pulled his dripping partner out of the water. Somehow they made it look graceful.

"I guess we had nothing to do with it," Eldred remarked.

"At least the vidsters missed my undignified exit from the water, hauled up by two burly Elutians, who had apparently volunteered to help the Nat Regs."

"They *volunteered*?"

"Well, for a small gift afterwards. That's only fair as they see it. Anyway, it seems they're mad at Omnia for stirring things up in the District and making business suffer." Marlo wiggled his toes under the covers of his hospital bed to make sure they still worked.

"How did the vidsters get these images? I thought there were no float-cams."

"I suspect they were hiding in the bushes on the other side of the river just waiting for something to happen. They got great shots of the warehouse blowing up, too. How's the baby doing?"

"Yelling a lot." Eldred shrugged. "Oslani was no help at all."

"Well, it's a Terran baby. It might not be a good idea to feed it Merculian baby milk."

It was the day after the mission and an unnatural calm hung over the city. The thick pall over the River District had dissipated and now the denizens went about trying to repair their losses, helped by crews of cleaning 'bots and aid workers sent in by the Civic Leaders. Eleven people had died in all the chaos, four Terrans, five Merculians, one mixed race, and one

Elutian, who had been forced into the river and couldn't swim. There had also been hundreds of people swept into detainment centers to be interrogated later. At least all of Marlo's team had managed to get out relatively unscathed and had all been checked out thoroughly.

After Eldred left, Marlo swung his legs over the edge of the bed and winced. But there was nothing seriously wrong, and he wanted to get back home to check on Cushna. Who knew what he had been up to. Mostly, he longed to spend some time with Calian who had not been allowed in to see him for security reasons. It was now late afternoon and the only person he had been allowed to talk to who was not a Healer was Old Livid. Apparently vidsters were clamoring at the gates to talk to him and to Triani, who was still across the hall. Eulio and Beny had been sent home to rest.

"Well, you pulled it off," Old Livid began, sounding almost resentful, "although I don't see how Triani got mixed up in it."

Marlo started to explain but Liviano interrupted. "I don't give a hot damn. Look, I know communications got pretty scrambled out there. I want you to know I couldn't control Donera or the Nat Regs who apparently got the idea you were either dead or incommunicado in some way so began their advance early. I did support the last-minute plan to bring in the Black Circle because they're military, armed to the teeth and mainly Terran, and they obey orders from us, most of the time."

"I think that was a good idea, chief."

Liviano frowned. "Well, things quieted down once they arrived. The bad news is Omnia and his top henchmen have disappeared. So, the end result? Nothing is settled but at least things have calmed down. For now."

"What about Stendi?"

Old Livid shrugged. "I don't think he'll start anything. We left his territory alone. For now." He got to his feet and looked out the window for a moment.

Marlo wanted to ask about Johnny Diaz and his brother but realized his boss probably wouldn't know.

Old Livid turned around. "Next time, don't save any babies. They just make things more complicated." And with that, he marched out of the room.

This comment reminded Marlo that he wanted to begin the search for the baby's surviving parent. There had been many images of the infant, one with him clutching it to his chest with a wild look on his face as if he was afraid someone would take it away from him. Somebody would be bound to recognize the child soon.

As he made his way to the door he winced, feeling sudden pain in parts of himself he usually didn't realize were there. In the fevered pitch of all the action in the River District yesterday he had been unaware of the bruises, jarring bumps, and deep cuts on various parts of his anatomy, not to mention the fall into the water from a great height. Now that he was moving around, they were making themselves known. Fabulous. He had a lot of work to do. He should feel elated, he thought, stepping onto the disk-lift. He had completed his mission successfully, if more messily than intended. Instead, he was feeling a bit of a letdown. Perhaps it was just the thought of all the work ahead of him, he decided. Or maybe he was just tired.

Boothby had been released early and although she complained of a bad headache she was waiting for Marlo at the back entrance in order to avoid the avid vidsters.

"I knew you wouldn't stay overnight," she remarked, leaning over to take his arm. "I came to drive you home."

"Thanks."

When they reached the door of his small house, Marlo hesitated. He was almost afraid of what he would find inside. He opened the door and ushered Boothby ahead of him. He looked around, baffled. There was no one here. Everything seemed to be just as he'd left it, only tidier, as he looked closer. And cleaner. Cushna must have been bored. Marlo looked in the sleeping chamber. No one. Even Cushna's brown bag had disappeared. Well, that was a relief!

Marlo pulled out his special store of pink biscuits, delighted to find there were still a few left and held out the box to Boothby.

She shook her head. "I've been trying to contact Rosian but he's not answering. I know he's not at my place because I dropped in there before going to get you."

Marlo had a sudden premonition. "Oh dear," he said softly.

Boothby headed for the door. "I'm going over to his place now. See you later."

Marlo raised a hand in farewell and stifled the urge to warn her. But what was the point? She would find out soon enough what it was like dating a Merculian with Rosian's easy charm and roving eye. Poor Boothby. He sat down in his favorite chair, closed his eyes and began munching on the rest of the pink biscuits as he waited for Calian to arrive. In his mind's eye he saw the river, cold and greenish blue, flowing fast as he struggled to steer himself awkwardly across with one arm while clasping the large baby tightly with the other. He could still feel its warm body squirming in his grasp, hear the indignant screams when they reached the bank and he released it enough so it could get a good breath. Poor thing. Someone must be crying for it somewhere. He had heard the Terran embassy had offered to take it in, but the Merculian response had not been too warm, for some reason. Perhaps the baby was mixed race? That hadn't occurred to him in his stunned state. Tomorrow he would pay a visit and find out. Maybe by then someone would have stepped forward to claim the poor thing. It must be returned to its parent as soon as possible.

Calian arrived soon after. He had been working all week on the other side of town at a Play Garden outlet, where he was doing an overhaul of their old games and adding a few new ones. They were keeping him busy, but he had insisted on time off to be with Marlo, starting that evening.

"I haven't had time to cook but luckily I have some leftovers that should be tasty," he said. He dropped the bowls he was carrying onto the table, wrapped his arms carefully around Marlo and cuddled in beside him. The chair groaned with their combined weight. "You're a hero, you know," he said, drawing away and smiling down at Marlo.

"Purely by accident."

"Do you want children of your own? You looked so natural holding that one."

Marlo shrugged. "Perhaps. Sometime. I haven't really thought about it."

"Hmm." Calian slid to the floor, pulled Marlo down with him and began to nuzzle his neck.

"Do I taste heroic?"

"Extremely." Calian smoothed back Marlo's hair and began kissing his forehead.

Marlo lay there, savoring the warm emotions flowing from his lover, the best cure for all his aches and pains.

A loud clapping interrupted them as Eldred burst through the front door. "We found him! Oh. Sorry. Shall I come back?"

Reluctantly, Marlo eased out from under Calian and sat up, leaning against the chair. "Wait. You went back to work? Who did you find?"

"The baby's father! His name's Anthony Peralta and he arrived about two and a half years ago."

"So we have his address."

"Yes, but it's a fake."

"And no one caught that at the SpacePort?"

"River District addresses come and go, you know."

Marlo made a face and stared at a potted plant that was watching him with all six of its tiny blue eyes. Calian was busy preparing the food he had brought. He was humming softly.

Eldred cleared his throat "I think you should know the newshounds are gathering outside."

"Why? What do they want from me now?"

"Your opinion. You saved the kid, after all and there are already rumors in the Terran channels that you might want to keep him."

"What?"

"There *is* precedent," Calian said quietly.

"A couple of hundred years ago perhaps but this baby has a parent. And it's an alien."

"It's a he."

"I don't care. He should go back home!"

"I can quote you on that?" Eldred was half out the door.

"Yes! Goodbye!"

Eldred grinned annoyingly and with a parting wave, finally disappeared into the evening.

FORTY-THREE

"How's Rio?" Eulio asked, looking at Triani over his glass of mint wine.

"He has a sprained wrist, but he had a numb shot and insists on working with his dance coach anyway. I think he's right," Triani added, dipping his toes into the crystal waters of Eulio's pool. He leaned over and splashed water on his bare legs.

He had just arrived at the Adelantis-Benvolini home a few minutes ago, wearing knee-length leggings and a loose silk top that covered the cuts, scrapes and hideous purple bruises on his shoulder. He was restless, having been forbidden to dance until the more serious gash on his leg had healed.

"So he's the only one of us cleared to dance." Eulio sat up and poured more wine. "Want a buzzer?"

Triani shook his head. He still felt a little disconnected from everything after yesterday's traumatic events. Ordinarily the headlines that hailed him as Eulio's savior would have pleased him but today he found it irritating. He just wanted to get back to work and he couldn't, all because some criminals, one of them a vicious alien, had decided to fight a war over territory. It couldn't all be about Liola, shocking as his death was. And anyway, it had nothing to do with him! He kicked his feet, causing waves to ripple across the pool.

"Why don't you just jump in and get it over with," Eulio said petulantly.

"I can't because of all the medi spray and dressings." Triani stood up and slumped into a chair. "Where is his excellency the spouse?"

"Busy."

Triani shrugged and reached for the wine. "So what's the real story, Eulio? What did she do to you, that alien female?"

"Nothing. Well, apart from knocking me out with some cloth over my face back stage and dragging me off to her van, that is. I came to in her lair. Well, her studio. It's off by itself, as you know, and is soundproof, or at least she said it was so apparently no one knew I was there. Then she said she was going to paint me. Portraits all done with those alien oil paints that smell bad. Over and over and over again."

"And you just sat there?"

"You try dealing with a large muscular Terran! Every time I got up she pushed me back. Hard. She said she'd tie me down if I didn't keep still, that she had to get a portrait that was absolutely perfect before I could go. She gave me some drink that made me woozy. And before you say anything, I drank it because I was thirsty. The whole room smelled strongly of some sharp chemical, too, that eventually made me sick. That's when she got scared and dragged me outside and her friend came and took me to where you found me."

"Did she paint you in the nude?"

"Triani, not all people are sex obsessed! All she wanted, apparently, was a perfect portrait. She's a real fan and knows a lot about Merculian dance. Once she saw me perform, she became obsessed with me. She's quite mad, I think, but not violent or dangerous. She did try to give me things she thought a Merculian would like to eat but she forgot how much sleep we need. She seemed to be able to stay up around the clock. She even watched me while I slept!"

"Creepy."

"You know, now that I'm home I feel sorry for her. She's a wonderful painter but can't seem to be satisfied with her work."

"Artists seldom are." Triani slumped lower in his chair. "She has nothing to do with that baby, does she?"

"I don't think so. She never mentioned it. Look, I just went all through this with Marlo an hour ago. She's been arrested, poor thing, but they're turning her over to the Terrans to deal with because she's sick, so now you know. Could we talk about something else?"

"Fine by me. You'll be ready to dance soon since nothing too drastic happened to you physically?"

"In about a week. Mostly I need sleep. And exercise."

"I hear Evalindo's back," Triani said, changing the subject abruptly. "He's in quite a state since his cast is shrinking, and Nevon doesn't want to use the third string understudies."

"Why not give them a chance?"

"Because Nevon's afraid they won't pull in the crowds. He's all about bums in seats, remember?"

"Not all, but I see what he means. This is a very expensive production, but I would think any bums would be better than none."

"Politics," muttered Triani. "Who wins, who loses. My bet is he'll close the theater. It makes him look caring."

"Since when did you get so smart?"

Triani grinned. "Where I come from you have to be smart."

"By the way, did I tell you Orosin loaned a pile of credits to Evalindo to pay what he thought was my ransom to some brutes in the River District?"

Triani raised his eyebrows. "Do tell. How much?"

When Eulio told him, he whistled. "I guess he loves you after all. Do you think Evalindo will ever pay it back?"

Eulio smiled. "You don't know Orosin very well, do you?"

"Interesting." Triani got to his feet and retrieved his shoulder bag from the floor. "I gotta go. See you later."

Triani climbed into his air-car and headed for the theater. He was meeting Parla back home for lunch. Things were going very well in the bedroom after Triani's recent brush with death and he didn't want to jeopardize that. But there was still time for what he had in mind.

Nevon looked up from his desk when he clapped at the director's door and smiled. A careful smile, Triani thought, as he came in and sat down.

"Hi, sweetie. I hear you're closing the theater."

"You have very good sources. That's not public yet. Are you here to talk me out of it?"

The dancer shrugged. "You have your reasons."

"When are you available?"

"A few weeks. It could be sooner, though."

Nevon settled back in his chair. "And what would make it sooner?"

Triani flashed his most beguiling smile. "If Eulio and I come back the same night and perform opposite each other in *Night Bird*, it might be arranged quite soon."

Nevon rolled his eyes. "You seem to have forgotten things like contracts. With Evalindo. With you. With Eulio."

"Did you know about Evalindo's huge debts?" He told Nevon what he had just learned from Eulio. "Might that grease the wheels a bit, sweetie? He can't afford to get on your bad side now, can he?"

Nevon shook his head. "You are almost diabolical sometimes."

Triani just smiled. "Do we have a deal?"

"I'll let you know."

"One more thing."

Nevon sighed.

"Rio gets his solos back. He's ready."

"Sure. Why not?"

Triani leaned across the desk and kissed him. Just before turning away, he paused. "By the way, did you hear Rio's had an offer from Laurel Hill?"

Nevon put his head on one side and studied Triani's face. "Has he accepted?"

Triani shrugged. "Not that I know of."

"Maybe you should tell him to come to me first."

"He didn't go to Laurel Hill, Nev."

"I see."

"Up to you, sweetie." Triani turned and swept out of the room.

FORTY-FOUR

Because of all the publicity and the relentless pursuit by newshounds, Beny had gone out the back way and walked down the path to meet his old friend Thar-von. The Serpian was waiting on the bench they now considered theirs, since no one came this way anymore. Beny smiled at his best friend, glad to see him after what seemed a long time.

"I hear our Raiders rounded up so many Terrans and others your people had to spread them around four buildings." Von smiled slightly, as if he found this amusing.

"Well, we don't usually have such an abundance of criminals. I hear several Serpians ended up in your embassy."

"You can have them back any time you want."

"Or you can just send them back to their home planet. I'm sure they've done something drastic enough to warrant that?"

"Probably. They are *Rebel* Raiders. But that's not my department."

"A pity you couldn't find Omnia."

Von bristled. "We were not there officially."

"I know, I know! I didn't mean…I'm just sorry nobody could find him, that's all." Beny studied his toes. He had to be more careful what he said to Von now. They were no longer just two cadets back at the Academy, helping each other with astrophysics problems. However, he did wonder how much others might have known about the Omnia crew.

"Von, if you can't answer this or prefer not to, that's fine. I just wonder if you have come across anything about this Omnia person… lately."

Von was silent for a few moments. Beny looked at him warily, but the navy-blue eyes just stared thoughtfully into space. Beny was just getting a little worried when the Serpian began to speak.

"The job of an embassy is interplanetary affairs, Ben. We

don't concern ourselves with Merculian internal matters."

"I know, but––"

Von held up a large pale blue hand. "That doesn't mean we don't notice things. Nor does it mean that other embassies are quite so...meticulous about this unspoken rule."

Beny stared at him thoughtfully. He ran through the list of alien embassies in Cap City in his mind, but none had given them much trouble by interfering in Merculian internal affairs. Or did he just not know? Why should he know? He thought of the Round Chamber. What might they know about such things? He sighed. He would have to go back.

"Omnia is Terran." Beny paused.

"Indeed."

There was another long pause. Thar-von got to his feet. "A great deal of money comes in and out of embassies," he said, adjusting his dark tunic. "There are even some who have one job title and do another, I hear. Perhaps they would like two salaries, as well."

"But not a Serpian."

"It is enough for us to do one job well. Now I must go." He bowed and turned around quickly as if anxious to get away. Beny was about to shout a thank you after him but decided it was better not to. He lay down on the bench and looked at the sky. And then he remembered. Anyone inside any embassy had diplomatic immunity. Bloody damn.

When he arrived back at the garden gate, he found Eulio had dozed off. He was still holding a dance shoe in one hand and a file in the other. He had apparently begun breaking in a new pair so that it was just the way he liked it. Beny never understood why the shoemaker couldn't do this but apparently they couldn't. Beny was about to tiptoe away when his spouse wakened with a jolt.

"Where are you going?" For a moment, a look of fear flashed in his eyes, then disappeared.

"I'm right here," Beny said quickly, patting Eulio's knee.

"I think Triani is up to something."

"Nothing new there, then." Beny sat down and rested his feet on Eulio's lap.

"What did Thar-von have to say?"

Beny brushed back a lock of hair. "I think he was trying to point me in the right direction without...well, you know."

Eulio shook his head in irritation. "Why can't he just tell you whatever it is?"

"You know he can't do that."

"Are you trying to find out the baby's *tatsi*?"

"The baby's not really the problem. I want to find that scum of Terran earth Omnia."

"Isn't that Marlo's job? Or those other Regulators. They'll get him."

"Not if Omnia has the kind of help I suspect he has."

Eulio sighed dramatically. He picked up his pale pink shoe and began to shave away a part of the sole on the inside edge. "Orosin, you don't have to stay by my side every minute of the day you know. I'm fine, now. I just want to get these shoes ready and then try them out in my studio. So go and do...whatever you're dying to do. Shoo!"

Beny stood up and kissed him. "Just don't leave the house."

Eulio paused and stared at him coolly.

Beny felt himself flush. "Alright. Just let me...or someone know if you do. Please."

Eulio nodded and began to work again.

Bloody damn, muttered Beny as he made his way to his tiny office beside his music studio. This smothering urge must be the result of being caught up in all that dangerous chaos in the River District. It was just pure luck that nothing had happened to Eulio in their frenzied escape. Now, finding the one who had caused all this mayhem with his cruelty and dangerous drugs and ruthlessness would be the only way to end it. And it had to end. Soon. His first thought had been to contact *Tan* Pamiano but something held him back. He dearly loved his *tan* but experience had taught him that some things were best done alone, relying on his own experience and contacts. If he put a foot wrong he didn't want to involve his relative. Besides, Pamiano might try to talk him out of getting involved.

He spent some time in his office tracking people down, and at last chatted at length with two Merculians whose task it was to keep an eye on all things Terran for the Inner Chamber. They had nothing much to offer except that there seemed to have been a lot more money cycling through Embassy contacts than usual, and much of it was in the last few days. When they tried to trace the money trail back to the point of origin, they ran into a blank wall. None of the sources appeared to exist.

The last few days. Omnia was getting ready to escape! Thar-von's oblique tip had come just in time.

Encouraged, he pulled down his vid-screen and began the careful process of inching his way into the Terran Embassy files. Their data base was surprisingly easy to get into, but he wasn't sure what he should be looking for. Someone helping Omnia. But how could he tell? What would give him away? The place to start was the list of employees, he decided, but once he had that, he could find no obvious link. Of course, none of the names mentioned by his contacts were listed. He hadn't expected them to be but the longer he searched the more determined he was that the link existed. Thar-von would not have mentioned what he had without reason. And there was the large amount of credits, too.

Baffled for the minute, Beny pushed the screen up out of sight. Marlo should know about the embassy anomalies. But just how to tell him was another problem. Beny had obtained the info through back channels, using his own diplomatic cred and illegal entry into the embassy data base. How much did he need to spell out to get Marlo to act? Where did this slip into him breaking his solemn oath to the Merculian government? Did this not constitute one of the worst High Crimes?

At last, he went into his music room and began to play his *klavalo*. He played the loud, clashing music he called his thunder and lightning themes—the kind that involved the whole body to play and pushed out all thought. He was swaying, his eyes closed as the music crashed around him when he felt arms encircling him, felt warmth and calm seeping into him from the one he loved most in the world. He burst into tears.

"Did I disturb you?" he managed.

Eulio slid onto the bench beside him, keeping one arm around Beny's waist. "Dhakan heard you and thought something might be wrong. He's right, isn't he?"

Beny wiped his eyes and laid his head against Eulio's

shoulder. "I don't know where my loyalties lie sometimes, Euli. Apart from to you, of course."

Eulio said nothing for a moment. "The truth?" he suggested.

Beny sighed and sat up. "We don't always have the luxury of dealing with truth, even if we should find it."

"I see. This is about the mess in the District. You know that woman Gloria has nothing to do with all this. I don't want any harm to come to her and they promised."

"She did kidnap you," Beny pointed out, "but this isn't about her. Or you."

They were silent for a moment, holding on to each other as if on a raft in a rough sea. Then Beny stood up and began to pace.

"You've found out something."

Beny nodded. Legally, he and Eulio were counted as one person once they were married, so telling him just about anything would be like talking to himself. On the other hand, oaths taken in any sort of diplomatic situation were much stricter. No one at all was to know what he had heard using any sort of network set up for gathering information crucial to the governing of the city or the planet.

"You want to tell someone something so they can take action," Eulio said.

Sometimes it was as if he could hear Beny's thoughts. "What I know is…not explicit."

"If it would help rid us of this plague of evil, you must tell."

"But I don't know for sure!"

"Love, you swore to be loyal to our world. You swore to do good. Does anyone else have this information who might tell? Obviously you don't think so. Remember, you told me about the Round Chamber and that they knew so much they weren't telling. So you must."

Beny looked into Eulio's clear blue eyes for a steadying moment. He kissed him. "Thank you," he said. "I'm going to talk to Marlo." He knew Marlo probably didn't have the authority that might be necessary, but he could tell others. And it was a place to start.

FORTY-FIVE

"**H**ey, Marlo! Did you kidnap the baby?"
    "What's the kid's name?"
"Is it true the *mertsi's* still alive?"
"Is the child mixed race?"

Marlo stopped trying to outrun the newshounds. They were younger and much more fit than he was. Almost at the steps of Regulator HQ, he stopped and turned around, trying to catch his breath. "The answer to all of those questions is a resounding 'no comment.' When I have something to say, I'll tell you!"

Grumbling, they began to wander off.

Marlo realized he was being followed as he made his way up the steps. He turned around again. "I told you––"

"Excuse me, but I am not one of them. Allow me to introduce myself. I am Gelian Crisone Baltalini and I represent *Chai* Peralta, the Terran child's father." He bowed.

Marlo recognized the name of one of the city's most revered legal teams. He smiled broadly at the fragile-looking, birdlike Merculian, relieved that progress was in sight. "Come inside. We can talk in the visitor suite."

As they sat down in the pleasant room, Marlo loosened his sash to a more comfortable position and folded his hands. It was a bit of a surprise that someone who lived in the River District should have access to such expensive legal representation but if it concerned one's child, expense would be secondary he supposed.

"I'm glad you're here," Marlo began. "We were wondering how to get in touch with *Chai* Peralta, since we seem to have only an out-of-date address for him."

"I am here to arrange a meeting later on today where you can hand over Baby Joey to me. I have the release form right here, signed by his father." He tapped his shoulder bag.

"I'm sorry, *chai*, but that's not possible. His parent will have to be there in person, or we can't release the child."

"Perhaps I should have explained." He flicked an invisible piece of dust off his green collar with a long finger. "The poor man is unable to come to the meeting because he is convalescing after the unfortunate incident in the District a few days ago."

"In that case I can take the child to him, *chai*. It will be my pleasure."

The legal rep chewed his lower lip for a moment and then opened his shoulder bag and withdrew a paper. "Here is a legal document naming me as the child's temporary legal guardian, *Com* Bogardini. This cannot be dismissed."

Marlo glanced at the paper and felt a cool breath of warning travel up his arm, as if someone unpleasant had touched him. He forced himself to smile and stood up. "I will need to take this upstairs, *chai*. This is beyond my expertise, you understand."

The other Merculian stood up with a satisfied smile. "You have my contacts. Let me know the time and place for the transfer as soon as possible. His father will be so happy to have him back home." He bowed and left the room.

Marlo watched him go. He moved with a sort of dainty grace, his back as straight as a dancer. Then Marlo glanced at the paper in his hand. It was unusual to deal with actual paper documents and somehow this leant an air of extra seriousness to the whole situation. As if it wasn't stressful enough.

Marlo was just about to step on the disc-lift when someone called his name and he turned to see Benvolini beaming at him.

Flying farts. The last thing he needed was something else to hold him back now. Marlo did his best to beam back at Beny, but he was sure the mysterious musician could see through the effort. He turned around and led the way back to the visitor suite. "It's always a pleasure to see you," he managed.

"We just wanted to thank you for all the great work you're doing on this ghastly case. It's wonderful having Eulio back home."

"I'm just doing my job." Marlo looked down at his hands modestly and waited. Beny would not be here for a thank you call.

"I'm pretty sure saving alien babies is not in your job description." Beny laughed. "Perhaps it's written between the lines."

"Perhaps it is." Marlo was paying close attention now. "The baby's father is Anthony Peralta, by the way, and his legal rep was just here arranging to get him back."

"How interesting." Beny seemed to be watching the colorful play of light rippling across one wall. "Where is the father now?"

"Well, that's the odd part. I still don't know. He's somewhere convalescing, apparently, but Baltalini didn't say where."

"Crisone Baltalini?"

For once Marlo had caught Beny off guard and it made him feel a little better. He nodded. "You know the name?"

"He represents some of my family."

"He is, apparently, the temporary guardian of the baby." Marlo handed over the heavy stamped and signed document.

"Very impressive," murmured Beny, glancing through it. "Could I see Peralta's SpacePort entry file, by any chance? I do have top clearance."

Marlo knew he should have asked Beny to produce proof but that would waste even more time. Instead, he went to the smart wall and punched in a code to send the file to his comdev. This was highly unusual, but he sensed what Beny was doing was even more unusual and might account for the faint ripple of unease he picked up from his visitor. Perhaps this was the information he had come for.

The image of Anthony Peralta flashed on the wall, along with the particulars of his entry into the Cap City SpacePort almost two and a half years ago.

"He's blond," said Beny, surprised. "The baby has dark hair, but as I recall that's not so strange with Terrans. Was the *mertsi* blond, too?"

"Perhaps. I don't remember." Marlo was staring at the image of Anthony Peralta. Something about it bothered him.

"Do you have an entry file on any other members of the Peralta family?"

"I suppose so." Marlo glanced up and then went back to staring at the image on the wall. "Perhaps he's not a natural blond," he murmured, almost to himself. "His eyebrows are black."

And then it hit him. "That's Vince Omnia! I saw him just before jumping in the river. It's Omnia! I'll swear to it! We are NOT giving any child back to that murderer!"

Beny studied the image of the blond man. "I don't remember seeing him."

"You were already in the river. He's dark-haired now, anyway."

"Ah. Your famous memory for faces."

Marlo stood up in his agitation. "This changes everything!"

"Yes it does, and until...Well, until there's a plan in place to deal with this discovery, it's up to you to stall his legal rep without tipping your hand that we know who Peralta really is."

"No, no! Omnia needs to be detained at once! Forget the baby!"

"Do you know where he is?"

"If I did he'd be in detention by now!" Marlo looked at Beny hard. "Do *you* know where he is?"

Beny smoothed the creases out of one cuff. "Please sit down and let me explain some things to you."

Marlo frowned and bit back a curse. "*Chai* Benvolini, I appreciate that you're trying to help but I don't need anyone to explain my job to me, the job I have been doing with some success for many years," he added.

"It would never occur to me do such a thing, *Com* Bogardini." Beny was now leaning forward, the picture of distress. "I apologize deeply if I gave that impression. I appreciate how highly you are regarded, believe me. In fact, that was my reason for coming here today, to thank you––"

"Please, stop. My job is to detain criminals like Peralta, alien or not. Now, please tell me where he is."

Beny sat back and folded his hands. "I wish I could tell you, Marlo, but all I have is supposition. For instance, there is a Peralta working at the Terran Embassy. He might be a relation."

"Flying farts! So Omnia could be *there*? If he is, I have no jurisdiction to get him out!"

"But you can make sure he stays in while a plan is worked out by others."

"You think an appeal to the ambassador might work?"

"That's not really something I can comment on." Beny stood up. "I'm sorry you got the wrong impression of what I'm trying to do here, Marlo. All I can say is that it will be in the best interest of Merculian if you keep stalling Peralta's legal rep about giving the baby back."

"That baby is not going back!"

"Of course not, but we don't want Peralta to know that."

"Why?"

Beny folded his hands as if in prayer. "A criminal Terran like Omnia will have a detailed exit plan. He has, I suspect, done this before. The only thing keeping him here is that child. Apparently he adores his son. If he didn't, he would be gone by now."

"I can promise nothing. The Cap City Regulators are a large and sometimes unwieldy organization. We can't always move quickly or in the way you might like." Marlo sensed his companion's mounting frustration, but he didn't care. Using a poor innocent child as a weapon was repugnant to him. Besides, what right did Benvolini have to put all this on his shoulders?

"I understand, *com.* I see now I have made a mistake coming here like this. It was presumptuous of me." He got to his feet.

Marlo felt a stab of remorse. As he bowed Beny out the door he laid a hand on his sleeve. "I have to deal in facts," he murmured. "I cannot operate in a complete fog."

Beny nodded. "Let's hope the sun comes out soon." He smiled, but the smile didn't reach his eyes.

FORTY-SIX

Beny pressed both hands to his stomach in a vain effort to calm the turmoil within. Marlo's startling recognition of Omnia/Peralta added even more urgency to Beny's need for action. But what could he do? What power did he really have? His only value lay in his connections and his strength lay in knowing how to use them. He had misjudged Marlo, perhaps even alienated him. But thanks to him, he now had important information that had to be handed on to someone who could do something about luring the murderer into Merculian hands.

The most powerful group he could think of was the Round Chamber, but he had marched out of there in anger after a speech which had probably barred that door to him forever. He stopped rubbing his stomach and stood up from his place between the paws of the great dragon on one side of the entrance to the Regulator HQ. There was one person whom he might approach with this information. Perhaps the Round Chamber already knew about Peralta, but he couldn't assume that, and one of the White Hats mentioned by the friendly Aldisi was right here, hidden somewhere high up in this building. Beny took out his gold bracelet with links that looked like small mantino chips but were actually coded with his high security clearance. Slipping it on, he went back inside and stepped onto the disk lift. With relief he heard the three quiet beeps acknowledging his pass and it began to rise quietly to the floor near the top that was never seen by the rank and file going past on their way to the parking pad on the roof above. But it stopped for Beny, and the invisible doors slid open, revealing a quiet entry with several arched doorways on both sides. Beny stood in the muted light wondering which door might be the right one, but as he moved into the hall, one of them slid open. Beny paused, took a deep breath and walked through the door with the apparently confident stride that had come in handy in the academy.

There were no windows here. The room was lined with screens flashing data and images but as Beny advanced, they flickered out of sight. A small Merculian was hunched over the slab of pinkish float-stone obviously used as a desk.

"You have strong nerves coming here, *Marquan*," this person said, his voice surprisingly strong in one so old.

The use of his old-fashioned title made Beny cringe inwardly. He was pretty sure it was not used as a compliment. "I was in the neighborhood, Excellency."

The old Merculian cackled. "Ahah. So convenient, situated as we are on the way to so many places of interest." He pushed the slab of desk aside and it floated against the wall, revealing the old Merculian's shriveled legs in their bright red striped stockings. "I assume you are here to tell me something about this current mess."

"I am."

"It will have to wait. Come. I have an air-car parked above." He moved his cramped hand over a button and the cushion he was sitting on rose and wafted him over to the door, across the hall and onto the disk. Beny rushed to keep up. "I can walk but it's tiring. I'm old. I like to take it easy."

"Quite right." Beny had been unaware of this problem since he had only seen him from the waist up in the Round Chamber.

"You are not universally liked," remarked the oldster, boosting himself into his air-car.

"Few people are," Beny replied, unfazed. "With the exception of my spouse," he added.

"Some say you have been promoted too fast, that your record, while successful in several difficult missions, shows you have made many mistakes along the way."

"And yet, here I am."

"Well, you do have some powerful friends in the Chamber. Get in. Sit. The afternoon session will be starting soon."

Beny wondered which side this oldster was on. He swung himself into the car which took off almost at once. As they swooped towards the Chamber, Beny finally remembered the councilor's name.

"Will they allow me to speak at such short notice, *Chai* Torelio?"

"They will. Hand me that bottle on the shelf there."

Beny handed it over. It had what looked like a medical label on it. Torelio took a long swig. As they skimmed closer to the Round Chamber building, Beny began ordering his thoughts into what he hoped would be a persuasive argument leading to action, forcing himself to ignore Torelio's odd hostility. He had met it before, though usually not expressed in such a forthright manner. What mattered was that he was getting back into the Round Chamber and would be able to speak, if he could count on his odd companion.

Everything happened without incident: Beny picked up his white hat, gloves, and speaking egg from the usual place and followed Torelio in his softly humming float seat into the Chamber. Neither of them said a word. Beny stepped aside and sat down on the same chair he had occupied before, looking around at the murmuring Merculians who filled the room. There seemed to be more of them than there had been the last time he was here. Something big must be on the agenda. He dropped his eyes, realizing he had been staring at a friend of *Tan* Pamiano's whom he hadn't seen there before. Better not to show any signs of recognition. Bloody damn! He pushed his egg to the front of his desk where it flashed its message to the assembly. 'This person would like to speak,' it said quietly. Somehow everyone seemed to hear, or maybe just saw the flashing message.

Beny glanced at Torelio who was now seated to his left halfway around the circle. The old Councilor sat canted to one side, talking to his neighbor, his longish grey-steaked hair falling over half his face. The lights dimmed and silence dropped like a cone over the room. Beny swallowed and took a deep breath.

Since it was an afternoon session much of the ritual was curtailed, and they were soon ready to work their way through the agenda which began scrolling across Beny's desk as he read it. Sure enough, the whereabouts of Vince Omnia was right at the top. But at the moment, they were concentrating on the Terran ambassador, who was not in Merculian's good books, having made several diplomatic mistakes that upset quite a few influential people. But to Beny it seemed mostly a matter of slips in protocol, like the far too valuable wedding gift the man had given him and Eulio. Patience.

He touched his egg and it glowed brighter, emitting a low hum. After a moment, there was silence and the egg lit up completely, signaling it was his turn to speak.

Beny got to his feet and squared his shoulders. "Excellencies: it has come to my attention that the foul criminal Vince Omnia, otherwise known as Anthony Peralta, may be hiding out in the Terran embassy where one of his relatives is on the technical staff. The relative's name is Terry Peralta. Large sums of credits have been flowing in and out of the place lately which suggests the villain plans to escape and soon.

"Ordinarily I would say 'good riddance' and wave good-bye to such garbage, but he has tortured and murdered a young Merculian citizen as well as making many others sick with his alien designer drugs and used some of our young people in strange sex-for-hire schemes which are repugnant to us. Not to mention the drink he distilled in his *brams* and distributed through many of our entertainment centers which has poisoned some of our younger city dwellers.

"I was invited to join you partly because of my knowledge of Terrans, having lived in an environment where they were in the majority for a number of years. In my experience, they are usually good people, but they can, at times, be very bad as is seen in their history. However, I never knew anyone as evil as this man. I can extrapolate from what I have observed to tell you this; Omnia will have had exit plans in place almost from the beginning. I can tell you that he has in all probability done this sort of disappearing act before and he has large sums of credits gained from his highly illegal operations already moved off planet.

"The only thing that can stop him leaving is his love for his baby. It seems he adores the child, and he has sent his legal rep, a highly respected Merculian, to *Com* Marlo Dasha Bogardini to arrange the transfer of the child to him. I propose that we use this event but hold off on actually doing it as long as possible, meanwhile making sure Peralta remains inside the embassy." He paused, looking around at the faces in the Chamber, most of whom looked angry, but at him or his words Beny wasn't sure.

"The Ambassador is aiding this criminal?" asked one, incredulous.

"I doubt he knows, Excellency."

"Hah," exclaimed Torelio.

"The Terran Ambassador is not the hick he appears," remarked another.

"But why would he risk doing this? He's a wealthy man."

Beny smiled. "There is a Terran saying that one can never be too rich or too…thin, I think it is." But Beny thought back to the reception held to show off the expensive painting the man had given them as a wedding gift. Whatever happened, there would be a big shake up at that embassy once this was over.

Debate and discussion were spirited. Some of what Beny had said they already knew but not about the proposed handover of the baby who quickly became the focal point of a rapidly emerging plan that shocked Beny with its duplicity. On the other hand, how else does one catch such a slippery bastard? No one had any idea how he planned to get off the planet, so they had to act fast before he disappeared again.

"The child is our only leverage with this cretin," Torelio said at last, his remarkably strong voice making itself heard over the babble. "We must promise to give the child back if Omnia leaves the planet. Then we will pick him up as soon as he is out of the embassy and fling him in detention until his trial."

"There is that warrant that just came in this morning from Rozemar," another voice chimed in. "Shall we ignore it?"

"It took them long enough," remarked Beny's neighbor.

"He was using yet another name there."

Torelio pulled himself upright. "No! We won't ignore it. Tell them they can have him once we've finished with him. Omnia will never be free again."

"What about the Regulators?" Beny asked, thinking of Marlo.

"Ahah. Let me worry about the Regulators." Torelio waved his hand in the air as if stirring a large pot.

Beny couldn't help smiling just a little.

FORTY-SEVEN

Marlo was off the case, at least as far as dealing with the baby was concerned. He had Beny to thank for that, he thought bitterly. Old Livid was right. These people were not his friends. On the bright side, this gave him more time to concentrate on all the other tasks he had to handle. Practically every team in the building was busy interviewing the motley crowd swept up in the River District raid and all these reports came to Marlo to sort out. Many were simple wrong-place-at-the-wrong-time problems, easily fixed as long as they had a guarantor to step forward and take them home. Some were more problematic in that they had a record of disturbance in the city, but if it was not too severe, he let them go, too. The Serpians he sent to be looked after by their embassy, and they would probably be sent back to Serpianus to stand trial. There was a rumor that several Elutians had spent more than an hour trying to bribe their way out, an effort their jailers found highly entertaining. Marlo tracked down the rumor, found it was true and sent the Elutians on their way with a caution. He even accepted a large yellow buckle, which made them feel better about the whole transaction.

"Don't want them to lose face," he explained to the guards. He trudged back to his office, where he hung the buckle on his wall.

An hour later he came across a vaguely familiar name right in the HQ detaining rooms. Max Kolinski. A Terran ballet dancer. He called for the man to be brought to the quizzer.

"I remember you," Marlo began, "and I'm sorry you got caught up in this. What were you doing in the River District?"

"I wasn't. I was in a Snack House nearby and got swept up when the riot broke out. Can I go now?"

"Do you have a guarantor? Someone to speak for you?"

The Terran frowned in thought. "The rest of the ballet company I'm with has already gone back to our ship. We're leaving tomorrow morning to go home so I really need to get out of here."

Marlo shook his head. "It doesn't work that way," he said. "Can you think of anyone, anyone at all who can vouch for you?"

The Terran pushed his wavy blond hair off his forehead. "Triani," he said, his face brightening. "He knows me."

Marlo sighed with relief. "Just wait here a moment while I check."

But when Marlo contacted Triani, the dancer laughed.

"Well, sweetie, I barely know the guy. No way can I guarantee anything about him."

"*Chai* Triani, he really needs your help."

"What do I care? I told you I barely know the bitch. Tell him to ask his girlfriend." And he broke the connection.

Marlo went back and sat down opposite Max. "I'm sorry. He says he can't guarantee you and to ask your girlfriend."

"Jesus! That little——" He stopped himself. "My girlfriend isn't here. I only mentioned her to Triani because he was coming on to me so strong and I wasn't interested. Now what do I do?"

"Look, if you consent to a temp chip placement in your arm you can go, pack your things and get out to your ship, but you must do this within 3 hours."

"Thank you! I'm so out of here! Thanks again." He reached across to shake Marlo's hand in the Terran manner and almost ran out of the room, followed by the techie who would give him the follow-chip.

"I thought this guy was a friend of Triani," remarked Eldred, who had been watching from the observation room.

Marlo sighed. "Sure, up to the point where the Terran rejected his advances. Triani doesn't like rejection."

"Probably not used to it," Eldred remarked. "Look, Charlo sent this through. He wanted you to come down, but I talked him out of it. Remember when he and his team built up the 3D images from the DNA of the two Terrans who raped that poor kid Liola?"

"That was stellar work."

"Thanks to that we've identified one of the Terran bodies from the explosion. He was found under a collapsed wall."

"So, one down, one to go. I'll thank Charlo when I get a minute."

"Wait, the second one's dead, too. He was picked up with the wounded in the riot, but he died this morning."

"Good." Marlo sat down and looked out the window. It was a good result but not the sort that gave him joy. He would rather have the rapists on trial for what they did––a High Crime on Merculian, right up there with murder. Still, they were gone, dealt with by fate.

He pulled up his never-ending list of detainees and noticed another familiar name at once.

"I need to speak to this one," he said, pointing out the name to Eldred.

When the man arrived, he looked much older than he had the last time Marlo had seen him. Marlo felt his heart go out to the man who had lost his daughter, but he reminded himself sternly of the other things Frank Diaz had been doing. He was not the innocent visitor Marlo had thought at their first meeting.

"It's so good to see a friendly Merculian face," the man exclaimed, smiling at Marlo as he sat down. "How are you?"

Marlo sat back and folded his hands. "What is your game, Mr. Diaz?" He watched the smile fade from the man's face.

"So, you're a real cop after all," Frank remarked, looking down at his paint-stained hands.

"Your people tend to underestimate us."

There was a pause while Marlo leaned back and watched as Frank began to pick at his thumb.

"Things got out of hand because Omnia always overdoes things. He's out of control!"

"What is your place in all this?"

"You've got to believe me, we had no idea things would go this way!"

"And yet you say, 'Omnia always overdoes things,' so not totally unexpected."

Diaz sighed. "My family are artists. It was all so simple at first, so innocent. I began copying famous paintings and selling them to people we knew, always adding or changing one detail so it wasn't a real counterfeit. It was almost like our student days back on Terra when we copied the great masters in museums as an exercise to learn their techniques. On Rozemar I was approached to do a faithful copy of a Viedermere. I was offered a lot of credits which I needed at the time for my daughter, who wasn't well, so I thought, why not? What difference would it make? It was for someone far away; I would never be connected to it. And then…then I met Omnia who threatened me with exposure if I didn't keep it up. The deal was his gang stole paintings, I copied them, they returned my copy and sold the original to billionaire collectors all over—I don't even know who or where they were. It was lucrative and some members of my family are very good at it, especially my daughter. She was the best, but she got too ambitious and…Well, you know what happened to her, poor girl. You mess up with Vince and you don't get away with it. That's it. That's our story."

"Why did you come to Merculian?"

Diaz shifted his position. "Things on Rozemar were getting …difficult. By this time, we were more closely associated with Omnia's crew, and he had made things too hot to stay there. My second spouse is Merculian, so it seemed a good idea to come here. We came to the River District because Maderi has relatives here and he could buy land, since he's a Merculian citizen. What Omnia didn't know was that Merculian doesn't allow aliens to own property so he himself couldn't buy anything. He didn't care. They came and forced their way into the District, eventually controlling over half the area. But as usual, Omnia wasn't satisfied and…" He shrugged. "When he killed that poor Merculian kid because he was spying for his *tan*, well, a lot of us rebelled, even some of his faithful followers."

"Wait. What do you mean Liola was 'spying for his *tan*'?"

"Yeah, apparently the kid's *tan* is Big Stendi. Anyway, the way it was done was way too much. It turned our stomachs."

"Flying farts," murmured Marlo. He wondered if Frank knew his own son had been a spy for Merculian.

"What will happen to me and my family? Some of them are

mixed race. We want to stay here."

"I doubt that what you want will carry much weight, Mr. Diaz."

"Even if I can tell you where Omnia is? How he plans to get away?"

"Then you will definitely stay, I can guarantee that." Marlo smiled. "So, you're a real dyed in the wool Snaker after all."

"Not really, but my younger brother is." He smirked.

"I see." Marlo got up and walked out of the room. As the door snapped to behind him he leaned against the wall and reached into his pocket for one of the honey squares he had slipped in this morning. He needed a jolt of sweetness to steady his nerves. As he chewed, he thought about the difference between this man and the grieving father he had met all those weeks ago and felt so sorry for. He had had no inkling then of any connection between this older artist with his modest market-stall selling sweet paintings of Terran and Merculian landscapes and this man with a direct connection to the Snakers, with his smirk and his barely hidden distain for the Cap City Regulators.

Marlo put his hand on the wall, opened the channels to Old Livid's office and explained what was going on. He could hear his chief breathing, then the click as different connections were made so that everyone who needed to know would hear what Frank Diaz had to say. "This better be good, Marlo," Liviano said quietly, just before making the final connection. "Otherwise, heads will roll."

Marlo touched his head reflexively and assured his boss this would be good.

And it was.

They learned that Omnia had an aunt who was the captain of her own inter-steller cargo cruiser. The ship was fast and small enough not to attract much attention. What she carried in the hold was of dubious origin, but she had never been caught with anything anyone could prove was illegal. Except once, and she had argued her way out of that one. Her one claim to honor was that she would have nothing to do with weapons of any kind, or so she said. Her ship was due to dock in the Cap City

SpacePort in the next few days. No one would have noticed if Frank Diaz had not spilled the secret plan, since the *Midnight Sun* had been here before and all its papers were in order. No one would have noticed a few Terrans wandering back to her dock space since they would have been listed as part of the crew. And Omnia would have disappeared.

"What about the baby?" Marlo asked. "Would he leave without his son?"

Frank shrugged. "I doubt it, but the kid's small enough to fit in a large carryon bag and could easily sleep through it all with the help of knockout drops."

Marlo shuddered.

"Is that all you want? I've told you everything I know, and I need to go find my family."

"No."

"You said we could stay!" Frank's face flushed with anger.

"Yes I did, but I didn't say you would be free." Marlo got to his feet and walked out.

FORTY-EIGHT

The city still reeled from the shocking events of the last week, but things were slowly getting back to normal. In the River District, crews of workers had descended to help clean up the place, parts of which now looked better than they had before the explosions. Many of the injured had returned home and the vidsters were now chasing other news. Someone had leaked the story that Triani was having a hot affair with a mixed-race designer and this meant Parla was also pursued, although when cornered, all he would say was "no comment." It seemed everyone had forgotten the baby.

Beny and the White Hats, however, had not. Since Eulio was now back at the theater rehearsing with Triani for their debut dancing together in *The Night Bird*, Beny felt free to sit in on all the meetings as plans were discussed, discarded, checked out, and eventually decided on. At last, they had chosen a few high-ranking Regulators to carry out the top secret operation to lure Omnia into the open and arrest him. *The Midnight Sun*, captained by Omnia's aunt, had been allowed to dock and was now firmly anchored in Level 2, Bay twenty.

Contact had been made with Omnia through his legal rep, who had been coerced into being the go-between. Omnia was offered the chance to be smuggled out of the embassy in a supply cart used regularly to transport large packages to and from Terran vessels. Once at the loading dock. Marlo would meet him and hand over his son. In exchange, Omnia would pay a large sum, supposedly bribes to all the people involved, and agree to never return to Merculian. Beny had assured them that a Terran criminal like Omnia would think it suspicious if large bribes were *not* involved in the plan. The group was under the leadership of the White Hat speaker Frandori Solinar Porferindo.

Marlo was excited to be involved in the clandestine plot, although it was hard not to be able to let Calian in on it. His job was to hold the baby. He looked around at the intent faces of the small group gathered in this nondescript building by the SpacePort for the final briefing late the next afternoon; Euvi, his friend from the DDD unit, Donera, three Regulators from Special Ops, and a few Nat Regs. The time arranged for the top secret event was early next morning, when Omnia would climb into the Embassy supply cart, setting the whole plan in motion.

"And when he arrives here," Donera said, indicating the tunnel opening on the wall-map with his pointer, "my Specialists will immobilize him."

"How?" asked Beny.

"Stun shot."

"Do I hold the real baby Joey?" Marlo asked, anxiously.

"Yes. Euvi will be with you. He doesn't look very threatening."

"I should carry some baby blankets or something," Euvi suggested.

"But Omnia won't actually get the baby," Marlo went on, still anxious.

"No! You stand at the other end of the tunnel in the light, here, where he can see you clearly. He'll start towards the baby, we stun him and clap restraints on him here. But, if he doesn't fall, the Nat Regs jump down from above and grab him. It's doubtful we'll need them though," he added.

"Are you sure he'll be alone?" someone asked.

There was a pause. "We're not positive," Frandori admitted. "We've tracked several of his top henchmen who are already on the ship. We can deal with them later. However, the surveillance cams at the employee entrance to the embassy went down about the time we suspect Omnia got there so we don't know if his bodyguards went in with him or not."

"Wait! If there's no float cam footage, how do we even know Omnia is in there?" exclaimed someone else.

"Eyewitness."

"Perhaps we should use the Black Circle for this?"

There was another uneasy pause. "They're mostly Terran mercenaries. Can we trust them?"

"Well, what about the Serpian Raiders?"

"No," Beny said. "This is an internal matter. They won't interfere."

"We're fine," Donera said. "We can do this ourselves."

"Just remember we want Omnia alive." Frandori said sternly.

Donera stood up, one hand on his dagger. "We've got this!"

"Yes!" the others chorused.

Marlo looked over at Beny, who smiled encouragingly.

Marlo had no idea how Euvi had talked his way into this group, or even how he had found out about it, but the next day, as he stood in a shaft of early morning sunshine clutching the large Terran infant in his arms, he was glad his friend was at his side holding some baby things. He had been up well before sunrise after an uneasy night of pacing and short naps interrupted by vivid dreams of disasters featuring him trying desperately to save the baby, now grown to the size of a bloated adult, who kept floating away just out of his grasp. The excitement he had felt on being selected for this mission had now vanished, replaced by acute anxiety, tinged with fear. All his senses on high alert, it seemed to him even the air smelled different now. He could almost taste it, sharp and bitter on his tongue. As he stared around him, the tunnel looked longer and narrower than it had in the diagrams back in the briefing room, with little space for him to dodge out of the way should Omnia manage to get by the Regulators.

Behind him rose the glittering SpacePort, just now beginning to stir into life and start the day. Although they had alerted the Port Manager, they had wanted everything to go on as usual, so that things would look completely normal to Omnia. The only thing unusual was the presence of the half-dozen hand-picked Nat Regs just out of sight in the loading shaft above the tunnel, ready to drop down through the hatch when needed, and Donera and his three backups, hidden behind the hastily constructed camouflage wall that blended completely into one side of the passageway.

Marlo threw back his shoulders. The baby was just waking up. His big brown eyes stared up at Marlo for a moment, then he took a deep breath and let out a great wailing cry.

"Oh no, no, dear. Not now," whispered Marlo. He thrust a finger in the baby's mouth. Luckily the finger still had a bit of powdered sugar on it and Joey sucked at it contentedly for a few moments. And then, as Marlo hitched him up higher in his arms, he felt the wetness. Nothing he could do about that now.

"Did anyone think Omnia might be armed?" Marlo whispered to Euvi.

"Well, if he is he won't shoot *you*," Euvi pointed out.

In the distance they heard the hum of the approaching cart on its invisible rail as it slowed down before passing by the other end of the tunnel.

"This child is getting very wet." Marlo grabbed a baby blanket from Euvi and tried to stuff it between himself and the baby. The kid wailed again, and this time did not stop no matter what Marlo tried.

"Eewe, he smells," remarked Euvi. He stiffened. "Heads up. Someone's coming!"

Marlo clutched Joey closer in spite of his wailing protests and watched in mounting horror as a hairy-faced muscular Terran male rushed towards him, head swiveling, stunner drawn. The bodyguard, apparently making sure all was as agreed. Marlo swayed and felt Euvi beside him clutch his belt to steady him. The man's laser sharp eyes swept over him and the baby, but he kept going, passing so close Marlo could smell his sweat. The man made some sort of a sign, raising his left hand above his head and then rushed down the ramp, disappearing into the docking area where the ship was waiting.

Before Marlo could catch his breath, he saw Omnia. The gaunt Terran strode towards him, his dark eyes burning with intensity.

"Give me my son!" he bellowed, while still halfway along the tunnel.

Marlo said nothing. As he watched, Donera and his three companions, stunners drawn, leaped from their shelter and surrounded the Terran. But repeated stuns didn't seem to make much impression on the man as he struggled desperately to get by them and grab his baby son. He kept shouting, "Let me go! I have safe passage!"

"Fuck that," muttered Euvi.

Then Marlo saw a third male. Another bodyguard! Moving with amazing speed for one so big, he rushed towards Omnia, zigzagging from one side of the passage to the other. He paused long enough to shoot the Merculian who was attempting to put restraints on his boss. The man was taking careful aim on another Merculian when a high whine buzzed in the air, and he fell with a cry.

"Euvi!" exclaimed Marlo in astonishment.

"Well, someone had to do it," muttered Euvi, slipping his weapon back in his belt. "I just wish it was Omnia."

Donera shoved the body to one side, kicked the weapon out of the way and made a determined grab for the Terran, forcing one arm up behind his back. Instantly Omnia twisted around and threw the Regulator over his shoulder onto the ground.

Suddenly a Merculian all in black and gold burst into the fray and thrust a long dagger into Omnia's chest. Marlo almost dropped the baby. Donera staggered to his feet and lunged for the assassin, but he twisted out of reach, rushing past Marlo and jumping off the edge of the ramp to disappear into the maintenance area below. From there Marlo knew, he could easily lose himself in the labyrinth of twisting passages which eventually would lead him to the outside and safety.

By now the Nat Regs had managed to yank open the hatch cover and drop down into the middle of the scene. Donera, streaked with blood, swore volubly. "Get after him, you assholes!" he shouted. For a moment no one moved, apparently stunned. After a moment of confusion, the Nat Regs finally dashed off in hot pursuit in an effort to redeem themselves. But the executioner had a head start and obviously knew the area. It was doubtful they would catch him.

Marlo pulled himself out of his shock and thrust the squalling baby at Euvi, who now smelled almost as bad as he did. He raced down the tunnel hoping Omnia was still alive.

The man was deathly pale. "My son! Joey?"

"Did that Merculian say anything?" Marlo leaned over the dying man. But he was too late.

"Did any of you hear him say anything?" he repeated.

Donera nodded. "He said one word— 'Liola.'"

Black and gold. The colors of mourning. Flying farts. Marlo got up from his knees and, ignoring the blood on his leggings, called Charlo. "One dead, one wounded," he said. "Come at once. Code 66."

Forty minutes later there was no sign that anything had happened in the tunnel leading to the loading dock and the small group who had been involved in the mission was on their way to a final meeting.

"One size does not fit all," Marlo grumbled as he struggled into the pale pink jumpsuit handed out to the blood-stained group as they arrived for their debriefing. He finally managed to get most of the ties done up and hoped no one would notice that the ones around the waist were nearly popping open. He sat down quickly beside Euvi, whose wiry body looked small in the suit that puffed around him. Only Donera managed to look as if the awful thing had been tailored just for him.

Frandori looked as if he had just eaten something very sour. "Today will not go down in history as one of our finest moments," he said at last. He peered keenly into each person's face and enquired coldly if anyone had any clue how Big Stendi had managed to get wind of this top secret operation? "That assassin obviously had detailed knowledge of the plan!" he thundered.

They looked at each other, each face more innocent than the last.

"We don't deal with Stendi or his minions," Donera said, equally coldly.

Marlo, too, shook his head. He had an inkling, but he had no intention of saying a word, now or ever. He knew how much Euvi secretly loved Jarodin, the dainty undercover who had suffered so much to find out what went on at Omnia's sex-fueled Flash parties, and Euvi and his drug unit had many contacts in Stendi's world.

"As for the National Regulators, they will deal with their own," Frandori went on. "Suffice it to say, I ask myself of what use all their vaunted training if they couldn't manage to open a door in time to be useful."

"*Chai*, if I may explain—"

"You may not."

"But it was stuck," muttered the Nat Reg resentfully, nursing his sprained wrist. "You didn't tell us the hatch hadn't been used in decades."

Frandori glared at him, and he subsided. "We're lucky we sustained few casualties. Our one wounded trooper will be fine in a few days. You were all so close to Omnia the shooter was obviously afraid to hit his boss by mistake."

After a moment, Frandori turned to Marlo, thanking him for getting the After Death team there so fast. "The body will be turned over to the Terran Embassy. They can do whatever they do with such things. We're satisfied and will never mention this person's name again."

"What about the baby?" Marlo asked. "Where is he now?"

"He's fine. He is to be adopted by a couple in the Terran Embassy."

"And the *Midnight Sun*?" Donera asked.

"We're letting the ship go, but they'll be barred from docking anywhere on Merculian ever again."

"And the...ah...executioner?" Euvi asked.

There was a tense silence.

"He got away," Beny said at last. "No one seems to know who he is."

And we don't want to know, Marlo thought, but decided to keep that to himself.

Although everyone had been so careful at the SpacePort not to leave a trace of what had happened, they had forgotten the old security cam in the tunnel, and it wasn't long before images of Omnia's last moments flashed across the city. Then it was as if the whole metropolis breathed a collective sigh of relief. People in the Pleasure Gardens began to dance. Singing broke out in the Meshdravi district. Some residents rushed outside to celebrate with their neighbors, while in the River District, people wandered about cautiously, hardly daring to believe they no longer needed to worry about inadvertently crossing some invisible boundary that could threaten their lives.

And Cushna finally went home.

Marlo went home, too, driven in an unmarked air-car to avoid the vidsters he knew would be lying in wait. He was exhausted, mentally, physically, and emotionally. He needed to be alone for a while. For once he was glad that Calian would not be coming until noon. Because of the top secret nature of this mission, he had had to send his cheerful lover away to avoid letting something slip in a thoughtless moment. Marlo tore off the horrible pink suit and pulled on his comfy loose knit grey pants and top, then sat in his sleeping chamber chewing his way through the paltry few cinnamon swirls left over from last night. He was thinking about the images that still flashed through the news outlets. Strange how the face of the black and gold clad person remained mostly in shadow. Strange, too, how the actual stabbing part seemed to be missing.

He lay back and gazed at the innocent-looking childish flowers that had hidden their secret of the route to the River District so well. He wondered what other secrets they might hide.

He yawned. It had been a long exhausting day and it was still not even noon. He hoped Calian would decide to ignore his instructions and come with lunch early.

FORTY-NINE

Triani stood in the large reception room of his country estate, hands on hips, shouting at his new employee.

"More to the right! No! The other right, you moron! Why did I hire you?"

"You said I had good legs, *chai.'*

'Too bad you don't have a good brain. Now get out!" He stood back to admire the new award he had just received from the Merculian Dance Association for his contribution to the field of dance interpretation. It looked good on his wall. Perhaps it needed a spotlight? He was pondering this when something in the news stream that had been running in the background caught his attention. He waved his hand to bring up the volume.

"...thus ending the reign of terror in the River District and Cap City in general. To repeat, the Terran criminal known as Vince Omnia is dead."

He paused the stream and looked at the image of the man who had killed Liola and pushed his sibling Rio into such despair. A gaunt dark face with a look of utter surprise in his eyes stared back at him. And then he thought of the horrifying image of the young Liola... He turned on his heel and went in search of Rio. He found him sitting on the floor in the practice studio, listlessly going through a box of dance shoes.

"Come here. I want you to see something." Triani went to the wall and activated the news clip he had just seen.

Rio got to his feet slowly and stared. "Play it again. Stop! I know him." He pointed at the image of the face of the Merculian. "That's Liola's *tatsi*! I met him at the Memory Circle. So he paid that monster back for what he did! Good! They didn't catch him, did they?"

"Apparently no one knows who he is. And I don't think

anyone wants to find out, either."

"I won't tell them. He doesn't live in Cap City anyway. He was just here for the Memory Circle, like I said."

Triani nodded absently. He switched off the news and looked at his sibling more closely. Rio was wearing dance clothes. That was a very good sign. "You going to warm up? If you wait a minute I'll join you. We can try the opening of *Prindi* if you want." He was expecting resistance, but Rio surprised him.

"I'd rather do *Dream*, okay?"

"If you're sure. There are lifts, you know."

Rio turned on him with a flash of his old spirit. "Afraid I'll drop you? I won't."

"Glad to hear it." Triani pulled off his spangled tunic and slipped into a red sleeveless top he had left draped over the bar at one mirrored wall.

Rio began a series of stretches. "Nevon offered me a contract yesterday," he said quietly.

Triani paused. "And?"

"It's not good enough, yet. I'm a principal with five years' experience."

Triani laughed. "Go get him, Rio!"

It didn't occur to him till much later, however, that now he would no longer be the youngest principal in the company.

EPILOGUE

In the Adelantis-Benvolini household Eulio turned the large oil painting to face the wall.

"I cannot have this thing in our house any longer!" he shouted. "It has to go."

"It was a wedding gift," Beny objected but his voice carried no conviction.

"I don't care if it was a gift from the High Priest himself. It has to go!"

Beny put his arms around his spouse, pulling the warm body against his own. "I know, dear, but can't we just wrap it up and leave it in the back of a cupboard?"

"No. I don't want anything trailing clouds of filth from the Snakers polluting the air we breathe. It has to go!"

Beny didn't say anything.

"Oro, this isn't even the same painting the Ambassador gave us!"

Beny let Eulio go and clapped his hands. "You're right! We can give it away to the Terran Museum! Will that be alright?" He looked at Eulio anxiously.

"Anything! Tell them to come and get it right now!"

Beny made the call, and they wrapped the painting up together and set it outside the front door, ready to be picked up.

"And they can take this big thing, while they're at it," Eulio said, handing over a huge ugly serving bowl with bilious yellow lizard-looking creatures all around the rim.

"Ah, no, Euli, dear. That's from the Elutian ambassador." Beny set the enormous platter down on the table.

Eulio grimaced. Whipping a long lace cover off one of the ceremonial chairs, he wrapped the serving dish up and stuffed it carefully behind everything else in the storage cupboard.

He turned and smiled at Beny. "There, all done with nobody insulted. Elutians never drop in unannounced."

"To think I nearly lost you," Beny said, tears in his eyes.

"Glad you married me?"

"Come closer and I'll prove it." Beny wrapped his arms around Eulio and together they fell back onto the yielding cushions.

ABOUT THE AUTHOR

CARO SOLES's novels include mysteries, erotica, gay lit, science fiction and the occasional bit of dark fantasy. She received the Derrick Murdoch Award from the Crime Writers of Canada for her work in the mystery field, was short listed for the Lambda Literary Award, the Aurora Award and the Stoker Award. Caro lives in Toronto, loves dachshunds, books, opera and ballet, not necessarily in that order.

Curious about other Crossroad Press books?
Stop by our site:
http://store.crossroadpress.com
We offer quality writing
in digital, audio, and print formats.